The Dirty Dozen

"Six years ain't taught you nothin', Harry, and I ain't gunna expose my town no more to you. You're worse'n smallpox!"

"Thanks," said Destry, "because I can feel the compliment behind what you say. Thanks a lot, old timer."

"Clarence Ogden dead!" said the sheriff. And here I ride alongside of the killer! What would they think in the East about that?"

"Eastern thinkin' never raised Western crops," observed Destry, "But about the Ogdens, you know them that live by the gun shall die by the gun. That's Bible, or oughta be!"

"You sashay right on outa Wham," said the sheriff.

"Not me," answered Destry, "except that my game ain't here any longer, I guess. All the birds have seen the hunter, and they all have flown, I reckon?"

The sheriff looked grimly at him.

"D'you mean to take all twelve?" he said. "One by one?"

"I mean it!"

DESTRY
RIDES
AGAIN

Max Brand®

LEISURE BOOKS 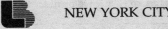 NEW YORK CITY

A LEISURE BOOK®

March 2009

Published by special arrangement with Golden West Literary Agency.

Dorchester Publishing Co., Inc.
200 Madison Avenue
New York, NY 10016

ISBN 10: 0-8439-6182-1
ISBN 13: 978-0-8439-6182-9
E-ISBN: 1-4285-0645-4

Visit us on the web at www.dorchesterpub.com.

Destry
Rides
Again

Chapter One

"Lil' ol' town, you don't amount to much," said Harry Destry. "You never done nothin' an' you ain't gunna come to no good. Doggone me if you ain't pretty much like me!"

So said Destry as he came from the swinging doors of the First Chance and now leaned against one of the slim, horse-eaten pillars that supported the shelter roof in front of the saloon. The main street of the town of Wham stretched before him, until it wound itself, snakelike, out of view. It had gained its title in yet earlier days when it was little more than a crossroads store and saloon where the cowpunchers foregathered from east and west and south and north; and meeting from all those directions, often their encounters were so explosive that "wham!" was a really descriptive word. It had grown to some prosperity, and it was yet growing, for the cattlemen still came in, and, in addition, long sixteen-mule teams pulled high wheeled freight wagons out of Wham and lugged them up the dusty slopes to the gold mines of the Crystal Mountains.

But still Wham had not grown too fast for the knowledge of Destry to follow it. It was held in the cup of his memory; it was mapped in his mind; he knew every street sign, and the men behind the signs, from the blacksmiths to the lawyers, for Destry had grown up with the place. He had squirmed his bare toes in the hot dust of the main street; he had fought in the vacant lots; and many a house or store was built over some scene of his grandeur. For the one star in the crown of Harry Destry, the one jewel in his purse, the one song in his story, was that he fought; and when he battled, he was never conquered.

His wars were not for money, and neither were they for fame; but for the pure sake of combat in itself, he used his fists, and never wearied or shifted with ambidexterity to knives or guns, and still was at home with his talents. To him, Wham was a good and proper name for a city; it expressed his own character, and he loved the town as much as he esteemed it little.

Having surveyed it now, he took note of a new roof, white with fresh shingles, as yet unpainted, and went strolling down the street to examine the newcomer. He had turned the first bend of the way when he met Chester Bent.

"Why, doggone my eyes," said Destry gently, "if here ain't lil' ol' Chet Bent, all dressed up pretty and goin' to Sunday school agin. How are you, Chet, and how you gettin' on? Where you get them soft hands of yours all manicured?"

Chester Bent was by no means "little"; he had a spare pair of inches from which he could look down at Destry and twenty-five pounds to give weight to his objections, but in the younger days he had fallen before the rhythmic fury of Destry's two-fisted attack. It had been no easy victory, for under the seal-like sleekness of Chester Bent there was ample strength, and behind his habitual smile was the will of a fighter. Three times they met, and twice they were parted with blood on their hands; but the third time they had battled on the shore of the swimming pool until Chester fell on his back and gasped that he had enough. Therefore, having conquered him, the hard hands of Destry were averted from him, and he became one to whom Destry spoke with a sort of affectionate contempt.

It made no difference that Chester Bent was a rising man in the town, owning a store and two houses, or that he had stretched his interests to include a share in a mine of dubious value; to Harry Destry he remained "lil' old Chet" because of the glory of that day by the swimming pool. And in this, Destry was at fault, since he failed to understand that, while many things are forgotten by many men, there is one thing that never is forgiven, and that is the black moment when man or boy is forced to say: "Enough!"

Chester Bent merely smiled at the greeting of the cowpuncher.

"What you-all doin' here in front of the shoe shop?" went on Destry. "Waitin' for a pair of shoes, Chet?"

"I'm driving out the west road," said Bent, "and I promised Dangerfield to take Charlie out and deliver her; she's in collecting a pair of shoes."

"Is Charlie in there? I'm gunna go in and see her," announced Destry. "You come along and hold my coat, will you?"

He marched into the shoe store, and found a perspiring clerk laboring over a pair of patent leather dancing slippers which he was trying to work onto the foot of a pretty sixteen-year-old girl whose hair was down her back, and the end of the pigtail sunfaded to straw color.

"Why, hullo, Charlie," said Destry. "How you been, and whacha done with your freckles?"

"I bleached 'em out," said Charlie Dangerfield. "Whacha done with your spurs?"

"I left 'em in the First Chance," said Destry, "which they're gunna hang 'em on the wall by token that a man has been there and likkered."

"You lost 'em at poker," said she.

"Who told you that so quick?" asked Destry.

"It don't have to be told, or wrote either," said the girl, "and it don't take any mind reader to tell where you've been. Did you spend your whole six dollars, too?"

"It was five and a half," said Destry. "Who told you that?"

"I know you been out at the Circle Y about six days, that's all."

"I tell you how it was, Charlie. It was a pretty hand as you ever see; it was four sevens pat; and I stand, and Sim Harper draws three, and doggone me if he didn't raise me out of a right good slicker, and my old gun, and a set of silver conchos, and a brand new bandana, nearly, and my spurs, and then he lays down four ladies to smile at me. D'you hear of such luck?"

"You can get all kinds of luck off the bottom of the pack," said Charlie Dangerfield. "That's where Sim mostly keeps his."

"I wasn't watchin' too close," said Destry. "I gotta admit that when I seen the four of a kind it looked to me like a hoss and a saddle, and a pack and a fishin' rod, and a month of fishin' up the Crystal Mountains. I was feelin' the trout sock the fly, and how come I could watch Sim's hands at the same time?"

"Did you lose your hoss and saddle, too?"

"Would I of got to my spurs without that?" asked Destry. "You've kind of slowed up in the head, Charlie, since you lost your freckles. Freckles was always a sign of brains, ain't they, Chet?"

Chester Bent was idly running his glance over the names on the rows of shoe boxes, and he shrugged his shoulders for an answer.

"Lil' ol' Chet is day dreamin' and raisin' his interest rates to nine per cent," suggested Destry. "Look here, George"—this to the shoe clerk—"tell me what's the size of that shoe?"

"Five, Harry," said the clerk.

"D'you aim to get that slipper onto that there foot?" asked Destry, "or are you just wrestlin' for the sake of the exercise?"

"Fives ain't a bit too small," said the girl. "The last time I——"

"You musta been to the Camp Meeting and got saved," declared Destry, "and swallered the miracles down and everything, because you sure are askin' for a tidy little miracle right along about now!"

"You ain't amusin', Harry," she told him. "You're jes' plain rude, and ignorant!"

"About most things, I certainly am, but feet is a thing that I can understand, and shoein'. Fetch down a pair of number sevens, George, because I ain't gunna send this here child home with blistered heels."

He reached down and took the stockinged foot in his hand. The foot jerked violently.

"Whoa, girl," said Destry. "Steady, you sun-fishin', eye-rollin', wo'thless bronc, you! Don't you kick me in the face!"

"You're ticklin' my foot," said the girl. "Leave me be, Harry Destry, and you go and run along about your business. I don't want to waste no time on you, and Mr. Bent is plumb hurried, too."

"I'm aimin' to save the time of *Mister* Bent," said Destry. "George, you go and fetch down them number sevens. But look here what she's been doin' to herself, and crampin' up her toes, and raisin' corns on the tops of the second joints. Doggone me if this old hoss ain't gunna be spoiled for me."

"For you?" asked Bent, now standing by to listen.

"Sure," said Destry. "When she gets filled out to these here feet, I'm gunna marry her. Ain't I, ol' hoss?"

"Bah!" said the girl, and wriggled with mental discomfort, because she felt her face growing hot. "You jus' talk and talk, Harry Destry, and you never say nothin'!"

"Hello, Chet!" called the store owner, letting the door slam as he walked in. "You seen the sheriff?"

"Have I seen what?" asked Chester Bent, without raising his eyes.

"He's been lookin' for you mighty busy. He's just down the street."

"Ah," said Chester absently, "he'll maybe find me, by and by! Are you gunna marry him, Charlie?"

"Why for should I marry such a lazy, shiftless thing?" she asked, looking at Destry with indignation.

"Because I plumb love you, honey," said Destry. "And don't forget that you're all promised to me."

"I ain't any such thing," she declared.

"Are you forgettin' that day that I carried you across the Thunder Creek——"

"Chet!" she exclaimed in furious protest. "Listen at how he carries on, teasin' a poor girl. He wouldn't take me all the way over till I said I'd marry him."

"And you kissed me, honey, and sure said you'd always love old wo'thless Harry!"

"Harry Destry," said the girl, "I wasn't no more'n hardly a baby. I wasn't more'n twelve or thirteen years old. I'd like to beat you, Harry, you wretched thing!"

"You were never a baby," said he. "You were born old, and knowin' more than any man would ever know. Now there, you see how neat that fits?"

The number seven, in fact, fitted like a glove on the long, slender foot.

Tears came up in the eyes of Charlie.

"Oh, Harry," she said, "ain't it monstrous big? I'm gunna grow up six feet high, I guess!"

"I mighty sure hope you do," said Destry. "Because it looks like I'm gunna be a tolerable ailin' man the most of my days, and never take kindly to work."

"How come you lost that Circle Y job?" she asked him, forgetting his illimitable personalities. "I'll tell you how. You been fightin' again!"

"Why, how you talk!" said Destry innocently. "Who would I be fightin' with over to the Circle Y, where they ain't had nothin' but scared greasers and broke-down nigger help for years?"

"They gotta rawboned Swede over there lately," she said, "that looks like he could lift a thousand pound. I bet it was him."

"Oh, Charlie," said Destry, "you was born old and wise! What a hell of a life I'm gunna lead with you, honey!"

"How's the Swede?" she snapped.

"Tolerable sick," said Destry. "Tolerable sick and run down. Which his stomach is kind of out of order, and that's got his eyes all involved up, so's he's hardly able to see. He ain't got no appetite, neither, and if he had, he ain't got the teeth left to bite with. But the doctor is gunna get him a new set of celluloid, and pretty soon he'll be better than new!"

"If I had you," said the girl, "I'd keep you muzzled and on a leash. I'd never loose you excepting at loafer wolves and such. That's what I'd do, if I had you!"

"Oh, you're gunna have me, honey!" said he. "Lemme help you out the door, will you?"

"You run along and help yourself," she advised him, "but don't you help yourself to no more redeye!"

"Why, Charlie, I ain't hardly had no taste of it!"

"You do your tastin' by the quart," she observed, "but even if you can fool the bottle, you cant fool me! Come on, Chet! Mighty sorry that I've kept you so long!"

They went out to the hitching rack, where Bent's span of matched bays were hitched in silver bound harness to a rubber tired buggy whose blue spokes were set off with dainty stripes of red.

"I'm gunna drive," said the girl, and leaped into the driver's place.

"You ain't gunna kiss me good-by, Charlie?"

"I'd slap you, you impident thing!" she said, grinning at him. "Listen at him talk, Chet!"

"Say, Chet," said Destry, "now you're gunna take my honey away from me, mightn't you leave me something in her place?"

Chet Bent looked up the street with a nod.

"There's Pike's bull terrier loose again," he said. "He'll leave another dead dog along his trail before the day's out!"

"Will he? He will!" said Destry, turning to watch, and as the wind blew open the flap of his coat, and as the girl sat up to watch the white streak across the street, neither Destry nor she saw the swift hand of Bent slip a thin package into the inside pocket of the cowpuncher's coat.

"About leavin' something—even trade rats do that!" said Destry.

"They leave rocks and stones," said Bent, smiling.

"And gold, I heard tell once!"

"Did you hear tell? Well, here's something. Make it last, Harry, will you?"

Destry was counting it, entranced.

"Forty—fifty—I'm gettin' plain dizzy, Chet!—sixty—seventy—this ain't real, but all sort of dreamlike!—seventy-five—eighty—who's put the new heart in, Bent? Is it your fault, honey?—ninety—a hundred—a hundred dollars——"

"You better start a bank account," suggested the girl.

"Wait a minute, Chet!" cried Destry. "What've you done that you wanta repent it as hard as all of this? Have you got religion, Chet? Have you sold a salted mine?"

He followed them a few steps along the sidewalk as Bent, laughing, started up his team.

Then Destry turned back to survey the town, which had taken on a new aspect.

"I'm gunna buy me a bronc and a saddle and git," said Destry. "Cowboy, buy yourself some spurs, and hump! Because money don't rain down every day, nor ham and eggs don't grow on the cactus, nor Chester Bent unlimber his wallet wide open like this! I'm gunna get reformed and start to work!"

So he said, frowning with resolution, but at this point he saw the swinging doors of the Second Chance saloon, and he felt that no atmosphere was so conducive to serious thought and planning as the damp coolness of that barroom.

So he passed inside.

Chapter Two

If alcohol is a mental poison, at least it did not show in Harry Destry by thickness of speech, or uncertainty of hand and foot. His eye grew brighter, wilder, his head was higher; his hand was more swift and restless before he ended the first fifty that Bent had given to him.

A hundred dollars, in those days, could be spread thick over many slices of good time, and Destry was both spreading and eating, and taking friends with him. No one knew how trouble started; they rarely did, when Harry Destry went on the warpath, but already there was a commotion in Donovan's Saloon when the sheriff rode up beside the whirling, flashing wheels of Chester Bent's buggy and raised his hand. Bent drew the horses back to a walk, and they went on, switching their tails, stretching their necks out against the uneasy restraint of the bits, and eager to be off again at full trot.

The sheriff brushed some of the dust from his black moustache, of whose sheen and length and thickness he was inordinately proud; then he said: "Chet, I wanta ask you a coupla questions. Where was you Wednesday night?"

"Wednesday night?" said Chester Bent, calmly thoughtful. "Let me see! I was doing accounts, most of the evening. Why d'you ask?"

"Because the express was held up that night, and the mail was robbed," said the sheriff.

He looked earnestly into the face of the younger man to see if there was not some change of expression. In fact, Chester Bent grew pale, with purple spots faintly outlined on his sleek cheeks.

"And seventy-two thousand dollars was taken," said the sheriff, "as maybe you know!"

"Great Lord!" murmured young Bent, aghast, and added in a rapid muttering: "And poor Harry Destry spending money like wildfire all over town——"

He checked himself, and glanced guiltily at the sheriff.

"Whacha say?" asked the sheriff, his voice high and sharp.

"Nothing, nothing!" said Chester Bent. "I didn't say anything at all. I wonder if you're suspecting me of anything, sheriff?"

"I'm not suspectin' nobody. I'm askin' questions, as the law and my job tells me to do. That's all!"

It was perfectly apparent, however, that he had heard the remark of Bent, as indeed that gentleman expected him to do, and now, with a mere wave of his hand in farewell, he spurred his horse into a gallop up the road, and every clot of sand and dust which the mustang's hoofs flicked upwards, like little hanging birds in the air, spelled mischief for Destry.

Of course all things went wrong at once, for as the sheriff came swiftly down the main street of Wham, he heard loud shouts, frightened yells, gunshots before him; and then he saw a hurried crowd pouring out from the mouth of the Donovan Saloon.

He stopped one frenzied fugitive, who ran at full speed, and made a spy-hop every few strides as though he expected that some danger might fly harmlessly past him under his heels.

The sheriff reached from his horse and caught the shoulder of the other, spinning him around and staggering him.

"What's wrong in there?"

"Destry's wild again!" said the other, and shot ahead at full speed.

The sheriff did not rush at once into the saloon. He was as brave a man as one would find in a hundred mile ride, but still he knew the place for valor and the place for discretion. He halted, therefore, at the swinging door, and called out "Destry!"

"Wow!" yelled Destry. "Come on in!"

And a forty-five calibre bullet split a panel of the door.

The sheriff stepped a little farther to the side.

"Who's there?" asked the sheriff. "Who's raisin' hell and busting the laws in this here community?"

"I'm the Big Muddy," answered the whooping voice within. "I got snow on my head, and stones on my feet, and the snows are meltin', and I'm gunna overflow my banks. Come on in and take a ride!"

"Is that you, Destry?"

"I'm the Big Muddy," Destry assured him. "Can't you hear me roar? I'm beginnin' to flow, and I ain't gunna stop! I'm rarin' to bust my banks, and I wanta know what kinda levees you got to hold me back. Wow!"

Another shot exploded, and there was a crash of breaking glass.

At this, the man of the law gripped both hands hard.

"Harry Destry," said he, "come out in the name of the law!"

"The only law I know," said Destry, "is to run down hill. Look out, because I'm fast on the corners.

I'm the Big Muddy River, and I'm runnin' all the way to the sea!"

The sheriff deliberately turned on his heel and departed. He merely explained in a casual way to bystanders that there was nothing to be done with fools of this calibre except to let them run down and go to sleep. And Wham, though it was a reasonably tough town, agreed. It had experienced the flow of the "Big Muddy" many a time before this and knew what to expect from Destry.

So, when Destry wakened in the raw of the chilly morning, with an alkaline thirst eating at his soul, he found that he was resting peacefully in jail, with the sheriff drowsing comfortably in the chair beside him. A guard was near by, with a grim look and a riot gun. Said the sheriff, while the eyes of Destry were still hardly half open:

"Destry, you robbed the Express!"

"Sure," said Destry, "but gimme a drink, will you?"

"You robbed the Express?"

"I did if I get that drink. If I don't get that drink, I never seen the damn Express."

"Give him a drink," said the sheriff.

The drink was given and disappeared.

At this, Destry sat up and shrugged his shoulders.

"You know you're under arrest," warned the sheriff, who was an honest man, "and whatever you say may be used against you. But you've confessed to robbing the Express!"

"Did I?" said Destry. "I'll rob another for another drink. Who's got the makings?"

He was furnished with Bull Durham and brown wheat-straw papers.

"Now then," said the sheriff, "you better tell me just what you did! How'd you go about it?"

"How do I know?" replied Destry, inhaling smoke deep into his lungs. "If I robbed the Express, all right, I done it. But I don't remember nothin' about it!"

"Look here," said the sheriff. "You recognize this?"

He presented that small packet which he had taken from the inside pocket of Destry's coat.

"How can I recognize it when I ain't seen what's inside of it?"

"You know mighty well," declared the sheriff, "what's in this here! Confess up, young man. It's gunna make everything easier for you in front of the judge and the jury. And even if you don't confess, they'll snag you, anyway!"

"Let 'em snag," said Destry. "I been workin' too hard, and I need a good rest, anyways! Was the Express robbed last night?"

"You know mighty well that the night was Wednesday!"

"Do I? All right. I just wanted to be sure what night it was that I done that robbin'. So long, sheriff. I'm gunna sleep agin."

He dropped the cigarette butt to the floor and allowed it to fume there, while he impolitely turned his back upon the sheriff and instantly was snoring again.

Chapter Three

". . . that Harrison Destry, residing in, near, or in the region about Wham, in the state of Texas, did on the night of Wednesday, May the eleventh, at or about fifteen minutes past ten o'clock, wilfully, feloniously, and injuriously delay, deter, and cause to stop the train entitled . . ."

Harrison Destry raised his head again and became lost in the labors of the big spider which was at work in the corner above the desk of the judge. The sun struck a mirror so placed against the wall that a bright beam was deflected into this very corner, and there the spider, unseasonable as the time was, busily pursued the work of constructing his net for flying insects. So distinct did the work appear in the bright light, and so keen was the eye of Destry, that he saw every glistening cable as it was laid, all threaded with globules of glue. He lost the voice that was reading.

Presently he was recalled to himself by the voice of the judge asking if he had selected a lawyer to represent him. When he answered no, he was briefly informed that it was well to have the advice of counsel from the first; that already he had been informed of this several times, and that it was specially valuable before the selection of a jury.

"I'm broke," said Destry. "What's your honor got on hand in the way of a good second-rate, up-and-comin' lawyer for me?"

His Honor was none other than Judge Alexander Pearson, whom perhaps six people in the world were permitted to address as Alec. The rest were kept at arm's length, and through all that range he was respected and dreaded for his justice, which he doled out with an equal hand, and for his knowledge of every individual, and of every individual's eccentricities and history almost from birth. It was possible to make promises about future conduct to some judges, but Alexander Pearson was too well able to tell of the future by the past.

"Counsellor Steven Eastwick," said the judge, "is here at hand, and I am sure is capable of giving your case a scholarly and careful handling. Counsellor Eastwick is newly a member of the bar, but I am sure——"

"Hello, Steve," said the prisoner. "Poker, sure, but not courtroom cards, if you play my hand! Thanks, your honor. I'll handle this deal better than Steve, to suit myself."

The judge went on in his even voiced way: "Counsellor Rodman Wayne is also newly one of us. Mr. Wayne, I am sure, would also be adequate and if——"

"Roddie never learned how to swim, till he was chucked into the water off of the dam by Clacky Fisher and me," said the prisoner. "And this here water is a pile too deep and fast for Roddie to look good in it, your honor. Got anybody else?"

"I think that in the hall there is——"

"Gimme the gent in the hall," said the prisoner. "He looks good to me!"

The judge overlooked this sanguine carelessness and gravely asked that Counsellor Christian McDermott be asked to step into the court if he was in the adjoining hall.

"Good old Chris!" said young Mr. Destry. "He'll help me a lot!"

He turned toward Chester Bent, who sat on the

first bench among the spectators, and said aloud: "Chris is so nearsighted that he never seen a joke till he got double lenses, and then the first thing he laughed at was himself in a mirror!"

"Mr. Destry," said the judge quietly, "there are certain rules of decorum which must be observed in a courtroom. Here is Mr. McDermott. Counsellor, are you willing to undertake this case?"

Mr. McDermott was. He had really almost given up the practice of law, and spent his time pottering around forty acres of apple trees up the valley toward the mountains. His one real labor of the week was to scrub the food spots from his large expanse of vest on Sunday mornings so that he could go spotless to church at noon. But for the sake of dignity, he occasionally appeared at the court and picked up a small case here and there.

He now came in, looked over his glasses at the judge, under them at the prisoner, and through them at the faces in the crowd, to several individuals among which he nodded greetings. So the selection of the jury began.

It proceeded with amazing swiftness. The only objections were those made by the assistant district attorney, Terence Anson, who was usually called Doc, for no good reason at all. His peremptory challenges did not need to be used often. He objected to Clarence Olsen, because the latter was known to have been pulled out of the creek by Destry years ago, and therefore he might be presumed to have some prejudice in favor of the prisoner, and three other men, one of whom had taken shooting lessons from Destry, and two others had been partners in the cattle business and were helped by Destry in trailing down a band of rustlers who had run off a number of cows. Aside from these four, he also used several peremptory challenges, but none were made by McDermott. He turned in each instance, anxiously, toward his client, but every time Destry merely shrugged his shoulders.

"It ain't much use to try for anybody better," said Destry.

And in a brief half hour, twelve men were sitting in the jury box. There was this remarkable feature which they possessed in common—they were all old inhabitants of Wham, and had known the prisoner for years, and all of them looked toward him with a singular directness.

Mr. McDermott regarded them with anxiety.

"D'you know," he said to his client, "that just from a glance at their expressions, I'd say that not a one of them is particularly a friend of yours?"

"There ain't one of 'em," said Destry, "that wouldn't skin half his hide off if he could put me in jail for life. But that don't matter. In this here town, Chris, I got nothin' but enemies and friends. Less friends than enemies, though. And I wouldn't have it no other way. What good is a hoss to ride that don't have kinks to be took out of its back of a morning? I got the chance, Chris, of a grit stone in a mill race. But what's the difference? I been needin' a rest for a long time, and a chance to think! But let's see what they got agin me?"

He soon learned. The trial proceeded headlong, for the ways of the judge did not admit of great delays. First Terence Anson in a dry, barking voice—he was a man who was continually talking himself out of breath—and having coughing fits while he recovered it—touched not too lightly on the past of Destry, and announced that he was going to prove that Mr. Destry was a man likely to have committed this offense, capable of having committed it, and in need of the money which it would bring in to him. After probabilities, he was going to prove that Harrison Destry did in person stop the Express, hold up the messengers, take their weapons from them, and, passing on through the train, remove the valuables from the entire list of the passengers, escaping with their personal property and the contents of the mail!

Mr. McDermott, when he made his own opening address, was somewhat handicapped for lack of material. He could not very well disprove the known fact that Harrison Destry was a trouble maker and a fighter by taste, cultivation, and habit. But he launched into certain vague generalities which had obscure references to the rights of the individual and the uncertainty of circumstantial evidence, and sat down with his case as well ruined as it could have been by any given number of spoken words. So, puffing and snorting, he waited in his chair and observed the opening examinations of the witnesses.

They were very few.

The engineer of the train was called, and stated that the person who had held up the train had been about the size of the prisoner—or perhaps a little larger. And the voice of the robber had been very much like that of the prisoner, except that it was perhaps a little higher. The two guards who had protected the mail delivered similar testimony.

Then there was the evidence of the owner and bartender of the First Chance saloon to the effect that Mr. Destry had come into his place equipped with very little cash, had lost that, lost even his gun and spurs, and had gone on down the street stripped of available cash. Yet when he had been loaned more money by Mr. Bent, instead of spending it with some caution, he had thrown away the fresh supply with more recklessness than ever! What did this prove, if not that he was confident of a reserve supply of negotiable securities which he could realize upon so soon as he left the town? In fact, a package of those securities had been found in his pocket, and what else could be desired as proof that he was the man?

There was no testimony which the defense could offer against this damning array, except when young Charlotte testified that as a matter of fact, she had seen Bent give the prisoner a hundred dollars. And the inference to be drawn by a very imaginative jury might be that the package of securities had been placed in the pocket of the accused man by someone with malicious intent to shift the burden of the blame upon the shoulders of Destry and so draw a herring across his own trail.

The jury, however, did not appear to be particularly imaginative. It looked upon the prisoner with a cold eye, and retired with an ominous lack of gravity, talking to one another before they were out of the courtroom.

As for Destry himself, he had no doubt at all of what would happen.

"What'll he do, McDermott?" said he. "Will he run me up for ninety days, or will he string me a whole year, d'you think?"

McDermott shrugged his shoulders.

"First offenders usually receive mercy, in some form or another," he declared.

"A year would be the limit, wouldn't you say?"

McDermott grew red and scratched his head.

"Otherwise," said Destry, "I would have bashed

my way out of their fool jail and never have stood for the trial at all!"

He gripped the arm of his impromptu lawyer.

"They wouldn't soak me for any more than that?" he asked.

Said McDermott: "The verdict's in charge of the jury, and the penalty must be assessed by the judge. I can't alter the law in your behalf, young man. But," he went on, "if you'll tell me where you've put away the rest of the stolen money and other properties, and make a clean breast of the whole affair, no doubt the judge would reduce the sentence that he now has in contemplation."

"You fat-faced, long-eared jackass," said Destry mildly. "D'you think that I've done this job? Or, if I'd done it, d'you dream that I'd come back here to Wham to spend what I'd made? Wouldn't I barge away for Manhattan, where I could get rid of such stuff for a commission? Of course I would! McDermott, go out and ask for a new set of brains. You make me tired."

He turned his back on McDermott as the jury entered. It had been out for two and a half minutes. He rose at the order of the judge. He stood guarded on both sides, and he heard Philip Barker, the foreman of the twelve good men and true say the fatal word: "Guilty!"

Chapter Four

At this point, there was a sudden leaning forward of all within the courtroom. The spectators leaned forward. The twelve good men and true themselves leaned forward in their chairs and watched the face of the judge with a hungry interest. Granted that the prisoner was guilty, what now would be done to him?

It was impossible to guess how hard the judge would strike, for sometimes he was unaccountably severe, and sometimes he was bewilderingly merciful. His very first sentence, however, put all doubts at rest.

He said: "Harrison Destry, you have been found guilty by a jury of twelve of your peers, and it is now my duty to pronounce sentence upon you, not for a first offense, in my estimation, but for the culminating act of a life of violence, indolence, and worthlessness!"

Here a clear, strong young voice cried out: "It's not true! He ain't any of those things!"

The judge should have ordered the disturbing element ejected from the courtroom, but he merely lifted a placid hand toward Charlotte Dangerfield, who had so far exceeded the proprieties of the courtroom, and continued as follows:

"I believe that I am not alone in having followed the events of your career with a fascinated interest since the days of your boyhood, Harrison Destry. You were not very old before I noticed that it was a rare thing to see you on the street without blood on your hands or on your face! If I passed youngsters of your age with discolored eyes, puffed and bleeding mouths, and battered faces, I could take it for granted that Harrison Destry was not far away. And usually I saw you, lingering in the rear of the defeated enemy.

"Such things are not taken seriously in a boy of ten. The ability to fight, after all, is perhaps the most prized of all the talents of man. And if I were to pick out the one cardinal virtue to be desired in a son of mine, I should name courage first, but that is not all!

"What is still a virtue at ten becomes a nuisance at fifteen. And when your hands were stronger, and you struck harder, there were more serious tales about your petty wars in the town, and on the range, as you began to work out as a cow-puncher and find men there as hard as yourself. In the iron school of the range you were molded. There you found men older and stronger than yourself, and almost as fierce. Now and again we had word that Harrison Destry had been beaten horribly. But before the next year rolled around we were sure to learn that he had gone far out on the trail of his conqueror and found him—in Canada—in Mexico—and defeated the former victor.

"At the end of each serious encounter, you usually returned to Wham, in order, one might say, to bask in the admiration of your fellow citizens, and it did not occur to you that it was not unmixed admiration with which they looked upon you. To be sure, they respected your bravery and envied your power of hand and quickness of eye, but when a man begins to use mortal weapons, as you did so young, it becomes less a matter for admiration than for fear, less of envy than of horror.

"And, from that moment, there were voices which announced that Harrison Destry would before the end have taken a human life! Some would not believe it, but eventually belief was forced in upon us.

"They were not entirely reprehensible affairs. The criminal, the brutal, the wasted and vicious lives were those who crossed you, and were those who fell. All seemed fair fight. And yet the time came when men shrank before you, Harrison Destry. In one word, the message went out that you were a 'killer' and all that that ominous term implies. That is to say, one who takes life for the pleasure he gains by the taking! Many a man has begun in that way, keeping within the bounds of the law; few have continued so to the end! They overstep, and an innocent life is taken.

"However, there was another change in you. You began as an industrious boy; you ended as a man who scorned any tool other than a Bowie knife or a Colt's six-shooter. You gambled for a living and fought for amusement. Your visits to the town became an often repeated plague. You roistered in the saloons. You cast a shadow over a community which has never been too peaceful!

"Consider the picture of yourself as at last it was presented to us! The proud, active, hard working boy is changed into the lazy, careless, shiftless, indifferent and tigerish sluggard! Now at last you have discovered a means of making a short cut to a fortune on which you could live for some time. You have taken that short cut. You have violently laid your hands upon the moneys of other people. You have interfered with a mail train. You have robbed the mail itself. For these acts the jury, composed of twelve of your peers, has found you guilty, and I heartily agree with the verdict. Under the circumstances, nothing but intolerable prejudice in your favor could have induced a single man among them to return any other verdict than this one.

"It is now my duty to lay on you a sentence in accordance with the nature of your crime and of your character. And after duly considering all of these things, I have decided that you must be sentenced to ten years of penal confinement at hard labor, in the honest trust that during that time you may have an opportunity to reflect upon your past and prepare yourself for a different future.

"If you have any remarks to make to qualify this judgment, I am ready to hear them, particularly since your legal adviser was summoned at the last moment and has had no fitting opportunity to work on your case."

It seemed that Destry hesitated, and considered for a moment what he should say, if anything. At length he drawled:

"What might be the meaning of 'peer,' your honor?"

"The meaning of peer," said the judge, "is equal. It is a portion of the law, Destry, that an accused man shall not be tried by those who are socially not his equal. That may be held to hark back to other times, when some men were free, and others serfs."

"And serfs, what might they be?"

"A serf was a man attached to the soil, or, more properly speaking, a man subordinated and tied to some social regulation which limited his freedom. But, on the whole, you may say that a serf is a man who is not free."

"These gents," said the prisoner, "you've said a coupla times are my peers. Is that right?"

"I take it there is no man among them who is not your social equal, Destry. At least, they are all free men!"

"Are they?" said Destry.

He turned toward the jury and made a few paces forward, and the guard followed him on either side, anxiously.

"You dunno these here gents," said Destry. "I'll tell you. That one on the far left in the front row, that's Jimmy Clifton—that little narrer shouldered feller with the flower in his buttonhole, as though he was walkin' out on Sunday with his best girl. Free? He's tied up worse than a slave and the thing that he's tied to is the women, I tell you! He can't walk out without feelin' their eyes after him, and the reason that he hates me—look at it in his eyes!—is because a girl that he wanted once turned him down to dance with me. If I lie, Jimmy, you tell the judge!

"Next to him, there's Hank Cleeves. By the look of his face, you'd never think that he'd ever been a boy, but he was. To be on top of the heap is his game and his main idea, and he's a slave to that. He's a serf. He's no free man, I tell you! This here Cleeves, I once socked him on the nose, and sat him down flat and quick. He said 'enough' that day, and that's why he says guilty this day.

"There's Bud Williams, too, him with the thick neck and the little head, that come down here aimin' to become the champion wrestler of the whole world. But you can't fight and you can't wrestle with the strength of your hands, because it's the strength of your heart that tells in the long run! And after him and me had it out on the gravel at the edge of the road, and his face was rubbed raw in the stones, he started hatin' me, and he never stopped from that day to this. Serf? There never was a worse serf than him! He envies the mules on the road, because of their muscle. He'd turn himself into a steam engine, for the sake of havin' so many hoss power!

"Next to him, I want you to look at Sam Warren, with his long neck, and his long fingers that are square at their tips. Look at him, will you? He could take any gun apart in the dark, and jump the pieces together again without no light. He loved to figger that he had every man's life inside the curl of his forefinger. He felt free and grand so long as he thought that was true. But when him and me had a little tangle, and he was sliced through the leg with the first shot, he sure was fed up quick and lay down to think things over. Your honor, he's a serf to the gun that he packs, and that's draggin' down under his left armpit, right this minute!"

Sam Warren raised his narrow length from his chair, in such an attitude that it looked for a moment as though he would hurl himself out of the jury box and at the throat of the other. And the prisoner said calmly: "If it ain't so, call me a liar. You set that gun up and worship it. You never get it well out of your mind. You dream about it all night, and when you look at your best friend, you pick out the button on his coat that you'll shoot at!"

"Mr. Destry," said the judge, in his quiet way, "you've insulted enough of this jury, I think. Have you finished?"

"I'll finish quick," said Destry. "Only, I wanta finish up first with these twelve peers of mine, as you call 'em. I want you to look at Jerry Wendell, whose God is his tailor, and Clyde Orrin, the handshaker, and Lefty Turnbull that's always hated my heart since I broke his record from Wham to the Crystal Mountains, and there's Phil Barker, too! How many times did Phil raise hell with his practical jokes, until along comes a letter askin' him to call on a girl after dark, and he found the dogs waitin' for him instead of her? He ain't forgot that I wrote that letter to him, and he'd hang me up by the neck today, if his vote would do it! There's the Ogdens, too, that took money for my scalp and cornered me to get it; they lost their blood and their money, that day, and they want to see me holler now. Then there's Bud Truckman and Bull Hewitt. I dunno why they want to stick me, but maybe I've give them a dirty look, some time."

He turned back to the judge.

"Twelve peers?" said Destry. "Twelve half-bred pups. If peers is equals, I'd rather be tried by twelve bullfrogs in a marsh than by them twelve in that jury box! But let 'em set down and think this here over! When my ten years has come up, I'm gunna call on all of these here, and if they ain't in, I'm gunna leave my card, anyway!"

"Destry," said the judge drily, "you'd better finish, here."

The jury sat back, trying to look scornful, but obviously worried, in spite of themselves.

"Here's the last thing," said Destry. "What you've said is plumb true. I been a waster, a lazy loafer, a fighter, a no-good citizen, but what I'm gettin' the whip for now is a lie! I never robbed the Express!"

Chapter Five

Short speeches linger a long time in some memories; and the final speech of the prisoner remained in the mind of the townsfolk long after he was sent away to stripes and bars for ten years. There was one other detail of that day in the courtroom about which men and women and children talked, and that was how young Charlie Dangerfield slipped through the crowd and got to Destry as he was being led away toward the cell from which he would depart to the prison. There before the crowd she threw her arms around his neck.

"I believe in you, Harry!" she cried. "And I'll wait for you, too!"

Wham smiled when it heard this story, for Charlie Dangerfield was only sixteen, but as the years went by and it was noted that, though she would laugh and talk with any man, and dance with the first comer on Saturday nights, yet she discouraged all tokens of a serious interest; and when she grew up from pretty child to beautiful woman, and still preserved the integrity of the fence around her, then Wham scratched its chin and shook its head.

It respected her the more; the more worthless the man to whom a woman is devoted, the more she is admired and beloved by all other men. Their own self-esteem and their right to expect the affection of a wife is thereby, as it were, given a groundwork and an assurance.

More than this: The very girls of Wham, the unmarried ones, the green and hopeful virgins, found it possible to have an actual affection for beautiful

Charlie Dangerfield, since, no matter how attractive she might be, or how she dimmed their stars in passing, she was no more than a passing moon, and never interfered with their affairs. The established youth of Wham quickly learned to waste no hopes on Charlie; only the strangers who arrived, attracted by her face and her father's rapidly increasing fortune, flocked for a moment around the flame, singed their wings, and flew lamely away.

Therefore, when the news came to the town that Destry had been allowed to leave the prison, and that his ten years had been shortened to six by good behavior, the first thought of everyone was for Charlie Dangerfield. How would she take this second coming of her hero, now aged from the penitentiary?

Now, on computation, they figured that, if he was twenty-five when he was committed, he could only be thirty-one now. Old in shame, then, if not in actual years—a jail-bird, a refugee still from society. He who has been through the fire must bear the mark on his face!

On the evening of that same day, however, on which the news came to the town of Wham, there was a secret meeting to which came Jerry Wendell, and Clyde Orrin, and the Ogden brothers, and Cleeves, Sam Warren, Bull Hewitt and Bud Williams.

Sam Warren, being the most celebrated shot in the town, presided at the meeting, sitting at the head of the table and regulating the discussion. They talked frankly, as only those talk who are faced by a common danger.

The first suggestion was made by Jerry Wendell, who urged that they should hire a gunman for the work of clearing Mr. Destry permanently from the slate.

It was not waved aside, this murderous thought, but seriously taken in hand, and only after some moments of talk was it decided that it was probably foolish to kill a man who would soon have himself in jail again. Clyde Orrin summed up the verdict on this point.

"Prison never makes a gent better; it always makes him worse! He'll raise the devil before he's been in Wham a day, and the sheriff will be waiting for him with both hands full of irons!"

This being taken for granted, it was decided at once that all eight of them should leave the town of Wham for a little hunting excursion into the mountains. Before they returned, doubtless Destry would be again in the hands of the law!

This proposal hardly had been concluded before there was a rap at the door of the hotel room in which they were sitting, and Chester Bent walked in.

They looked on him without pleasure, but Chester Bent, leaning on the end of the table, a little out of breath, and hat still in hand, smiled on them all.

"My friends," said he, "I know you're surprised to see me here. I wasn't a member of the jury that called Destry guilty and sent him to prison. You know that I was his friend then, and am his friend now, and I suppose that he'll come to stay at my house when he returns. Now, I want to assure you all that I shall do my best to keep Destry from taking any steps that are too rash and bold. But I also want to say that I doubt my ability to keep him in order. I hope that you won't misconstrue what I have to say. I give you my word, I'm your friend, as well as his. I'm here to ask how I can serve you, because I take it for granted that you all realize that you will be in danger from the instant that Destry arrives this evening!"

This was putting the cards on the table with a vengeance, and the eight sitters at that table looked on Mr. Bent with a real enthusiasm, at once. He was a man worth attention in Wham, by this time. For one thing, he had increased his wealth at least six-fold in the time during which unlucky Destry had been in jail. Indeed, it was at about the same time that Destry was taken away that Wham received proof of the business talent of Bent by the amount of cash which he had on hand ready for investment; and, by placing it well in mines, in the buying of shares in a lumber company that operated in the Crystal range, and by picking up random bits of real estate here and there, Chester Bent had now established himself in a position which was hardly second to that occupied by any man in the town or the range around it. He had not piled up such a huge fortune as Benjamin Dangerfield, to be sure, nor as a few of the great cattle barons and the mining millionaires, but Chester Bent was rich, and he was among the few influential men who had to be called in for consultation whenever any important move was made by the controlling spirits of the community.

For all of these reasons, the eight men at the table listened greedily to all that he had to say. Destry, singlehanded, was bad enough, if he were even a ghost of his old self. Destry, backed by such a man as this, would be the equivalent of ruin to them all.

They told him with equal frankness that they had determined to withdraw from the town, and he received the suggestion with pleasure. He would send them word, he assured them, of the time when it was safe for them to return to Wham!

That afternoon they left; that evening, Chester Bent was walking up and down the platform of the station waiting for the westbound train. It drew up, stopped, and half a dozen passengers dismounted; baggage and mails were thrown off, train lanterns swung, and the long line of cars started away, the observation platform swaying out of sight at high speed around the next curve in another moment.

But no Harry Destry!

Then a hand fell lightly on the arm of Bent, a tentative and timid touch, and the young man turned and looked down into a face as sickly white as the belly of a frog.

It was Harry Destry at last, but Bent had to look at him twice before he could recognize the former gunman of Wham, the cynical, reckless warrior whose exploits had broken heads and glassware in every saloon up and down the main street of the town. He seemed both thinner and smaller, like one who has diminished from a great reputation of the past and grown down to a lesser size, a lesser fact.

Such was the Harry Destry who returned to Wham!

A strange gleam of joy appeared in the eye of Chester Bent, and it was not all the pleasure of welcoming home an old friend. Yet he wrung the hand of Destry with a feverish eagerness.

"You're coming home to live with me," said Bent. "I've fixed up a room for you——"

"I've got no claim on you, Chet," said the other. "I reckon I jus' better slide on out of the town and—"

"What are you talking about?" said Bent. "Look yonder—that phaeton under the pepper trees, yonder. There's Charlie Dangerfield waiting for you, man. She would have come up and met you; she wasn't afraid of doing that in front of everyone, y'understand?—but I thought it would be better if she met you quietly. You know how the papers pick up such things? Richest rancher's daughter greets return of ex-convict—you know what I mean, old fellow!"

He was half leading and half pressing his companion forward as he spoke. He had taken in his left hand the little satchel that contained the total possessions of Destry; his right was in the small of the convict's back, forcing him on. But here Destry paused.

"Rich?" said he. "Has Ben Dangerfield gone and got himself rich? Charlie never told me nothing about that in her letters!"

"I guess Charlie didn't want you to know what was waiting for you when you come home," said Bent, losing some of the polish of his higher school education in the excitement of the moment. "Because that's just what Ben Dangerfield has done nothin' else but do! He's gone and got himself to be the richest man on this range! The Dangerfield mine is so doggone rich that you could break a year's income for most men right off the lode and drop it into your pockets an' not weigh uncomfortable much when you walked home with it. Rich? They're made of money, now, and that means that you'll be made of money! Go ahead, there, and see Charlie, and kiss her. She's been waitin' six years for this minute, Harry!"

He paused when he was a few paces from the carriage, so as to let Destry have some privacy, but the instant that the support of his hand was withdrawn, it seemed as though the latter hardly could move forward. Slowly he drifted towards the phaeton; he stole his way along beneath the shadow of the thin branched pepper trees, through which the stars were gleaming. And, at the last, he stood fixed to the ground.

Charlotte Dangerfield was out of the carriage in a flash and had her arms around him.

"Harry, Harry, Harry!" she cried, her voice rising from a whisper to a moan. "What have they-all been doin' to you? What have they done to you, Harry?"

She kissed his white face, luminous in the shadows, and cold to the touch of her warm lips.

He did not stir in her arms, nor raise a hand to her.

"It's been six years of pretty much trouble, Charlotte," he told her.

And she thought that even his voice was changed, lowered to keep any other ear from hearing what he had to say.

At this, she fell into a bustle of activity, making plans, managing a good deal of excited laughter, as she turned him over to the hands of Chester Bent. He was to come out in the morning to the Dangerfield ranch; her father was wild to see him; in the meantime, he heeded a good night's sleep.

But before she left, Chester Bent had one opportunity to look into her eyes and see the horror there. It was no effort for Chester to be cheerful on the drive home to his house!

Chapter Six

He was anxious to have Destry under the steady light of a lamp when he got to the house, but it was not easy to get Destry into the light. In the dining room, he managed to turn his chair a little, apparently to give more attention to his host, but really so that he threw a shadow over his features, and with repeated and humble bowings of his head, he listened to all that Chester Bent had to say.

For his own part, Destry spoke little, and generally preluded every remark with an apology: "If you don't mind me sayin'"—or "Excuse me, Chet, but"—or "Of course what I say don't count—" And Chester Bent saw more and more literally how the heavy hand of the law had broken and hammered what had seemed such unmalleable metal.

They were in the library after dinner, that library which was the latest crown upon the life of Chester Bent, where dark ranges of volumes mounted in tier on tier toward the shadowy ceiling, where two or three large tomes generally could be seen opened face downward, as though the student had just been called from their perusal, and where the face of the desk was littered with papers, the token of the busy man. Enthroned against such a background, Chester Bent drew out his guest a little more, but it was difficult to go far. It was ten o'clock before the truth came out.

Destry wished to leave Wham!

There had once been a happy hunting ground for him in this village, but now he dreaded the familiar field. He sat with his head slightly canted to the side, listening to the booming chorus of the bull-frogs that saddened the marsh like the drone of bass viols. The longer he listened, the more uneasy Destry appeared.

"I've gotta go," he said to Bent. "I dunno why you should be so extra kind to me, Chet. But I couldn't stay here. I got piles of enemies in this here town!"

"You have friends, too, old timer!"

"I got friends. But friends, they don't catch bullets out of the air! They can't do that, Chet! I'm gunna go on. I wanta be a peaceful man; I don't want no trouble in the world, no more!"

He shivered as he said it, and Chester Bent had to glance slyly down to the floor to keep the flame of exultation in his eyes from being seen. Immediately afterward he allowed Destry to go to bed, but the big chamber which had been prepared for his accommodation was totally unsatisfactory to the new guest. In place of that, he preferred a little attic room, with one small window hardly a foot square.

He called the attention of Bent to it cautiously.

"What would you say, Chet? That a man could squirm through that in the middle of the night?"

"A man? Hardly a frog could get through there, a frog-sized frog, I mean to say!"

Destry sighed with relief, and went straightaway to bed; Bent returned to the library and there wrote the following letter to Jerry Wendell:

Dear Jerry,

Harry Destry is back, but so changed that you wouldn't know him! He has just gone to bed in an attic room, because it has a window so small that a man couldn't climb through it in the middle of the night.

His eyes are sunk in his head, and he has the look of a dog that's been over-disciplined. He's white and thin, and seems to have lost a few inches in height, which I suppose is simply another way of saying that he's not the man he used to be!

I don't think that you need be afraid of coming back to town, you and the rest; though perhaps you'd better send back a couple of the roughest of you to break the ground and make sure that he's really as harmless as he seems.

You can observe from this that I am trying to be your friend and a friend to all the rest, while I'm also trying to make poor Destry happy.

He hasn't said much about his prison life, but I gathered up a few references to dark cells, etc. I presume that he was pretty roughly handled at first, and it's broken his spirit.

I pity him from my heart, and so will you, when you see him.

> Yours cordially,
> CHET BENT.

He left the house to mail this letter at once, and, walking slowly home beneath the stars, he looked up to them and thought they burned more bright and beautiful on this night than ever before. When he opened the door of his house again, he stood for a moment staring into the dark, and conjuring up in it the picture of Charlie Dangerfield's lovely smile, and Ben Dangerfield's still more lovely millions! Then he went back to his library.

He curled up on the couch and went to sleep, but he kept the light burning, for it did well for the inhabitants of Wham, returning late at night, to see the lighted study windows of that rising young man. They then could tell one another that Chester Bent was a genius, but that genius was nine-tenths work! It increased their respect for him, but it diminished their envy!

It was after one before he put out the light, stumbled sleepily up the stairs to his room, and there fell at once into a profounder slumber, and into the arms of yet happier dreams.

In the morning, he took Destry out to see Benjamin Dangerfield. He walked with Charlie under the trees while Destry talked to his prospective father-in-law; all they heard of the interview was the loud voice of Ben Dangerfield exclaiming: "Whacha lookin' behind the doors for, Harry? Dust?"

Charlotte wanted to talk about Destry continually, but Bent dexterously shied at that subject and finally managed to keep it out of sight. In half an hour they heard Dangerfield shouting for them, and went back to find Destry standing with lowered head, tracing invisible patterns on the floor with the toe of his shoe. Bent heard the caught breath of Charlie, but even he dared not look at her.

Dangerfield himself was gritting his teeth, and he said in the presence of his daughter and Bent: "My daughter's old enough to run her own business. If she wants you, she'll take you, I reckon, and let her have you; it ain't no more affair of mine!"

Chester Bent did not need to look far back to a time when not even Dangerfield, no matter what his years or his millions, would have dared to speak in such a manner to Destry.

But that time was gone. He took Harry Destry back to the town, and the latter bit his lip continually, looking down into the heat haze that obscured the distant vistas of the roadway. Not one word passed between them until they came to the edge of the town, and there Destry asked to be let out, because he wished to saunter through Wham. His wish was obeyed, and Bent drove on back to his office.

All was well with him. He plunged into his affairs for that day, but as he worked, he dreamed, and his dreams were all of Charlotte Dangerfield.

A slice of gingerbread and a glass or two of milk made his lunch, so that he had not left his office since morning, when Charlotte herself came to see him late that afternoon, bursting impetuously into his office.

She had ridden at high speed all the way from the ranch. The flush of the gallop was high in her brown cheeks and the dust was in her hair as she stood before him, kneading the handle of her quirt in her gloved hands. But her eyes were desperate and sick, as they had been the night before at the station.

"I can't go on, Chet!" she told him. "I'm mighty miserable; I'm fair done up about it; but I can't go on after this day!"

He asked her what had happened.

"You don't know?" she cried. "The whole of Wham knows! Everybody's shrugging shoulders! Don't try to make me tell over again what's happened!"

He could guess; a prophetic foresight had told him everything when he let his companion out of the buggy that morning and drove softly on through the velvet dust of the main street; but he told her now that he had not left the office.

She had to take a turn up and down the room before she could speak again; and then she faced half away from him, looking out the window.

"He went into the Second Chance," she said,

speaking rapidly to get through the thing. "He asked for a lemon sour——"

"I'm glad he's stopped drinking, if that's what it means," said Bent.

She risked one glance at him over her shoulder.

"Oh, Chet," said she, "it means something else; you must know that it does, in spite of all this mighty fine loyalty of yours! Dud Cross came in. You know that wo'thless boy of Dikkon Cross? And Dud was full of redeye. He bumped against Harry, and when he saw who he'd nudged, he jumped half way across the barroom, they say. Then he saw that Harry didn't resent it; just stood there smilin', lookin' a little white and sick——"

She stopped here, but getting a fresher grip on her quirt she went on with a savage determination.

"That Dud Cross seemed to guess everything at one glance. He came back and—and damned Harry for running into *him!* Damned him! And—Harry—took it!"

She gasped in a breath.

"Dud Cross said he wasn't fit to drink with white men, real men, and told him to get out. And Harry went and—"

It was much even for Bent to hear, and he wiped his face with his handkerchief.

"Cross kicked him into the street. Kicked him! And Harry picked himself up and went home to your house. I suppose that he's there now! Chet, I want to do the right thing; but what *is* the right thing?"

It had come so swiftly that Bent could hardly believe in his good fortune, but he had sense enough not to appear to jump at the opening.

"I suppose I understand everything," he said

slowly. "It won't do, of course. You'll have to see him and tell him that it can't go on!"

"How can I see him and strike him in the face—a—a thing like that?"

"You don't have to see him. I think he knows, too. He expects it, surely, if he has any speck of manhood left in him. No, Charlie, you just sit down there at my desk and write him a letter. It will do perfectly. I'll tell you what. I'll take the letter along to him, and do any necessary explaining."

"Will you do that?" she asked.

She swung about and dropped her quirt and caught at his hands. "When I see what a noble way you have about you, Chet, standing by him, true to him—out of the whole town the only one that's standing by him, I feel pretty small and low. It's beautiful, the way you're acting! But oh, Chet, tell him very gentle and careful about how things stand. I wouldn't of let him down—only—only—he's *not* a man!"

Chapter Seven

Chester Bent took home this letter in the evening and gave it to Destry to puzzle out in the dusk of the library.

> Dear old Harry,
>   It just can't go on. I would have crossed the ocean for you, for the old Harry Destry, but I guess you can see that you've changed a good bit. I don't blame you. Six terrible years have gone by for you. You'll be your old self one day, after you've ridden on the range again for a while; and when you are, come back to see me. If you don't hate me too much, try to think of me as a friend. That's what I want to be, always.
>   CHARLIE DANGERFIELD.

Bent waited on the opposite side of the table.

"She didn't know what to do. She was afraid to see you, Harry. So she gave me this letter to take to you. I'm mighty sorry, because I can guess what it's all about!"

Destry, carefully thumbing the creases of the letter after refolding it, fell into a brown study, out of which he spoke, surprisingly, not of Charlotte Dangerfield at all. He merely said in a worried, depressed voice:

"The Ogden boys are in town, now, Chet. And I hear that Sam Warren and Clyde Orrin are back from the hills, too. You remember? They was all on the jury! They might think that I would do them some harm, and—and try to get at me first! Chet, I guess I better leave town!"

It was of course the wish which of all others lay closest to the heart of Bent; for now that the girl had broken with Destry, it was by all means best to get him away from the range of her impulsive pity, which might undo all that already had been accomplished.

"Perhaps you're right," said Bent. "Perhaps Wham is a bit dangerous for you. You know in the old days your gun was fitted into a mighty loose holster, Harry, and people don't forget that. You'd better go; I'll handle all the financing. I tell you what, old fellow, I'm not going to let you down, no matter what the rest of the world may do and say!"

He was not even thanked! Destry, as one stunned, fumbled still with his thoughts.

"Somebody said that more of them were coming back. I mean, Bud Williams, and Jerry Wendell. Eight of them, all together. Eight that used to be on the jury that sent me away to prison!"

"It might be a bad climate for you here," admitted Bent again. "Look here, old son. Leave right now, if you want. I have a bang-up good horse in my stable this moment. I'll fix you up with a pack, and you can be out and away—with a full wallet, mind you—and fifty miles over the hills before the day breaks!"

At this, Destry groaned aloud.

"Oh, Chet," he said, "what'd I be doin' outside in the open, where so many of 'em could be followin' me? What would I be doin' away in the hills, I'd ask you? They can read trail. They'd run me down. I'd be alone! Oh, God! Think of ridin' the hills and seein' the same buzzards circlin' in the sky that'll eat the eyes out of your head, before long!"

Even Chester Bent was a little aroused with pity.

He said sharply: "What in hell did they do to you in the penitentiary, man?"

"I'd rather not to talk!" said he, and Bent wisely did not press him to speak, for he felt that a hysterical outburst was close at hand.

In his own room, he scratched another note to dapper Jerry Wendell.

> Destry is badly broken up, and shaken. You fellows will handle him with gloves, I'm sure. He's helpless and harmless, and you'd pity him if you saw him. Charlie Dangerfield has broken her engagement with him—that's a secret that you're sure to find out by tomorrow—and he hasn't the spirit even to regret the loss of her! He can only think about his personal danger from you and the rest of the boys who served on the jury. I think it may be months before he becomes his old self again!
>
> CHET.

He added that last line after much deliberation, for it woud not fit in with his plans to allow Destry to be considered permanently harmless. Harmless he never could be, in the eye of Bent. Not that the latter feared that Destry ever could become his old self, but because he once had read that women truly love once, and once only, and the line had sunk into his heart. At this moment, Bent felt that he was closer than ever to Charlie Dangerfield, simply because she admired the manner in which he stood by the fallen man. If his dream was realized, and she became his wife, what would happen in her heart of hearts if she again met a partially recovered Destry on some future day? The mind of Bent was logical and sure. There must be no future for his guest!

He sent a house mozo to carry the message; then

he went down to find Destry and take him to the dinner table.

Destry was not there. He had gone out, Bent was told, to take a little air; but he was not in the back garden, nor in the front.

He had gone into the town, perhaps, tormented by fear, tormented even more by the fascination of lights under which other men were drinking and enjoying themselves. No doubt he wanted to see careless faces, and therein strive to forget his mental burden!

Whatever the reason, Harry Destry had gone down the main street, avoiding the lighted places, slipping from one dark side of the way to the other, until he came to the region of the saloons, and into the Last Chance he started to make his way when fate, which works with a cruel insistence in our lives, placed Dud Cross once more in his path, for Dud came reeling out as Destry approached the swinging door.

"The yaller dog's out and around agin!" shouted Cross. "Get back home and ask your boss to tie you up! Or you're likely to get et up here in Wham!"

He acted as he spoke. The wide-swinging palm of his hand cracked against the cheek of Destry and sent him staggering back against a hitching post. There he leaned, one side of his white face turning crimson, his eyes staring vacantly at his persecutor, and drunken Dud Cross lurched forward to rout his victim.

It was only luck that brought the sheriff there. Ding Slater stepped before Cross and pointed a forefinger like a gun in the face of the bully.

"You get yourse'f home!" said he, and Dud Cross disappeared like a bubble into the night.

The sheriff turned back to Destry with compassion and disgust equally troubling him.

"Harry," he said, "don't you go bein' a fool and

showin' your face around the streets. You take my advice. You better go home. You hear me?"

"Yeah," said Destry faintly. "Yeah, I hear you."

And he looked into the face of the sheriff with eyes so blank, so wide, so helpless, that Ding Slater could not endure the weight of them. He turned without pressing his point and hurried down the street damning impartially the stars in the sky and the penal system of that sovereign state.

Destry, as one drawn by powers beyond him, slowly went forward, pushed open the doors of the saloon, and entered.

It was a busy evening. A dozen men were lined up at the bar, and there was a gleam of eyes, a flash of faces as they looked toward the door and the newcomer. Then all backs became rigid and were turned squarely upon him!

He did not seem to understand but, taking his place at the farthest end of the long bar, he half cowered against the wall, ordered a drink, and then forgot to taste it, but looked aimlessly into nothing, while the subdued talk along the bar was picked up again, and carried on in its former tone.

Half of those men had drunk and roistered with him in the old days; their pity and their self-respect kept them from noticing the fallen hero now. Religiously their eyes dodged when they chanced to fall upon the face of Destry in the midst of laughter or in the midst of narrative.

The gay minutes went on; but shortly a pair of them departed. And then another pair, and another. There were other places to drink in Wham, where the depressing influence of Destry would not be felt, and the horror to which a brave man could descend be witnessed!

The bartender was not a callous man, but he was naturally irritated when he saw an evening fairly blasted before it had begun to blossom. He took the first occasion to say behind his hand to Destry: "You better finish your drink and move on!"

"Sure," said Destry, and looked at him with the same humble, but uncomprehending stare.

A man at the far end of the bar growled to the saloon keeper: "Leave him be, will you? He ain't right in the head!"

"He makes me sick," said the bartender, with more ferocity than he felt, and took three fingers for himself, and paid for it with a vicious punch at the cash register. However, the big man at the farther end resolutely moved down beside Destry and found himself at once embarked in conversation.

"I hear that Wendell's in town?" said Destry. "Where might he be livin', now?"

"Down two blocks, in the big house with the fir hedge in front."

"Yeah? Orrin's place is just opposite, ain't it?"

"No. Orrin's moved. He's down by the river, just left of the bridge. Cleeves has the opposite house."

"Yeah? Cleeves was a great pal of Williams."

"They used to be thick."

"Is Williams in town, too? Still here?"

"Still here. He's got a room in the Darlington Hotel where——"

He paused with his glass at his lips.

Destry turned to follow the direction of his companion's glance, and he saw just passing through the swinging door as dark a picture as he could have wished to see. For the Ogden brothers were at that moment kicking the door wide and stalking into the place, and the object on which their eyes fell and stayed was the face of Destry himself.

Some things are obvious as day. When the moose is bogged down in snow, and the wolves sit in a circle with red, lolling tongues, it does not need a prophet to tell that they will soon eat red meat. And it was perfectly apparent from the solemn entrance of the Ogden brothers that they had come for Destry and meant to have his life!

Chapter Eight

After that first glance, they paid no heed to Destry, but strode to the bar and ordered whiskey, and Destry remained in the corner, silent, looking at his dreams with open, empty eyes. The bartender, who had been through many phases of this mortal coil, observed him with the eye of a physician who sees symptoms of a fatal disease, against the progress of which there is no remedy. There were still five men in the room, and these drew back from the bar, not hastily, but by slow degrees, conversing with one another, as though their business required greater privacy than could be found under the bright light of the two kerosene lamps which flooded the bar and its vicinity.

Out of the chatter of conversation which had preceded the entry of the Ogden brothers, an approximate silence fell upon the room, as when, before a prizefight, the voices of the spectators are gradually hushed, and there remains a dead moment in which even the most casual murmur is audible, surprisingly, over several rows and the speakers grow embarrassed and glance about in the hope that no one has overheard their profanity.

So it was now in the barroom after the Ogden brothers had come in. They were two of a kind. That kind originates somewhere in the middle West, instantly understood by all who have been in that region, and understood by no others.

They were tall, but they were not awkwardly built. Their shoulders were broad, but their chests were not shallow. They stood straight, and their heads were high, and yet there was a trail of the eternal slime upon them. It appeared in their greasy complexions, their overbright eyes, wrinkled too much at the corners, as though by continual laughter, though the practiced observer knew that laughter had nothing to do with those lines. They had a way of smiling secretly, one to the other, conscious of a jest which was not apparent to the rest of the world, and they fortified themselves with this laughter; for laughter is a two-edged sword, and all of those who do not understand it are bound in the course of nature to be ill at ease.

At this very moment, they were smiling sourly at each other as they raised their glasses. They did not pledge the bartender with the accustomed nod and tilt of the glass; they did not turn the usual good-natured grin towards the others at the bar, but, instead, they raised their liquor swiftly, and swiftly they disposed of it. Then they put down the glasses with a clink upon the varnished wood of the bar and considered the thing that was before them.

They had come to kill Harrison Destry. That much was plain to themselves and to all observers; but they needed a bridge by which to pass from the commonplace to the greatly desired event. It would hardly do to turn on their heels and lay the new born coward dead!

With secrecy, with some shame, with great embarrassment, indeed, they looked slyly at each other and considered the means by which they would approach this fatal climax of the evening's work.

And still Destry gave them no excuse, no finger's hold, no faintest sham of a pretense to attack him. He stood with the same considerate gaze steadily upon vacancy, and spoke not a word, invited no comment, asked for no opinion. At last he said, timidly: "I'll take another."

The bartender noted with a real amaze that the glass of Destry was empty. He spun out the bottle, and when Destry had poured a moderate measure, the saloon keeper filled a glass for himself to the brim, for once more he needed a stimulant.

There was no conversation at all. One man had slipped noiselessly through the swinging door; the remainder stayed for the obvious purpose of seeing the killing of Harry Destry. Not that he was important now, but that he once had been a man of note.

Suddenly Jud Ogden said: "Destry?"

The latter raised his head with a faint smile.

"Yes?" he said.

No one could see his face, at that moment, except the bartender, and he underwent a strange convulsion that caused the liquor to tilt in his raised glass and to spill upon the floor half of the contents. Still under the influence of the same shock, whatever it could have been, he replaced his glass upon the bar, then changed his mind and tossed off the contents with a single gesture.

He coughed hard, but he did not take a chaser. With both hands gripping the edge of the bar, he remained frozen in place, looking not at the Ogden brothers, but at Destry, as though from him the important act was now to come.

"Destry," said Clarence Ogden, taking up the speech where his brother had left off, "they was a time when you done us wrong, you—Destry!"

"I done you wrong?" said Destry, as contemplative as ever. "*I* done you wrong?"

"You done us wrong," broke in Jud Ogden brutally. Silence once more fell over the barroom, and the spectators, secure within their shadow, looked at one another, knowing that the time had almost come.

"Well," said Destry, "I'd be powerful sorry to think that I'd made anybody in this town unhappy! I'd sure hate to think of that!"

He turned from the bar as he spoke, a shrill laughter forced and unconvinced, breaking from his lips.

The bystanders winced, and their lips curled. As for the Ogdens, they looked secretly at each other, as much as to say that they had expected this. Then Clarence Ogden turned bodily upon Destry.

"You lousy rat!" he said.

But Destry did nothing, neither did he stir a hand!

"That's a hard name," he said.

But, as he spoke, it became suddenly apparent to all who listened that he was not afraid! He, the coward, the nameless thing, turned a little from the bar so that he faced the Ogdens, and as he spoke, his voice was like a caress.

"That's a hard name," said Destry.

And his voice was unafraid!

It was as though a masked battery had broken out from a screen of shrubbery. The greasy faces of the Ogdens lost color; the spectators by instinct drew closer together, shoulder to shoulder, and stood wedged in a row.

And Destry went on: "What for d'you call me that, boys?"

The Ogdens in their turn were silenced.

They had come expecting to find a wild cat whose teeth and claws were drawn. It appeared that beyond all belief they might be wrong!

"I hear a mighty bad word from the pair of you," said Destry. "It sure hurts my feelings. Here I come in, askin' for a little quiet drink, and along comes the

Ogdens. Brave men. Big men. Pretty well known. They call me a yaller skunk, as you might say, for why?"

He smiled at the pair, and the pair did not smile back.

"It ain't possible," said Destry, continuing in the same subdued manner, "that you come here lookin' for a whipped pup and found a real dog in his place?"

His smile grew broader, and as he smiled, it appeared that the stature of Destry grew taller, that his chest expanded, his eye grew brighter.

"It ain't possible," said he, "that the Ogdens are gunna prove themselves to be a pair of mangy rats that wouldn't live up to what they said?"

He made a single light step toward them, and they drew back instinctively before him.

"It ain't possible that they're a pair of lousy fakers," said Destry. "It ain't possible," he added, in a louder tone, "that they're walkin' up and down the town in the attitude of great men and great killers without the heart to back up what they wanta seem to be?"

Fear? In this man?

The white face was lighted; the nostrils flared; the eyes of Destry gleamed with fire, and the audience shrank closer against the wall. If there was sympathy now, it was not for the one man but for the pair.

So action hung suspended until Clarence Ogden yelled, with a voice like that of a screeching old woman: "I'll take you, you——"

He yanked at his gun as he cried; he was dead in the middle of a curse; for out of the flap of his coat Destry had drawn a revolver, long barreled, gleaming blue; a fire spat from its mouth.

Clarence Ogden made a blundering step forward.

"I'd—" he began in a subdued tone, as though about to make an explanation, then sank slowly to the floor, a lifeless heap.

No one noticed his word at the end. His brother had reached for a weapon at the same instant, and fired. Only by a breath was he too late. By less time than it takes for an eye to wink, the second shot of Destry beat the bullet from his own weapon, and Jud Ogden spun in a circle and fell with a crash against the wall. Still he struggled to regain the weapon which he had let drop, sprawling forward like a frog on dry land.

Destry struck him across the head with the barrel of his Colt and leaned above him. Jud lay still. His great hand was fixed on the floor, seeming to grip at it as though anxious to rip up a board and reveal a secret. But all his powerful body lay helpless and unnerved upon the floor.

Destry stood up above his victim.

He said to the gaping row of witnesses along the wall: "I guess you boys all seen that I couldn't do anything to stop this here. I was tolerable helpless. They jus' nacherally insisted on havin' my scalp, as you might say! Terrible sorry!"

He stepped to the end man of the row, nearest to the door.

"Wendell, Jerry Wendell, you know him?"

"Yes," gasped the man.

"Where does he live? Tell me that! I've heard before, and forgot!"

He was told in a stammer, and started for the door.

When he reached it, he turned again toward the others and surveyed the two motionless forms upon the floor; and he laughed! Never to their death day would they forget the sound of that laughter. Then Destry was gone into the night.

It was the bartender who roused himself before any of the others, and running to the telephone, which stood at the end of the bar, he jerked off the receiver.

"One—nine—eight, quick, for God's sake!"

No man stirred among the frozen audience.

Then, finally the saloon keeper was crying:

"Is that you, Wendell? This is the Last Chance Saloon. You hear? The Ogden boys both jumped Destry in my place. They're both dead, I think, or dying! He's started for your house! Get out of town! Get out of town! He's been shammin'. It ain't the old Destry that's back here with us, but a devil that's ten times worse! Wendell, get yourself out of town!"

Chapter Nine

There was one habit of industry which Benjamin Dangerfield had clung to all his life, and that was rising at an early hour. To him the entire day was sick unless he saw the night turn gray and the pink of the dawn begin to blossom in the east. It was still not sun-up when he sat at his breakfast table with his daughter.

"I ain't showed you my new coat," said he, and rose and turned before her, a piece of ham poised at his lips on the end of a fork. "How does it look?"

"Mighty grand," said Charlotte. "Down to the knees you look pretty near as fine as a gambler."

For he had on common blue jeans beneath the coat, and the overall legs were stuffed into heavy riding boots, which never had seen a touch of polish or of other care than a liberal greasing in the winter of the year.

Mr. Dangerfield sat down again.

"How I look below the table don't matter; what I look above it is the thing that counts."

He patted his necktie as he spoke and brushed his moustache with his finger tips, sensitively.

"Sure," said the girl. "Anything that's comfortable is right, I guess. The dogs under the table wouldn't be comfortable if they had to go sashayin' around among broadcloth trousers. Neither would the cats."

"Suppose," said the father, "that you wanted to go and set on the corral fence and look at a hoss— would fancy trousers be any good for that?"

"They wouldn't," she answered. "They's just get all full of splinters."

"Or suppose that you got tired of walkin' and wanted to rest, would you go and set down on the ground in fancy pants?"

"No, sir, you most certainly wouldn't."

"Which you're laughin' at me the same," said he. "Speakin' of dogs, where's that brindle hound? I ain't seen him yet this mornin'."

"He's on the foot of your bed, most like," she answered. "You must of throwed the covers over him when you got up."

"I reckon I did," said he. "Mose, go upstairs and see if you can find me that wo'thless Major dog, will you?"

Mose disappeared.

"You look fair to middlin' miserable," observed Mr. Dangerfield. "Help yourself to some of that corn bread and pass it to me. It's cold! I'm gunna kill me a nigger out yonder in the kitchen, one of these days, if you don't bring 'em to time pretty quick!"

"How can I bring 'em to time?" asked the girl. "I've fired that good-for-nothin' Elijah six times, and you always take him back again!"

"In this family," said Dangerfield, "niggers ain't fired, I thank God!"

"Then don't you raise a ruction because you got indigestion. You can thank God for that, too!"

"It ain't the men in the kitchen, it's the women there that makes the trouble. I've fired that useless Maria, too," declared Charlotte, "but bless my soul if she don't start howlin' like a dog at the moon. Last time, she set outside my door three hours and give me nightmares with her carryin's on."

"You oughta cut down their pay," said Dangerfield. "I never seen anything like the way you throw money away on them niggers, the wo'thless good-for-nothin's!"

"Why, how you carry on!" said his daughter. "What diff'ence does it make to them, the money? Didn't they all keep on workin' all them years when they didn't get nothin' at all for pay?"

"Money is no good for niggers," said Dangerfield. "Money and votes ain't no good for them. Pass me some of that fish. They ain't hardly a thing on this table fit to pass a man's lips!"

"You've got a sight particular," said she, "since you've blundered into a few pennies; I seen the day many a time when we was glad to have just the corn bread on the breakfast table, without no eggs, nor ham, nor fish, nor milk, nor coffee neither."

"It ain't true!" said the father. "They never was a time, even when my fortune ebbed its lowest, when I didn't have coffee on my table."

"Yeah," drawled Charlotte. "But it was second and third boilin' most of the time, and I had to fla-vor it up with molasses to make it taste like something at all!"

"You gotta disposition," said her father, "like a handful of tacks. You got the nacheral sweetness of a tangle of barbed wire, Charlie. I ain't gunna talk to you no more this mornin'."

"Which I never asked you to," said she.

"Why don't you run along and leave me to finish my breakfast, then?"

"Because then I wouldn't have nothin' but niggers to bother," she replied, her chin in her hand.

"Charlie, if you're gunna be so downhearted about it, why don't you go and take him back, then?"

"There ain't anything to take back," said she. "He's only a handful of bubbles."

"Then why for are you sorrowin' so much?" he asked.

"Because I've lost my man," she said, "and only his ghost come back."

"You'll get yourself fixed up with another right now," said he. "You ain't never had no trouble collectin' young nuisances around you. That tribe of young boys has et up a drove of hogs for me, and a herd of cattle, and a trainload of apples and such; they've drunk enough of my whiskey to irrigate a thousand acres of corn; and all because you're close onto half as good lookin' as your mother used to be, Charlie."

"Thanks," said she. "You wanta see me tied up in one of these love-me-little-love-me-long marriages. But the fact is that I ain't gunna marry, never."

"If you ain't gunna get yourself a husband," said he, "you might get yourself some grammar; which a man would think that you never been to school, to listen at you talk!"

"I only dress up my talk once a week," said she, "and the rest of the time I'd rather go around comfortable and let the pronunciation take care of itself. What difference does it make to an adjective if it's used for an adverb? It don't give the word no pain; it's easier for me; the niggers understand me better, and everybody's happy all around."

"I've seen young Chester Bent look kind of odd at some of your language, though," observed Dangerfield.

"Young Chester Bent," she mocked, "wouldn't mind the language of a red Comanche if she had the Dangerfield money."

"There you go," said he, "puttin' low motives into high minds! That boy is all right!"

"Yeah?" she queried. "Who's that comin' across the field?"

"I don't care who it is," said her father. "What I want to say is that Chester Bent is about the best——"

"It's somebody tryin' to catch something or tryin' to keep from bein' caught,' said Charlotte.

Her father leaned to look through a gap in the trees that surrounded the ranchhouse, and he saw across the hill a rider flogging forward a horse so tired that its head bobbed like a cork in rough water.

"He's lookin' back," remarked the girl, "and the fact is that he's scared pretty bad. He's comin' here like a gopher scootin' for a hole in the ground."

"Who is it?" asked Dangerfield.

"Some boy from town," she replied, "because no puncher that's worth his salt ever rode so slantin' as that."

"Which Harrison Destry sure could fork a boss," remarked her father.

The rider disappeared behind the trees, but almost immediately afterward an excited negress appeared at the kitchen door saying: "They's a young gent here that wants powerful to see you, Colonel Dangerfield!"

It was the family title for him; it was a title that was spreading abroad, now that he was able to lend money instead of "borrowing" it.

He had no chance to invite the stranger to enter and share the hospitality of his house, for the man that instant appeared, shouldering past the fat cook. He was very dusty. Dust was thick in the wrinkles of his sleeve and on his shoulders. His hat was off, and his hair blown into a rat's nest; he walked with a stagger of exhaustion; his face was drawn, and his eyes sunken. Yet it was a handsome face; some said he was the finest looking fellow on the entire range, for it was Jerry Wendell.

He fell into a chair, gasping: "Lock the doors, Colonel! He's not three jumps behind me! He means murder! He's killed two men already, this night. He's hounded me across the hills. I've gone a complete circle around Wham, and he's been after me every minute!"

"Lock the doors and the windows, Charlie," said the Colonel with composure. "Hand me that riot gun, too. I loaded it fresh with buckshot yesterday. How many of them is there, Jerry, and who are they, and what the devil do they mean by chasing you right onto my ranch? There ain't anything to be afraid of. My niggers will fight for me. How many are there, though? Charlie, give the alarm—"

"There's only one," said Jerry Wendell. "*Only* one, but he's the devil. I'm not ashamed of running! You know who it is! You must have heard!"

"Nothing!"

"It's Harry Destry running amok!"

The riot gun crashed to the floor from the hands of the girl.

Jerry Wendell, his eyes rolling wildly at the windows, was crowding himself back into the most obscure corner of the room, as he continued, his voice shaking as violently as his body:

"It was all a sham! You see? Pretending to be afraid! Oh, what fools we were to think that Destry ever could be afraid of anything! He wanted to trap us all—every man that sat on that jury—oh God, how I wish I never had seen that courtroom or listened to that judge! He'll kill the judge. I hope he kills the judge."

"Straighten up," said Dangerfield slowly. "I've

seen Destry actin' like a yellow hound dog with his sneakin' tail between its legs, and you tell me that he's runnin' wild?"

"That's it! He waited till all of us were back in town. Then he trapped the Ogdens in the Last Chance. He—he—killed them both. He killed them both!"

Dangerfield stepped closer to him.

"Murder?" he asked.

"Murder? What else? What else?" screamed Jerry Wendell. "What else is it when a killer like him starts after an ordinary man, like me? Murder, murder, I tell you! And he'll never stop till he's got me here and slaughtered me under your eyes in your own house!"

Chapter Ten

Shame, after all, is a human invention; the animals know no touch of it. The elephant feels no shame when it flees from the mouse, and the lion runs from the rhinoceros without a twinge of conscience, for shame was unknown until man created it out of the whole cloth of his desire to be godlike, though the gods themselves were divorced from such small scruples on sunny Olympus. Poor Jerry Wendell in his paroxysm quite forgot the thing that he should be; fifty thousand years of inherited dignity were shaken out of him and he acted as a caveman might have done if a bear were tearing down the barricade at the mouth of the dwelling, and the points of all the spears inside were broken.

Every moment he was starting, his pupils distending as he looked at the doors or the windows. He was oblivious of the scorn of the Dangerfields, which they were covering as well as they could under an air of kind concern.

"Have you got a man at that door?" asked Jerry. "And that?"

"Yes."

"And that?"

"That leads down into the cellar. He won't try to come that way."

"No matter what you do, he'll be here!" said Wendell, wringing his hands. "*I* thought I could stop him, too. I had the message from the saloon in time; I had three good men posted; I was telephoning across the way for more help, and then I heard a step on the stairs—a step on the stairs———"

The memory strangled him.

"I ran for the back steps and jumped down 'em. I locked the kitchen door as I went out. I tore across the garden and vaulted the street fence, and as I jumped, I looked back and saw a shadow slide through the kitchen window.

"Then I found a horse on the street. I didn't stop to ask whose it was. I jumped into the saddle, thanking God, and started for the lights in the middle of the town.

"But he gained on me. I had to cut down a side alley. He was hard after me on a runt of a mustang.

"I got out of the town. Luckily my horse would jump. I put it over fences and got into fields. There was no sight of him behind me then, and at last I decided to circle back into Wham.

"Then I saw him again, coming over a hill—just a glance of the outline of him against the stars—and he's been on my heels ever since—ever since! He'll——"

"Sit down to breakfast," urged Dangerfield. "The corn bread's still warm. You look—hungry!"

"Breakfast?" said the other. And he laughed hysterically. "Breakfast!" he repeated. "At a time like this! Well, why not?"

He allowed himself to be put into a chair, but his hands shook horribly when he tried to eat. His soul and nerves were in as great disarray as his clothes; his hair stood wildly on end; his necktie was jerked about beneath one ear; in a word, no one would have taken him for that Handsome Jerry who had broken hearts in Wham for many a day.

He spilled half his coffee on his coat and on the tablecloth, but the rest he managed to get down his throat, and his eye became a little less wild. Instantly the buried conscience came to life again. He clutched at his tie and straightened it; he made a pass at his hair, and then noticed for the first time the downward glance of the girl.

He could read in that many a thing which had been scourged out of his frightened brain all during his flight. Ostracism, ridicule would follow him to the ends of his days, unless he actually met Harrison Destry, gun in hand. And that he knew that he dared not do. The cruel cowpunchers and the wags of the town would never be at the end of this tale; they would tell of the mad ride of Jerry Wendell to the end of time!

He said, faltering as he spoke: "I would have stopped and faced him, but what chance would I have against that jailbird? And why should a law-abiding man dirty his hands with such a fellow? It's the sheriff's duty to take charge of such people. Ought to keep an eye on them. I said at the time, I always said that Destry was only shamming. He drew us all back, and then he clicked the trap! He clicked the trap! And——"

Here he was interrupted by another voice inside the room, saying: "Hullo, Colonel! Morning, Charlie. I was afraid that I'd be too late for breakfast, but I'm glad to see that they's still some steam comin' out of that corn bread. Can I sit down with you-all?"

It was Destry, coming towards them with a smile from the cellar door, which he had opened and shut behind him silently before saying a word.

The three reacted very differently to this entrance. The Colonel caught up the sawed-off shotgun that had been brought to him; his daughter started up from her chair, and then instantly steadied herself; while Jerry Wendell was frozen in his place. He could not even face about toward the danger behind him, but remained fixed shivering violently.

Charlotte Dangerfield was the first to find her voice, saying with a good deal of calmness:

"Sit down over here. I'll get in some eggs and some hot ham. I guess the coffee's still warm enough."

"Thanks," said Destry. "Don't you go puttin' yourself out. I been trying to get up with Jerry, here, and give him a watch that he dropped along the road. But he's been schoolin' his hoss across country so mighty fast that I couldn't catch him. How are you, Jerry?"

He laid the watch on the table in front of the other, and Jerry accepted it with a stir of lips which brought forth no sound. Destry sat down opposite him. The host and hostess were likewise in place in a cold silence, which Destry presently filled by saying: "You remember how the water used to flood in the cellar when a rainy winter come along? I had an idea about fixin' of that, Colonel, so I stopped in and looked at the cellar on the way in, but they wasn't quite enough light this early in the day to see anything. You didn't mind me comin' up from the cellar door that way?"

Dangerfield swore softly, beneath his breath.

"You're gunna come to a bad end, boy," he said. "You leave your talkin' be, and eat your breakfast. Why you been gallivantin' around the hills all night?"

"Why," said Destry, "you take a mighty fine gold watch like that, and I guess a man wouldn't like to think that he'd lost it, but the harder I tried to catch up with Jerry, there, the harder he rode away from me. He must of thought that he was havin' a race with big stakes up, but I'm mighty sure that I didn't have money on my mind!"

His smile faded a little as he spoke, and there was a glint in his eyes which turned Jerry Wendell from the crimson of sudden shame, to blanched white.

"What you-all been doin' this while I been away?" Destry asked politely of Wendell.

"Me?" said Wendell. "Why, nothing much. The same things."

"Ah?" said Destry. "You alluz found Wham a pretty interestin' sort of a town. I was kind of surprised when I heard that you was gunna leave it."

"Leave it?" asked Wendell, blank with surprise. "Leave Wham? What would I do, leaving Wham?"

"That's what I said to myself, when I heard it," said Destry gently. "Here you are, with a house, and a business, and money in the mines and in lumber. Jiminy! How could Jerry leave Wham where everybody knows him, and he knows everybody? But him that told me said he reckoned you got tired of a lot of things in Wham, like all the dances that you gotta go to, and the dust from the street in summer blowin' plumb into your office, and all such!"

Wendell, confident that something was hidden behind this casual conversation, said not a word, but moistened his purplish lips and never budged his eyes from the terrible right hand of the gunman.

"Him that told me," went on Destry, "said that you'd got so you preferred a quiet life. Here where everybody knows you, you're always bein' called upon for something or other. They work you even on juries, he says, and that's enough to make any man hot."

Wendell shrank lower in his chair, but Destry, buttering a large slice of corn bread, did not appear to see. He put away at least half the slice and talked with some difficulty around the edge of the mouthful.

"Because them that work on a jury," he explained to his own satisfaction, "they gotta decide a case on the up and up and not let any of their own feelin' take control. Take a gent like you, you'd have an opinion about pretty nigh everybody in town even before the trial come off. And you might make a mistake!"

"There's twelve men on a jury!" said Jerry Wendell hoarsely.

"Sure there is," nodded Destry. "You seem to know all about juries—numbers and everything! There's twelve men, but any single one of 'em is able to hang the rest! One man could stop a decision from comin' through!"

Wendell pushed back his chair a little. He was incapable, at the moment, of retorting to the subtle tortures of Destry.

At last he said:

"I'd better be goin' back."

"To Wham?"

"Yes, of course."

"Well," said Destry, "that's up to you. Go ahead. I think they might be somebody waiting for you along the road, though. But a gent of your kind, old feller, he wouldn't pay no attention to such things."

Wendell stood up.

"I'm leaving now," he replied, with a question and an appeal in his voice that made the girl look up at him as at a new man.

"Good trip to you," said Destry.

"But first I'd like to see you alone, for a minute."

"Don't you do it," said Destry. "I know just what it must be like to cut loose from an old home, the way that Wham has been to you. Well, good luck to you!"

"I'll never come back," said the other, unnerved at the prospect.

"Likely you won't—till the talk dies down a mite."

"Destry!" shouted the tormented man suddenly. "Will you tell me why you've grounds to hate me the way that you do?"

"No hate, old fellow. No hate at all. Don't mix that up in the job. But suppose that we let it drop there? You have your watch back, I have a cigarette in this hand and a forkful of ham in that and a lot of information that I would like to use, one day."

Chapter Eleven

Wendell left that room like a man entranced, and behind him he would have left a silence, if it had not been for the cheerful talk of Destry.

"I come by the Minniver place, last night, lyin' snug under its trees, with the moon standin' like a half face just over the gully, where it splits the hills behind, and doggone me if it wasn't strange to see the old house all lit up, and, off of the veranda, I could hear the whangin' of the banjos, soft and easy, and the tinkle of a girl laughin', like moonshine fingerin' its way across a lake. But we had to go on past that, though it looked like Jerry would of wanted me to stay there, he seemed so bent on turnin' in. But I edged him away from it. Only, when we went by, I recalled that that was the first time that I see you, Charlie. You was fifteen, and your dad, he'd let you go out to that dance. D'you recollect?"

She looked at him, her lips twisting a little with pain and with pleasure.

"I remember, perfectly," said she.

"You can remember the party," said Destry, "but you can't remember——"

"Harry!" she cried at him. "Will you talk on like this about just nothing, when there's poor Jerry Wendell being driven out from Wham and cut away from everything that he ever was? Wouldn't it be more merciful to murder him, than to do that?"

"Why, look at you, Charlie!" said Destry, pleased and surprised. "How you talk up right out of a school book, when you ain't thinkin'!"

"Sure," said Dangerfield. "If Charlie wasn't always

watchin' herself, the boys would think that she was tryin' to have a good influence on 'em, and educate 'em, or something. Now and then I pick up a little grammar from her myself!"

"You can both make light of it," said the girl, too troubled to smile at their words, "but I really think that killing would be more merciful to Jerry!"

"So do I," answered Destry.

It shocked the others to a full pause, but Destry went on: "There ain't much pain in a forty-five calibre bullet tappin' on your forehead and askin' your life to come outdoors and play. I used often to figger how easy dyin' was, when I was in prison. Ten years is a long time!"

They listened to him, grimly enchanted.

"It was only six," said the Colonel.

"Time has a taste to it," said Destry. "Like the ozone that comes from electricity, sometimes, and sometimes like the ozone that the pine trees make. But time has a taste, and it was flavored with iron for me. What good was the six years? I thought it'd be ten, of course. I've seen seconds, Charlie, that didn't tick on a watch, but that was counted off by pickin' at my nerves—thrum, thrum!—like a banjo, d'you see?"

He smiled at them both, and buttered another slice of corn bread.

"This is something like!" said Destry. "I hope I ain't keepin' you from nothin', Colonel?"

The Colonel did not answer; neither did the girl speak, and Destry went on: "Nerves, d'you see, they ain't so pleasant as you might think. I thought jail wouldn't be so bad, and for six months I just sort of relaxed and took it easy, and slept, and never bothered about nothin'. 'It'll get you' says the others at the rock pile. 'Pretty soon it'll get you in a heap!' Well, I used to laugh at 'em. But all at once I woke up out of a dream, one night.

"In that dream, where d'you think that I was? Why, I was at the party in the old Minniver house, and there was all the faces as real as lamplight ever had made 'em, and there was sweet Charlie Danger-field, with her hair hangin' down her back—and her face half scared, and half mad, and half happy, too, like it was when I kissed her for luck.

"There I lay, wrigglin' my toes again the sheet, and smilin' at the blackness and sort of feelin' around for the stars, as you might say, when all at once I realized that there was nine layers of concrete and steel cells between me and them stars, and in every cot there was a poor crook lyin' awake and hungerin', and sweatin'. Why, just then it seemed to me like death was nothin' at all. I'll tell you a funny thing. I got out of my cot right then and went over to the knob of the door and figgered how I could tie a pillow case onto it and around my neck and then hang myself on that."

"Harry, Harry!" cried the girl. "It's not true! You're making it up to torture me!"

He looked at her; he smiled his way through her.

"I didn't do it, even then when I figgered on nine years and six months more of the prison smell. I didn't do it, honey, even when I seen then that death is only one pulse of life, even if it's the last one. Even when I seen then that every other pulse of life can be as almighty great as the second we die in—and here I was cut off from livin'—but I didn't hang myself, Charlie—not because I hadn't the nerve, but because I still seen you on the Minniver veranda, slappin' my face!"

He laughed, with his teeth close together.

"I laid there for five and a half years more, thinkin', and that's why I didn't kill Jerry Wendell, seein' that death is only a touch, but shame is a thing that'll lie like a lump of ice under your ribs all the days of your life. So Jerry's alive! You wanted to know, and now I've told you. Could I have another shot of that coffee, Colonel? You got the out-cookingest nigger in that kitchen of yours that I ever ate after!"

It was Charlotte, however, who went to the coffee pot and poured his cup steaming full.

"Ah," said Dangerfield, "you had a long wait, there. What busted into you to rob that mail, son?"

Destry laughed again.

"There's the joke, Colonel. It would of been pretty easy to lie close in jail, thinkin' of the good time I'd of had with stolen money the rest of my days, when I got out; but the joke was that I didn't steal the money. I was only framed!"

The Colonel suddenly believed, and, believing, he swore violently and terribly.

"All at once, I know you mean it!" said he.

"Thanks," said Destry, "but there was twelve peers, d'you understand, that wouldn't believe. They wouldn't believe, because they didn't want to. Twelve peers of what? Chinamen?"

The humor had died out of his eyes; they blazed at Dangerfield until the latter actually pushed back his chair with a nervous gesture.

"It's all over now. Harry," he said in consolation. "You're able to forget it, now!"

"I'll tell you," answered Destry. "You know how they say a gent with his arm cut off still feels the arm? Gets twinges in the hand that's dead, and pains in the buried elbows, like you might say! And it's the same way with me; I got five dead years, but a nervous system that's still spread all through 'em!"

"Are you fixed and final on that?" asked the Colonel.

"Fixed as them hills," said Destry. "You gunna leave us, Charlie?"

"I reckon that I better had," said she, standing up. He rose with her.

"You gotta headache, Charlie," said her father. "Maybe you better lie down."

At this, she broke out: "I ain't gunna be dignified, Harry. I'm not gunna put on a sweet smile and go out soft and slow, like funeral music. I'm gunna fight!"

"All right," said Destry. "You're the fightin' kind. But what you gunna fight about, and who with?"

"I'm gunna fight with you!"

"We've had a lot of practice," said Destry, grinning. "Fact is, we've had so much practice that we know how to block most of the punches that the other fellow starts heavin' at us!"

"Oh, Harry," said she, with a subtle change of voice, "I can't block this! It hurts me a powerful lot."

"Look at her!" said the Colonel. "Why, doggone me if she ain't about cryin'! Kiss her, Harry, and make a fuss over her, because if she's cryin' over you, I'll have to use the riot gun on you, after all!"

She waved that suggestion aside.

"What are you gunna do, Harry? Are you gunna take after them all, the way you promised them in the courtroom?"

"Look what they done?" he argued with her. "All the days of six years, one by one, they loaded onto my shoulders, and as the days dropped off, the load got heavier! I tell you what day was the worst—the last day, from noon to noon. That day was made up of sixty seconds in every minute, and sixty minutes in every hour, and the hours, they started each one like spring and ended each one like winter. I was a tolerable young man, up to that last day!"

He added hastily:

"Speakin' of time, I better be goin' along! I got a lot of riding to do today. I better be goin' along."

He turned to the host.

"Good-by, Colonel."

"Wait a minute, Harry! They's a lot of things to talk about——"

"I can't stay now. Some other time. So long, Charlie. You be takin' care of yourself, will you?"

He leaned and touched her forehead with his lips.

"So long again, Colonel!"

He was through the door at once, and instantly they heard a chorus of voices from the negroes hailing him, for he was a prime favorite among them. His own laughing voice was clearly distinguishable.

"Is that a way," said the Colonel, "for a young gent to kiss a girl good-by, when it's a girl like you, and he loves her, like he does you? He pecked at you like a chicken at a grain that turns out to be sand and not corn! Hey, Charlie! God a'mighty, what's possessin' you?"

"Leave me be!" said she, as he overtook her at the door.

He held her shoulders firmly.

"What's the matter? What's the matter?" asked the Colonel.

"You'll make me cry in about a half a minute," said she. "Will you lemme go, dad?"

"Hold on," said the Colonel, his eyes brooding

upon her with a real and deep pain. "Has *he* got something to do with this all? If he has——"

"Hush up," said the girl.

"But there ain't any call for carryin' on the way you are, Charlie. Everything's all right. He's busy. He's got his mind on the road. Everything's all right; ain't he come and started where you and him left off?"

"What makes you think so?" she asked.

"Why, he wouldn't of showed up here at all, except that he wanted to show you that he didn't keep your letter in his mind."

"He came here for Jerry Wendell, and that's all," said the girl.

"But he kissed you, Charlie. He wouldn't of done that!"

"Oh, don't you see?" said she. "He was only kissing me good-by."

Chapter Twelve

It was not yet prime of the day when Destry jogged his tired mustang down the main street of Wham again. He rode with his eyes fixed straight before him, but from their corners, he was able to feel the attention which followed him. The little, light rumor, which rises faster than dead leaves on the wind, which is more penetrating than desert dust, had whispered before him so rapidly that he was aware of faces at windows, at doors, always glimpsed and then disappearing.

Already they knew him thoroughly, and this made him sigh. For, if he could have gone about his work secretly enough, he might have struck them all, one by one, in this same town. But three were gone, in a breath, and nine remained. He looked forward to their trails with a drowsy, almost a dull content, like a wolf that trots on the track of a tiring moose, and knows that there is no hurry.

Sheriff Ding Slater came up to him at a gallop, turning a corner in the fine old slanting style, and raising a huge cloud of dust, like a gunpowder explosion, when he jerked his mustang to a halt. That dust, settling, powdered the moustaches of the sheriff a fine white. He shook his gauntleted hand at Destry.

"Young man," he said, "you been at it fine and early! You clear out of Wham. You ride right on through, and I'll see you out of town!"

"Come along, sheriff," said Destry. "It's a long time since last night, when I talked to you last!"

The sheriff fell in at his side.

"It's a dead man and a mighty sick man besides, since last night," said Ding Slater. "Six years ain't taught you nothin', Harry, and I ain't gunna expose my town no more to you. You're worse'n smallpox!"

"Thanks," said Destry, "because I can feel the compliment behind what you say. Thanks a lot, old timer. Have the makin's?"

"A dead man! Clarence Ogden dead!" said the sheriff. "And here I ride alongside of the killer! What would they think in the East about that?"

"Eastern thinkin' never raised Western crops," observed Destry. "But about the Ogdens, you know them that live by the gun shall die by the gun. That's Bible, or oughta be!"

"You sashay right on outa Wham," said the sheriff.

"Not me," answered Destry, "except that my game ain't here any longer, I guess. All the birds have seen the hunter, and they all have flown, I reckon?"

The sheriff looked grimly at him.

"D'you mean to take 'em all?" he said. "One by one?"

"I mean it!"

"I can use that agin you, young feller, if this comes up in court, as it's sure gunna do!"

"The law'll never get to the wind of me again," replied Destry. "I'm like a good dog. I've had the whip on my back, and I don't need two thrashin's to make me remember the feel of doin' wrong!"

"Of doin' wrong!" cried the sheriff. "Is it doin' right to shoot men down?"

"Self-defense ain't a crime, even in a Sunday School," said Destry.

"Ay," growled Ding Slater. "I can't answer back to that when it was two to one——"

"And they'd hunted me down!"

"They was huntin' a calf. They didn't know that a wild cat was under the skin. But leave the Ogdens out of the picture. What about the rest? Are they likely to come at you?"

"Them and their hired men," said Destry. "But let's not get down to particulars. Everything that I do, it's gunna be inside the law—plumb inside of the laws. You'll be helpin' me out, before long. You'll——"

"You got plenty of brass in you," complained the sheriff. "Help you out? I'll be hanged first!"

"I'm a sort of a special investigatin' agent," said Destry. "I'm gunna open locked doors and let in the light, like the parson said one Sunday in the prison. I'm gunna unlock a lot of private doors and let in the light, sheriff."

"Now, whacha mean by that?"

"There ain't a man on earth," said Destry, "that don't need to wear clothes. They's some part of his life that's a naked shame, and I'm gunna find that part. I'm gunna punish them the way that I was punished, only worse."

"You kinda interest me," said the sheriff thoughtfully.

"I bet I do," replied Destry. "If they was a fine-toothed comb run through your past, what would come of you, son?"

"There ain't a thing for me to cover up, hardly," said the sheriff. "But every man's a fool some time or other. But to get back to the others——"

"Sure," said Destry, smiling.

"I always wished you well, Harry."

"I guess you did."

"But whacha mean about punishing the others the way that you were punished?"

"Why, I was shut off from life behind bars. I'm gunna shut off the rest of 'em, but not behind the bars. They'll have life in the hand, but it'll taste like sand and cactus thorns when they try to eat it."

"You're talkin' right in the middle of the street," noted the sheriff.

"I figger on you tellin' them," replied Destry. "Murder is all that they're lookin' for now, though the case of Jerry Wendell might show 'em different. You go tell 'em all, Ding. The more doors they gotta watch and guard, the worse they'll be able to guard 'em. So long. You'll be wantin' to get to work sendin' out letters. You know the names! I gotta turn in here to see Chester Bent."

He halted his horse and looked fondly at the house.

"He's stood by you fine," agreed the sheriff.

"I wish that his house was ten times as big," said Destry with emotion. "I wish that they was marble columns walkin' down the front, and a hundred niggers waitin' for the bell to ring, and a hundred hosses standin' in his stable, and a hundred towns like Wham in his pocketbook. God never made no finer man than him!"

The sheriff went back down the street, and Destry turned down the short drive that led to the barn behind the house. There, with two other men in a green field behind the house, was Chester Bent, looking at a tall bay mare which one of the others was leading up and down. Bent came hurrying to meet his friend, and wrung his hand.

"I've heard about Jerry!" he said. "Ah, Harry, you've pulled the wool over my eyes, as well as over the eyes of the rest of the town. Wendell's come in, and gone again, looking like a ghost."

"If I'd told you," answered Destry, embarrassed,

which was a strange mood in him, "you would have started to talk me out of it!"

He laid his hand on the other's shoulder.

"I know you, man! Good for evil is what you'd say, and turn the other cheek, and all that kind of thing. But it ain't in my nacher. God didn't make me that way, and you could give me a bad time, but you couldn't change me. Not even you!"

"What is it now?" asked Bent, overlooking both the apology and the praise.

"They've scattered like birds. I'm gunna follow down one trail."

"You're set on that?"

"Out yonder I can spot one of 'em. That's Clyde Orrin, the great politician, the risin' man in the state, the honest young legislator, the maker of clean laws—him with the soft hands that are never more'n a half hour away from soap and water! I'm gunna call on Clyde's dark closet and look for spooks. Are you buyin' that mare?"

"I think so. Come and look at her. But about my friend Orrin—a perfectly harmless fellow, and a good man, you know——"

"Listen to me," said Destry. "A man can't live on bread alone. He's gotta have words, too. I can talk to you, old timer, but I don't wanta listen. Understand?"

Chester Bent took a handkerchief from his upper coat pocket and passed it gingerly over his face. Then he nodded.

"I'll stop thinking about you, Harry," said he, "and only remember that whatever my friend does must be right! Now come look at the mare for me. They want nine hundred dollars. And of course that's too much."

"Lemme try her," said Destry.

He took her from the hands of the dealers and swung into the saddle without a glance at her points. Down the pasture he galloped her, jumped a ditch, turned, took a wire fence, jumped back over it, and cantered her back to the group.

He dismounted with an unchanged face.

"You tried her over wire!" exclaimed Bent. "You might have ruined her, man!"

"Look at the old cuts," said Destry calmly. "If she ain't been able to learn wire from that much trouble, she ain't worth her looks!"

Bent drew him aside.

"What you say? Not nine hundred, Harry!"

"Listen," said Destry. "What would you pay for a pair of wings?"

"Is she as good as that?"

"Better! You can't talk to wings, and you can talk to her. She's a sweetheart, Chet, I wouldn't wish you on no other hoss than her!"

Which was how Fiddle came into the hands of Chester Bent; for his check was written in another moment, and she was taken to the stable by a waiting negro.

Then Bent walked back to the house and up to the room of his guest to watch Destry pack his roll. He pressed him very little to stay.

"I see it in your eye, man," he said. "I almost envy you, Harry. You're free. You have the open country, and ride your own way; I'm tied here to my business like a horse to a post; and I'll take no more of it with me in the end than the horse takes of the post. I feel like a tame duck in the barnyard, when it sees the wild flock driving a wedge across the morning, and letting the music come rattling down. I'm still young enough to understand that music, but after a while I'll get used to clipped wings and not even dream of better things at night. Harry, is there one last thing I can do for you?"

"Lend me a fresh mustang—you keep a string of 'em—and take mine in change. It's a hand picked one, and I haven't ridden the velvet off it, yet!"

Bent went out to give directions for the saddling of the new mount, and Destry, finishing his packing, swung his pack over his shoulder and went down the stairs to the front door. He found the stable boy and note waiting for him beside the new mare, Fiddle:

Dear Harry,
    It's a sad thing to shake hands with a man I may never see again. I couldn't have the heart to stay here and say good-by. Take Fiddle with you. I saw in your eye what you thought of her, and I want you to take with you something that'll remind you that I'm your friend.

                                        Chet.

Chapter Thirteen

Chester Bent did not write one note only, that morning, but as soon as he had hurried down to his office, he scribbled rapidly:

Dear Clyde,

This is haste. Destry has come to see me. He's not satisfied with Clarence Ogden dead, and Jud Ogden a cripple for life. It makes no difference that Jerry Wendell has been disgraced and made a laughing stock. He's determined to keep on the trail until he's killed or ruined every man of the twelve of you.

You know that I'm the friend of Harry. I suppose you also can guess that I'm yours. I've tried to dissuade him, but he's adamant. I couldn't budge him a whit.

He's off now, and on a fast horse. But I'm sending this message on to you, in the hope that you'll get it in time. I don't know how to tell you to guard yourself. It may be your life he's after. It may be only some other scalp that he'll try to lift, but this thing is sure—that if he has his way with you, you'll *wish* for death before the end!

I don't need to point out to you that I run a most frightful danger in sending you this letter. If it, or any knowledge of it, should come to the hands of Destry, I suppose he'd turn on his trail and come back to murder me, friendly though we are.

However, I can't resist the chance of warning you that the sword is hanging directly over your head, old fellow, and not even a thread to keep it from falling. Take care of yourself. Remember me to your good wife.

                                        Adios,
                                CHESTER BENT.

When he had written this letter, he rang a bell, and when his secretary came, he said to her: "Send for that scar-faced Mexican who was in here the other day."

"Do you mean Jose Vedres?" she asked.

"I mean Jose."

She hesitated, looking rather shocked, but she was a discreet women who had reached the age of forty, guarded against all scandal by a face like a hatchet and a voice like a whining cat. She was attached to Bent by more than a personal devotion, and that was a slight sharing in his secrets. She knew ten per cent inside the margin, and that was more than any other human had mastered of the ways and the wiles of Chester. She knew enough, in fact, to wish to know more, and Bent was aware that she never would leave him so long as the hope of one day having him at her mercy was shining before her eyes. For that very reason he let her look around the corner now and then, just far enough to be able to guess at the direction he was going to take.

She sent for the Mexican at once, and the man came in a few moments, a venomous looking specimen of his race, slinking, yellow-eyed, with nicotine ingrained to his very soul.

Bent gave him the letter.

His directions were short and simple; he merely added at the end:

"If that letter gets to any hands other than those of Clyde Orrin, I'm a dead man, Jose. And if I die——"

He made a slight but significant gesture to conclude, and Jose nodded. He understood very well that his own life was so neatly poised in a balance that it would not take more than the fall of his friend to undo him.

He bowed himself, accordingly, through the door, and, from the window above, Bent watched him as he pitched gracefully up into the saddle, and sent the mustang scurrying down the street.

"Life insurance," said Chester Bent, and striking all of this affair from his mind, he turned back to his business of the day.

Jose, in the meantime, took a short cut from the town, crossed the fields beyond, and soon was headed up the valley.

He did not follow the river road, for, though it was far better graded, it wound too much to suit him. Instead, he chose to take a straighter though more rugged way which skirted along among the trees and through ground that rose and fell gently, like small waves of the sea.

In the first copse he paused, drew off a riding boot with some difficulty—for his boots were the one pride of his life in their fineness and tight fit—and, cutting threads at the top, he divided the outer leather from the lining. In this space he inserted the letter which had been intrusted to him. Afterward, with a fine needle and waxed thread, he closed the seam which he had opened. His precautions did not end here, for he actually threw away the needle and the thread remaining before he remounted and continued his ride.

No animal on dangerous ground could have traveled with a keener and a quicker eye than Jose. It searched every tuft of brush before. It scanned the shadows thrown from the patches of rocks that outcropped. It probed the groups of trees before he was near them. And yet all precaution cannot gain utter safety.

As he shot the mustang down a grade, he heard the easy rhythm of a long striding horse behind him, and, looking back, he saw a long-legged bay swinging down the hill, and in the saddle rode Harrison Destry.

Jose did not spur ahead. One glance at the gait of the horse behind him convinced him that flight was folly. Besides, no one but a fool would present a broad target, such as a back, to Destry. The Mexican drew rein, and was merely jogging as the other came alongside at a similar gait—a soft, smooth gait in the mare, the fetlock joints giving so freely that Destry hardly stirred in the saddle with the shock of the trot.

"Hullo, Jose," said he. "You're makin' good time for a hot day."

"You, too," said Jose, countering.

"Not for this mare," replied Destry. "She don't run; she flies. A flap of the reins sends her thirty mile an hour and she takes a hill from the top to the bottom with one beat of the wings. The buzzards and the eagles have been blowin' behind me in the wind of her gallop. Doggone me if I ain't been pityin' them. Where you bound, Jose?"

"Up the valley," said Jose, with a courteous smile.

He had another manner for most, but Destry was on a special list with him.

"Likely it's the heat comin' on in the flat," suggested Destry. "When the summer comes along, I reckon that you wanta get up to the high pines, Jose. It's a mighty savin' on the complexion, eh?"

This irony apparently missed the head of Jose entirely, for he answered:

"There's nothing to do in Wham. No jobs for Jose! I go up over the range and try to change my luck!"

"I tell you the trouble with your luck," said Destry. "You try too many things. Runnin' up a pack with two crimps in it is a fine art, Jose, and you oughta be satisfied with one. It works on the suckers, and the wise ones will spot your game, anyway. You aimin' at a range-ridin' job?"

"Yes."

"That's why you left your pack behind?"

Jose's eyelids fluttered down, but instantly he looked up again with his smile.

"You know poker is no man's friend, señor. It left me a naked man, this mornin'!"

"What color is your hide, Jose?" asked the other.

"Señor?"

"Stop your hoss, drop your gun-belt, and strip. I wanta look at you!"

"Señor Destry——" began the other.

"Jose, Jose," protested Destry, as one shocked, "you ain't gunna stop and argue, are you, when you see I'm so hurried? And when the sun is so hot? Jus' you climb down off that hoss, and drop your gun, and strip for me! It'll cool you, no end."

Jose made a pause that lasted only a half second. In that half second he had taken count of his chances and figured them accurately as one in five. He was a good gambler, a brave gambler, but he was not a fool. So he dismounted at once and undressed after he had obediently unbuckled his cartridge belt and allowed it to fall, together with the holstered gun which it supported.

Then he stood in the glare of the sunshine, looking sufficiently ridiculous in his nakedness, but with the great Mexican sombrero still on his head.

Destry went over the clothes with care. He found two packs of cards, which he examined card by card. He found a pair of knives, one long handled, one short, as for throwing. He found a bandana, Bull Durham and papers, a box of matches, a travel stained envelope with the name of Señor Jose Vedres inscribed upon it in feminine writing, childishly clumsy.

This he opened and scanned for a line or two.

"She loves you, Jose," said he. "Then she's like the rest of 'em. Optimists before marriage, and hard thinkers afterwards! Nothin' but a profit in girls, and nothin' but a debit in wives. I guess you ain't ever married, Jose?"

"No, señor. Are you ended?"

"Before I've had a look at the gun, and the boots? Not me, son! Something was blowin' you up the valley away from the town too fast for my good. Everything that runs out of Wham, just now, is likely to have something to do with me, and why shouldn't I take a look?"

He began to thumb and probe the coat, lingering for a time over the shoulder padding; then he picked up the gun, which he took to pieces with lightning speed, and left unassembled again on the fallen coat.

"So's you won't begin target practice at my back till I'm a half mile away, anyway," said Destry.

He took up the boots, next, removed the inner lining, and then with consummate care and attention tapped on the high heels, listening with his ear close to them.

"It's a mighty delicate business," said Destry. "Maybe they's a hollow in here, but I reckon not. Besides, I've wasted enough time. I'm gunna make a short cut, Jose!"

His voice roared suddenly; his Colt leaped from its scabbard and leveled at the Mexican.

"What sent you out of Wham, and who was it that started you on your way?"

"Myself, señor, and no other!"

"Then get down on your damned wo'thless knees and say your last prayers. I'm gunna have the truth out of you, or stop this trip!"

Jose shrugged his lean, crooked shoulders.

"The saints have stopped their ears to the prayers of poor Jose, señor," said he. "In heaven it is not as on this sad earth of ours; good deeds are better than good words; so I have stopped praying!"

Destry put up his gun in one flashing gesture.

"You're dead game, old son," said he. "You're straight enough to follow a snake's track, I reckon. So long. And don't hurry along too fast, because it might be that I'll meet you where you're goin'."

Chapter Fourteen

Mrs. Clyde Orrin agreed with her husband perfectly in the major issue. That is to say, she felt that a "diplomatic" attitude was all the world deserved to see, but whereas Clyde Orrin brought home his official manner to the supper table, Mrs. Orrin felt that there was a time when one should be oneself.

"What great big thought has my boy tonight?" asked Mrs. Orrin at the table, noting a slight vacancy in the eye of her husband.

"Nothing—nothing at all," said Clyde Orrin. "Nothing of any importance."

"Don't come that stuff," said Mrs. Orrin, who had risen from the chorus to be the bride of this rising young politician; she enjoyed letting a little of the old times appear on her tongue when they were alone. "What's eating you, Clyde?"

"Children," said he.

"Children? Oh, rot! There's tons of time for them."

"I don't know. One has to form a habit pretty young."

"I see what you mean," she said. "You think I can run this house, and put up a front with your vote-getting friends, and go gadding to teas and such, picking up alliances for darling Clyde, and then I'm to tear home and stay up all night rocking the cradle of Clyde junior. Is that the idea? It ain't as catching as mumps, honey, if that's what you mean!"

He drummed his pink, soft fingers against the top of the table, and did not answer.

"Look here, sweetheart," said Mrs. Orrin. "Don't be such a great big strong silent man when you come home here to me. Let the office be your Rock of Gibraltar, darling; but when you get in here climb down off yourself."

"Why, dear," he said, "I didn't mean to hurt your feelings."

"I don't mean baby-talk, either," declared Mrs. Orrin. "But if it's a young Clyde that you want squalling around the house, just say so. I'm perfectly willing. There's nothing I'd like so well as to chuck all of this political rot and start a real home. You know it, too! But you have to pasture this girl on the long green, honey, if you expect her to start raising a family. I'm not cook, sweeper, window-washer, bell-ringer, duster, marketer, tea-pourer, handshaker all at the same time even for Darling. D'you follow me, or do I just seem to be saying one of those things?"

Her husband looked down at his plate, and knew that his face was softly, gently thoughtful, though there was almost murder in his heart. Still, he was rather fond of his wife; he knew that she was endlessly useful; twice she had saved his scalp from the tomahawk of a furious political boss, and numberless times she had saved him from time and trouble by being gracious on the street and off it. Moreover, the sharp definition of her character was a relief to him. After the haze of political diplomacy, small and great, in which he lived and breathed all the day, it was a great rest to see the naked truth inside the doors of his house. However, he was convinced that he had married beneath him, and this conviction he knew that his wife secretly shared. Because of that, he guessed shrewdly that his domestic happiness was founded upon sand.

"Suppose that we drop the talk about children,

then? I don't want to make you uncomfortable. Only someday——"

"Sure," said she. "Someday is the time, in the Sweet Sometime on Someplace street. It's not children, though, that's occupying your mind tonight. What is it that's eating you, my great big brave, noble boy?"

"Don't you think," he suggested, "that we could at least try to be polite to one another, even when there's no one listening?"

"I *am* polite," said she. "I'm telling you how big and strong and wonderful you are. Pass me the celery, Clyde, and put the official manner in your inside coat pocket, will you?"

Her husband considered her with the gravity of the fabled basilisk, but his wife answered his gaze with the most ironical of sweet smiles. They understood each other so extremely well that it was doubtful if they could ever remain friends very long. Suddenly he put the thought in words.

"No matter what I may be outside; at home, I'm only a fool and a worm!"

"No matter how I may get by away from here," she retorted, "the minute you come home I'm back on the stage and showing my knees. If I lived with you a thousand years, you'd never stop being afraid that I'll some day make a bad break."

"Come, come," said he, "you know that's not true! I know what I owe you!"

"Not love, though?" said she.

He got up from his chair hastily and went around the table to her, but she held out her hand and warded him away.

"I don't want any perfunctory pecks, and I hate reconciliation scenes because they're so sticky," she said. "Being reconciled always makes a girl cry; I suppose because it's better to cry over a husband than to laugh at him. Go back and sit down, Clyde, and I'll try to take you seriously."

He returned to his chair, very pink and haughty, but Mrs. Orrin, who felt that she had gone far enough and who really thought that she might be able to drive even this somewhat flabby carriage to some political height, now softened her eyes and her smile.

He regarded her dubiously.

"You know how to pull in your claws and give the velvet touch," he told her. "Now get ready to put the claws out again. Listen to this! It's a letter from William R. Rock about the T. & O. business."

"Go on," she said. "I knew there was something for mama to hear."

He took the letter from his pocket, unfolded it, looked darkly at his wife, and read slowly, aloud:

Dear Orrin,

I've just read a copy of your last speech, the one of the seventh. It made me smile, but not on the side of the face you think. You want to get this in your head, young fellow. You're not in there to make the legislature laugh at us but to make it laugh with us. We've retained you for something more than an after-dinner speech. Ten thousand a year is higher than we've gone in this state for some time, and we want returns on our money. You know what we expect. We want a tax reduction and a fat one. You've been fiddling around for a long time and drawing pretty pictures, but now we want to hear from you in headlines. We want you to chuck the funny business and work up a little public sympathy for the T. & O. We want you to make the people feel that we're done for and will have to get out of business unless we're given a helping hand. The state needs us more than we need the state. That's your line, as I laid it down for you months ago.

Now, then, Orrin, come to life and wake up that legislature. We've made enough alliances for you; all you need to do is to start pulling a few of the strings that we've placed in your hands, and the thing will go through. Besides, if you father a really big piece of legislation like that, it'll bring you before your public and double your strength with the voters.

Don't make any mistake. Keep in our saddle and we'll ride you a long way. A governorship, perhaps, or the U.S. Senate. But only if you play our game. The Old Man was down here yesterday and he's not satisfied with you. This is a friendly tip. Get back into harness and help us pull our load and we'll not forget when we get to the top of the hill. You've been paid what you're worth in advance, but if the tax cut goes through, there'll be a bonus, anyway. I don't know just what. Ten thousand more, at least. Put that in your pipe and smoke it, and I think you'll enjoy the flavor of the weed.

Now, boy, this is straight from the shoulder. Personally, I believe in you! I'm with you and behind you every minute that you play our game with us. But when you chuck us and start going for yourself, we're going to plow the ground from under your feet as sure as God made little apples.

Yours truly,
W. R. Rock.

He read it out to the signature, slowly, dwelling a little on every offensive phrase, and as he finished her first remark was: "You poor simpleton, couldn't you remember the gist of that without bringing it home? Burn it in the fireplace this minute! That's a bomb that would blow you to pieces if the newspaper got hold of it! The *News-Democrat* would love to have that! Can't you see a photographic reprint on the first page?"

"How long would I last with you," he asked curiously, "if things went bust?"

"I don't know," she said. "I'm in here working with a wise man, not with a sap. Burn that letter, will you?"

"It has to go in the safe," said her husband.

"Suppose that the safe is cracked?"

"What yegg would waste his time on a safe like that?" he asked her. "I'm not rich. There's not a hundred dollars in cash in it, and as for my papers, who am I? No, I need this letter to refer to. It may be that they'll try to double cross me. Here's their definite promise of a ten thousand bonus."

"Would they pay any attention to it?"

"There are certain quarters—not newspapers!— where I could show this and do them a lot of harm if they were to try to hold out on me. They'd know that. One reason Rock made this so strong and open was to scare me into burning it. But I'm made of tougher stuff than that."

She hesitated, glancing at a corner. Then she snapped her fingers.

"I think you're right!" said she. "You *have* a head, Clyde darling, and I can see it, once in a while. Better go down and put it away now!"

Here the front door bell rang, and they looked at

each other with big, frightened eyes; then Orrin himself went to answer the call.

He let in the yellow eyes and the smoked skin of Jose Vedres, who stood before him, sourly smiling, a letter in his hand. Orrin, without a word, tore it open and read.

"Wait here!" he said to the messenger, and hurried back into the dining room.

He flung the letter down on the table, before his wife, merely muttering:

"Read this, Sylvia!"

Sylvia read, and then, refolding it without a word, she puckered her smooth brow.

"It's like something in a play," she said at last. "I ought to say: 'Has it come to this, Clyde Orrin?'"

"It's come to this," said he.

"You look pretty sick," said she. "But what could this man-eater get by clawing you?"

"What did he get by clawing poor Jerry Wendell?"

"True," she answered. "You'd better call in the police."

"For what?" he asked.

"For the safe! It has your soul locked up in it. And after all, it's a pretty good idea to keep a soul inside of a steel skin."

"You're not worried, Sylvia?" he asked her grimly.

"Darling," said she, "my heart's in my throat!"

But he knew, as he listened and watched her, that already the woman was preparing herself to see the ruin of her husband.

Chapter Fifteen

One of the strings which lay in the hand of Clyde Orrin connected with the detective branch of the police department and it was for that reason that Detective Hugh McDonald was installed in the little basement room which contained the Orrins' safe. It was a small, bare room, without an electric light, and even after a chair had been installed, and a lamp furnished, the place was not much more inviting. However, Mr. McDonald had sat through longer nights in worse places.

He first looked to the small window and assured himself that the bars which defended it were solidly sunk in the concrete of the sill and window jambs. He shook them with all his might, and still they held. Then he drew down the whitened glass pane, which shut out all sight of the interior to one passing outside. Next, he regarded the door, locked it, shoved home the bolt, and told himself that no agency other than spiritual could effect an entrance to this chamber. After that, he opened his magazine and resumed the narrative which had been interrupted by this call to duty.

To make surety a little more sure, he laid his Colt across his lap; it was a special guaranty against sleepiness, because it would be dangerous to allow that gun to fall to the floor.

Dimly, overhead, he heard the last sound of people going to bed, the creak of a stairs being climbed, and the screech of a chair pushed back from a table. Then silence gathered the house softly in its arms.

It was two o'clock when there came the tap on his

window. He looked at his watch, made sure of the hour, and then approached the window carefully, standing to one side, where the lamp could not throw his shadow upon the whitened glass. He was in no humor to throw away chances, for he had not forgotten the strained face of Clyde Orrin when the latter told him that in spite of one or twenty detectives, that room would be entered and the safe opened, if so be that the feared criminal decided to do this thing. Hugh McDonald had smiled a little at this fear; he was used to the tremors of the man of the street.

Now he said: "Who's there?"

"Jack Campbell," said a voice, dim beyond the window. "Open up and let's have a chin, will you? I'm froze out here and wanta thaw out my tongue!"

Mr. McDonald, hesitating, remembered the strength of the bars beyond the window, and his doubts departed.

But first he returned to the lamp and turned down its flame until there was only the faintest glow through the room. After that, he raised the window and peered cautiously out into the darkness. At once a face was pressed close to the bars, a face that wore bristling moustaches which quivered and stood on end as the fellow grinned.

"Who are you?" asked McDonald.

"I'm Campbell. I heard there was another Campbell down here on the job."

"I ain't a Campbell," said the McDonald with reasoned bitterness, "and what's more, I wouldn't be one. I ain't a Campbell and there ain't a drop of blood in me that ever seen Argyleshire, or ever wants to see it. I ain't a Campbell, and I never had a Campbell friend, and what's more, I don't never expect to have one. If that ain't enough for you, I'll try to find another way of sayin' it!"

"Campbell or McDonald," said the stranger at the bars, "there's only one country between us."

"You don't talk like it," said McDonald.

"Don't I? What chance of I gotto talk Scotch when I never was there, but a Scotchman's a Scotchman from London to Yuma, and don't you mistake."

"You talk like a man with a bit of reason in him," admitted the McDonald. "But what are you doin' out there?"

"I'm the outside gent of this job," said the other.

"I didn't know there was goin' to be an outside man," said McDonald.

"There wasn't," replied the Campbell, "but along comes Orrin back to the office and makes another howl, and gets me put on the job to be outside watchdog! What's in there, anyways?"

"Nothin' to eat," said McDonald.

"And me with my stomach cleavin' to my backbone."

"Where'd you come from?"

"Up from Phoenix."

"I never seen you before."

"Because you never been in Phoenix."

"Have they put you on regular?"

"They've put me on for a try, but if they don't give me no better chance than this, what good will a try do me, I ask you?"

"Search me," said McDonald. "What can you do?"

"Ride a hoss and daub a rope."

"Humph!" said the McDonald. "Well, I wish you luck. I'm gunna go back to my chair. You can set on the outside of the window sill, if that's a comfort for you!"

"Thanks," said the other. "But put these mous-taches straight, will you?"

"What?"

"Look at 'em," said the other. "I dunno whether they're tryin' to make a fool out of me, or not, but they stuck these on me like a detective in a dime novel. Look at the twist in 'em, already, but I got no mirror to put 'em straight."

"What difference does it make? It's dark. No-body's worryin' about your style of moustaches."

"It makes me nervous. It don't cost you nothin' to put these right for me, and it keeps me from feelin' like a clown. Look at the way they got me fixed. A wig, too, and the damn wig don't match the mous-taches. They're makin' a fool out of me, McDonald."

"Some don't take much makin'," said the McDon-ald sourly. "Wait a minute, and I'll give those whis-kers a yank for you."

He stepped close to the bars as he said this, and when he was near, the hand and arm of the other shot through a gap. In the extended fingers of the Camp-bell appeared a small rubber-housed bag of shot which flicked across the side of the McDonald's head.

The detective fell in a noiseless heap to the floor!

After this the "outside" man fell to work with a short jimmy which easily ripped the bars from their sockets. He was presently able to pull the whole framework back, and, entering the room through the window, he closed it carefully behind him.

Next, he secured the fallen gun of the man of the law, "fanned" him dexterously but failed to find anything more of interest on his person, and then gave his attention to the safe.

He turned up the flame in the throat of the lamp's chimney, so that he would have ample light, and then fell to work with wonderful rapidity running a mold of yellow laundry soap around the crack of the safe door.

Then, into an aperture at the top of the mold, he let in a trickle of pale, viscous fluid from a small bottle which he carried.

He was engaged in this occupation when the form on the floor stirred and groaned faintly. The other calmly went to him, selected a spot at the base of the skull, and struck with the bag of shot again. The McDonald slumped into a deeper sleep.

A moment later the fuse was connected, lighted, and the intruder stepped back into a corner of the little room and lay down on his face. The next instant the explosion took place, not a loud roar or a great report, but a thick, half stifled sigh that shook the house to its foundations.

The lamp had been put out by the robber before; now he lighted it again and by that flame he viewed the contents inside the open door of steel. In the very first drawer he found what apparently contented him—a letter which began:

"Dear Orrin,

I've just read a copy of your last speech—the one of the seventh——"

He glanced swiftly through its contents and placed the envelope in his pocket. Then he canted his head to listen to the rumble of footfalls coming down the stairs.

He was in no hurry. He even delayed to lean over the unconscious detective and slip a hand under the coat and over the heart of the McDonald. The reassuring though faint pulsation made him nod with satisfaction, and, raising the window, he was gone in a moment more into the outer night.

Still he was not ended for that evening, but hurried to the street, across it to a narrow alley, and down this to a hitching rack where a tall bay mare was tethered. He mounted, and cantered her out of the little suburb village into the adjoining capital city, itself hardly more than a village, conscious of its three paved streets and its gleaming street lamps!

He gained the center of the town, where he tethered the mare again in an alley and shortly afterward was climbing the dingy stairs that led to the rooms of the *News-Democrat*.

The reporters were gone. It was far too late for them, but the editor remained, punching wearily at his typewriter while he held the press for a late item. He was an old man. He had sunk to a country level from a city reputation. His head was gray, his eyes were bleared with the constant perusal of wet print, the glamour and the joy of the press almost had departed from his tired soul, but still a ghost of his old self looked through his glasses at Destry as that robber stood smiling before him, rubbing the crooked moustaches with sensitive finger tips.

"What're you made up to be?" asked the editor, grinning.

"I'm made up to be scandal," said Destry. "You take a look at this and tell me what *you* think?"

The editor glanced at the first few lines, half rose from his chair, and then settled back to finish. At the conclusion, he glanced fixedly at Destry for a few seconds, then ran to a tall filing cabinet from which he produced a handful of specimens of handwriting. With a selection from among these, he compared the signature at the bottom of the page.

After that, he allowed everything except the letter

to fall fluttering and skidding through the air to the ink-painted floor while he rushed to a telephone.

Destry started for the door, and heard the editor screaming wildly:

"Stop the press! Stop the press!"

Then, as Destry was about to disappear, the editor's voice shouted after him: "I want your story! Where'd you pick this up?"

"Out of his safe," said Destry.

"Hey? Wait a minute! You mean that you robbed his safe?"

"Out of a feelin' for the public good," said Destry. "So long. Make it big!"

"Make it big! It makes itself! It's the whole front page! It's the T. & O. going up in smoke——"

But Destry waited to hear no more. He hurried down the stairs to the street, only pausing at the first dimly lit landing to take from his pocket a card containing a list of twelve names. Three of these already had been canceled. He now drew a line through the fourth.

Chapter Sixteen

The slope was long, dusty, and hot, and Destry jogged up it on foot, with Fiddle following close at his heels, stepping lightly with the burden of his weight removed from the saddle. When they came to the crest, the man paused to roll a cigarette and look over the prospect before him and behind. In front was a steep declivity which ran down to the cream and brown froth of a river in spate, the water so high that it bubbled against the narrow little wooden bridge that spanned the flood. Then, turning, Destry scanned the broader valley behind him.

He could see the cattle here and there, single or in groups, like dim smears of pastel; but only one thing moved to the eye of the fugitive, and that was a puff of dust which advanced gradually across the center of the hollow. He knew that there were six riders under that veil, and the thought of them made him look carefully at his mare.

She had done well, she had done very well indeed to hold off the challenge of relayed pursuers but she showed the effects of the labor, for her eye was not as bright as usual, and though it was as brave as ever, it was the luster that Destry wanted to see back in it. She had grown somewhat gaunt, also, and the ribs showed like faint streaks of shadow under the gloss of her flanks.

She needed rest. She could not endure the continued strain of the race which already had lasted for thirty-six hours since first the handful of riders had spotted him on his way back from the capital and had launched their early sprint to overtake him.

Since her legs were not long and strong enough to distance all pursuit, Destry calmly sat down on a stump and considered the problem gravely, unhurriedly. There was only one salvation, and that was in his own mind.

He could, for instance, nest himself somewhere among the rocks and open fire pointblank on them, when they came struggling up the slope within the range of his rifle, but he knew that he who kills is bound to be killed. Moreover, even if he dropped two or three of them, enough would remain to keep him there under observation; and more men, more horses, were sure to come up from the rear. Aware of this, Destry lighted a second smoke, and with the first whiff of it, he saw the thing that he should do.

He went down the slope at the calmest of walks, therefore, and crossed the little bridge with the mare at his heels. The water had now risen until some of the spray dashed continually upon it and got the surface of the floor boards slippery with wet, yet Fiddle went over with a dainty step and stood at last on the farther side with her fine head raised and turned back toward the ridge of land they had just crossed, as though she knew that danger was coming up behind them.

Destry led her on up the steep way that twisted snakelike among the rocks above. When she was safely upon the shoulder of the table land that appeared here, he put her behind a nest of pines and went back to the edge of the plateau. The bridge was now a hundred feet directly beneath him, and over the ridge which he had just passed tipped the pursuit—six riders, six horses, one rushing behind the other, and their shout of triumph at the view of him went faintly roaring down the wind to Destry's ears.

There were masses of detached boulders lying about, fallen from the upper reaches of the high ground, and one of these monsters he rolled end over end, until its three hundred pounds pitched over the verge, landed not a foot from the bridge, and burst like a shell exploding.

Another great shout went up from the pursuers, but Destry had learned how to find the range and he heaved another boulder to the brink with perfect confidence, regardless of the shots which the six were pumping at him. Bullets fired from the saddle on a galloping horse are rarely more dangerous than a flight of wild sparrows. He carefully deliberated, then heaved the stone over.

This one, falling more sheer, struck a projecting rock-face half way in its descent, and glanced outward. Almost in the center of the bridge it struck, and broke the back of that frail structure as though it were built of straw. The water completed the ruin. The bridge seemed to rise with muddy arms, and in a trice all the timbers had been wrenched from their lodgment and carried swiftly down the water.

So the link was broken between Destry and the six.

He waved his hat to their shaken fists and brandished guns, then returned to the mare and rode her at a walk through the pines, up to the crest, where he appeared again, faintly outlined against the sky, then dipped from view beyond. He was in no slightest hurry.

At the first runlet which crossed his way, he refreshed Fiddle by sluicing water over her stomach and legs, and letting her have a few mouthfuls of grass; then he loosened the cinches and went on, walking in front of her, while she followed grazing here and there, then trotting to catch up with him—sometimes galloping a quarter of a mile ahead, and there pausing to feed greedily, until he came again.

In this manner he walked straight through the heat of the day, and in the early evening, when the sun was beginning to bulge its red cheeks in the west, he came up to Cumber Pass. Through it lay the way to Wham, split cleanly between two lofty mountains, and on the outer lip of the pass was a small hostelry. It had been a shambling little ranch house until the Pass was reopened. Now by the addition of a few shambling lean-tos it had been converted into a hotel, and even a second story had been built, looking like a straw hat on an oversized head on a windy day.

Destry paused here and spoke to a small boy who was seated on the top rail of the corral fence. On his head was a hat brim, without a hat He wore a shirt with one sleeve off at the elbow and the other off at the shoulder; his father's trousers were upon him, not cut off, but worn off at the knees. But this loose and shapeless attire nevertheless appeared to accent a degree of freedom and grace in the boy. He looked past a liberal crop of freckles and eyed Destry with as firm a blue glance as ever said: "Beware! I am a man!"

"The top of the evenin' to you," said Destry.

"How's yourself?" answered the boy.

"Kind of bogged down with a tired hoss. Is this a hotel?"

"You can see the sign," suggested the boy.

His eyes wrinkled a little as if he would have liked to ask some acrid question, such as whether or not the stranger could read, but he restrained himself.

"You ain't full up?"

"Full up with air. We got nobody yet for tonight," said the boy.

"Then I reckon I'll put my hoss up. Is that the stable?"

"It's the only one."

He slid down from the rail and accompanied Destry.

"She kind of runs to legs, I reckon," he observed.

"Kind of," agreed Destry.

"Them kind don't hold up very good," said the boy, "unless you get the kind that Destry rides."

"What kind has he got?" asked Destry.

"I'll tell you what kind. She cost nineteen hundred dollars, and she was cheap at that. A rich feller down at Wham gives her to Destry. Nineteen hundred dollars!" he repeated slowly. "That's a sight of money."

"It is," agreed Destry.

"Take thirty dollars a month and save it all—how many months——"

The eyes of the boy grew vague with admiration.

"Some people are pretty nigh made of money," he concluded.

"I reckon they are. Who was the rich man? One of them miners?"

"It was that big bug—that Chester Bent He's one of them that everything they touch turns to money, Pop says. He's got sense enough to want Destry for a friend, you better believe!"

"Why, I wonder?" said Destry. "I thought that Destry was in prison."

"Him? Ain't you heard that he's out?"

"I been up country."

"You been up pretty far!" said the boy, with a touch of suspicion. "You mean to say that you ain't heard?"

"No. About what?"

"Why, Destry's loose!"

"Is he?"

"Sure he is."

"Did he escape?"

"I'll tell you how it happened. He gets tired lyin' around that jail and he sends for the governor."

"Did the governor come?"

"You better believe! Would *you* come, if Destry sent for you? Well, I suppose that nobody'd be fool enough to want Destry to come and *fetch* him! You bet the governor come a hoppin'. Destry says: 'You look here, I'm tired of this here life.'

" 'What's the matter?' says the governor. 'Ain't they treat-in' you pretty good?'

" 'They can't make corn bread here fit for a pig,' says Destry, 'it's that soggy.'

" 'I'll have that fixed right away,' says the governor.

" 'Besides,' says Destry, 'they're a pile too early with breakfast, I tell you.'

" 'I'll give 'em word to let you sleep,' says the governor.

" 'They's only one thing you can do for me,' says Destry. 'I've tried your old prison, and it ain't no good. I want a pardon.'

" 'If they ain't anything else I can do to please you,' says the governor, 'here's your pardon. I wrote out a brand new fresh one before I come down. I suspected maybe that was what you'd want!'

"So Destry and him shakes hands, and Destry comes home, and then whacha think that he done?"

"I ain't got an idea."

"Plays scared-cat Even lets folks slap his face, some says! People begins to laugh. The jury that scattered out of town when they heard he was comin', they drift in back; and then bang! He's got 'em!"

"All of 'em?"

"Three of 'em, quick. He kills one, and he cripples another, and he chases another out of the country, and now he's gone over and showed that another one of 'em was just a low crook, all the time, and the police are lookin' for him. Pretty soon he'll have all twelve of 'em! That's the kind that Destry is! You don't seem to know much about him!"

"No, not much. He always kind of puzzled me a good deal."

"Well, Pop says it's like lookin' down a double-barreled gun to look at Destry's eyes. That's the kind he is. He could pretty nigh kill you with a look, if he wanted to!"

"Could he?"

"Pop says the same as a bird does with a snake, that's the way of Destry with a man he don't like. Just charms 'em helpless, and then he swallers 'em!"

The boy spoke with great gusto.

"That's a funny thing," said Destry.

"Sure it is, for them that ain't swallered."

"How can he do it?" said Destry.

"Pop says that it's practice. Teach yourself to look straight at things, and pretty soon you bear 'em down. I been tryin' it out at school."

"Have you swallered plenty of the other boys?"

"No, but I've had plenty of fights tryin' it and practicin' it out, and now it begins to work better, if I only had more boys my own size to use it on; but I've licked all of them in the school! Here's the barn. You snake off the saddle, and I'll throw her down a feed of hay."

Chapter Seventeen

"Pop" turned out to be a chinless, weary man, with a little work-starved wife as active as a squirrel. It was she who placed ham and eggs and country-fried potatoes before Destry, while Pop drew up his chair opposite and conversed with the new guest.

"You look plenty tired," said Destry. "Been puttin' in a hard day?"

"Me? I ben tired for years and years," said Pop. "I was took tired all of a sudden, once, and I ain't ben the same man since."

"I could tell you the year and the day," snapped the wife. "It was when we got married and you found out——"

"Ma," said her husband, "I dunno what possesses you that you keep comin' out with that, when it ain't a fact at all. I've argued you out of that twenty times, but you keep right on comin' back.

"Fact is," he said to Destry, "that a woman can make a pile of words, but not much sense. You know how it is! But it takes a man like Destry to come along and make 'em hop into their right place."

"Can Destry do that?"

"Him? Look what everybody says! That rich Dangerfield's girl, her that was gunna wait till Destry got out of prison, when he come back and pretended to be a yaller dog, she turned him down, and what did he do? When he showed himself and kicked the town in the face she was mighty anxious to be noticed agin. Did he do it? He didn't. He wouldn't give her the dust off his boots. Pride is what they like. You take a reasonable man like me, that likes to argue out a point, and they just wipe their boots on him; but when a Destry comes along and slaps their faces, they plumb like it. The snappin' of a black snake is the only kind of music that really makes them step. They's a lot of ways that a woman is like a mule!"

The wife turned back to her stove, merely shrugging her shoulders at this drawling harangue.

"Get me some wood, Pop," she said drily, at the end of it, "or if you won't, let Willie go out and fetch some in."

"Willie, you hear your ma askin' for wood," said Pop irately. "What you standin' around for?"

"Don't you tell nothin' about Destry," said Willie, "till I come back."

And as Willie vanished, with a great slam of the kitchen screen door, Destry asked: "You a friend of Destry?"

"One of the best in the world," said Pop with conviction. "Him and me always took to each other."

"Lazy men and thieves is always matched pretty good," said the wife, without turning around from her stove.

Her husband raised his head and stared at her back with dignified rebuke. Then he went on: "Destry and me, we been like twin brothers, pretty nigh."

"That's mighty interesting. I been hearin' that he didn't have many friends."

"And no more he don't. What would he be doin' with a lot of friends? He wouldn't be bothered. But now and then he goes and picks him out a gent and cottons to him, and that feller's his friend for life, like me. It ain't often that he does it But when he does, it's for life!"

"That's a strange thing," said Destry.

"I don't think he ever seen Destry in his life," said the woman at the stove.

Her husband laughed with a fierce scorn.

"Listen at her!" he suggested. "You'd think that I sat here and actually *made up* the things that I've heard Destry say, and the things that I've seen Destry do! That's what you'd think! You'd think that I was a liar, you would, to hear her carry on!"

"They is some things," said the wife, "that a body can be sure about, and don't have to stop with thinkin'."

Pop half rose from his chair.

"Woman," said he, "if shame can't shut you up, my hand'll pretty pronto do it!"

"Your hand!" she said. "Your hand!"

And this, or the connotations which the word suggested to her, sent her into a fit of subdued laughter which continued for some time; it was indeed against a background of laughter that Pop continued talking. He first winked at Destry and tapped his forehead, then hooked a thumb over his shoulder as though to indicate that his better half was slightly, but helplessly addled.

"He seems to be makin' a good deal of talk," said Destry. "What sort of a looking man might Destry be?"

"Him? He ain't so big," said the other. "Tallish, sort of. Might be three or four inches taller than you. That's all. Biggish in the shoulders. Run about thirty pound more than you, I'd say. But it ain't the size of him that counts."

"No?"

"I'll tell a man that it ain't! It ain't the size at all, that counts, but just the style of him. You see him settin' still, he don't look like nothin' much, but you see him rise up and walk—then you see something, man!"

"Like what?"

"Well, ever see a cat sleepin' by the fire?"

"Sure. Many a time."

"It don't look much, does it?"

"Nope. It don't. Only sort of slab-sided and all fell in togethers."

"But along late when it opens its eyes and the eyes is green and it goes and sharpens its claws on the leg of the table—it's kind of different, ain't it?"

"Yes. Now you come to put it that way, it *is*!"

"And ornery, and dangerous?"

"Yes, that's true, too."

"And all at once you're kind of glad that it don't weigh twenty pound instead of six?"

"Yeah, I've thought about that, watchin' a cat get ready to go out huntin' at night. I've even dreamed about it afterwards—me bein' the size of a rat, and the cat stretchin' a paw in after me, with the claws stickin' out like big sickles, and every one sharp as a needle!"

"Well, then, I don't need to tell you nothin' about Destry, because he's just that way, and when he comes around, the brave men, and the rough handers, and the gun slingers, and the knife throwers, they curl up small, and get into a corner, and hope that he won't reach out for them. And when he stands up and slips across the floor, slow and silky, you can see what kind of a machine *he* is!"

"Yeah?" said Destry, entranced.

"You bet! Snap off a man's head quicker'n a wink."

"You don't say!"

"Don't I? I do, though! Tiger, that's all."

"Aw, rot!" said the wife, with a sigh. "You gunna carry on all evenin'?"

The boy, who had brought in the armful of wood and had been standing by listening, agape with interest, now glanced out the window and called out: "Hey! Look see! They's that light winkin' off by the Cumber River! That one we seen a coupla times, lately!"

"What light? Oh, that? That's jest the sun hittin' on a rock face, as the sun goes down," said the father of the family. "I disremember when it was," he resumed his narrative, "when I first seen Destry——"

"It was one night when you was dreamin'," said the wife.

His face contorted into a ball, but gradually the anger relaxed a little.

"Like a pin bein' jabbed into you, the talk of a woman," said he, bitterly.

"But this here Destry, I guess he ain't done much damage to other folks," said Destry, suggestively.

"Ain't he though? Oh, no he ain't!" said Pop in soft derision. "I guess he ain't wors'n Billy the Kid and Wild Bill throwed into one. I guess he ain't!"

"I guess he ain't *twice* as poison as both of them throwed together!" crowed the boy, chiming in with a face brilliant with exultation at so much bloodshed.

"Why," said Destry, "appears like Billy the Kid killed twenty-one men, and Wild Bill done up about fifty, in his time."

"Sure, and what about Destry? He don't do it in front of reporters. He don't advertise none. He just slips up and says to a gent: 'You and me'll take a walk, tonight.' The gent don't think nothin'. Destry goes out with him, and they walk by the river, and Destry comes back alone. Yes, sir! That's the way it happens!"

"Murder?" said Destry, appalled.

"Murder? Why for would he murder? He don't have to. Is there any fun in murder? No, there ain't nothin' but dirty hands. It's the fun that Destry wants, not the killin'. If he kills, it's so they won't talk about him afterwards. But fast as a cat can snap off the heads of mice, that's the way with Destry. I know him like a brother."

"Must be kind of dangerous to have him around, ain't it?"

"Him? Not for me. I know how to handle him. Suppose I sent him word, he'd be up here in a jiffy. The gents around here, they talk pretty careful around me. They wouldn't want Destry to come up and look 'em in the eye. They wouldn't want that, I can tell you."

"No, I reckon that they wouldn't," said the wife. "But if they was only to say boo! at you, you'd start runnin' and never stop! G'wan and gimme a hand with the wipin' of the dishes, will you?"

"Son, you hear you ma talkin', don't you?" asked the father. "G'wan and do what she wants. You can hear me just as good from over there, I reckon?"

"Only," said the wife, "I'd like to know why that light off yonder winks so fast? That ain't like the way that the sun would be off of a rock!"

"What light?" asked Destry, rising suddenly from the table.

He went over to the window and looked out.

"Over yonder," said she, pointing to the range of hills.

"There?"

"Yes."

"I don't see anything just now."

"I reckon maybe it's stopped. Yeah. I guess it's stopped."

"Because the sun's gone down!" said Pop triumphantly. "They ain't no logic in a woman, partner. Logic will always put 'em down, I tell you what! And they got nothin' to do but little things, so's they're always tryin' to rig up little things into mysteries and they shake their heads and start wonderin' about nothin'——"

But Destry looked fixedly from the window across the darkening landscape and toward the blue of the eastern hills on which the light had winked. He would have given much to have seen the flashing of the light, for there was such a thing as a heliograph which could send messages jumping a score of miles as accurately as any telegraph.

The drawling voice of Pop began again, however, and lulled all his senses into a sleepy security.

Chapter Eighteen

Destry went to bed at once. He was a little particular in his selection of a chamber, taking a corner one in the second story, where the roof of the first floor jutted out beneath the window, but, having locked his door, he threw himself on the bed without undressing and was instantly asleep.

Pop, having heard the key turned in the lock, returned to the kitchen to his wife.

"Well," said he, "it sort of opened that young feller's eyes, didn't it, when I talked about Destry? I thought that they'd pop right out of his head."

"They sure did," joined in Willie. "I never seen nothin' like it."

The wife put down a pan she was washing, and with such recklessness that greasy dishwater spurted from the sink over her apron and far out on the floor.

Then she turned on her two menfolk. She was one of those excitable creatures whose emotions appear in their physical actions; now she gripped her wet hands and shook her head at Pop.

"You know who that there is?"

"Who? The stranger?"

"Yes—stranger!"

"Why, and who might he be, bright eyes?" sneered her husband.

"Destry!"

It had the effect of what is called in the ring a lucky punch. In other words, it caught Pop when he was walking into danger, not knowing that it was there. His head jerked back; his hair flopped under the impact; his knees sagged; his eyes grew glassy. Then he staggered toward his wife exactly like a half stunned boxer striving to fall into a clinch.

But she slipped away from him, holding him off at a distance while, with cruel eyes, she struck him again.

"It's him! It's that great friend of yours! It's Destry himself!"

Willie rushed to the rescue.

"Him? You could cut Destry in two," he declared, "and make a coupla men better than him!"

"Oh, of course Willie's right," said Pop. "As if I didn't know Destry when I seen him! This here Destry? You wanta make me laugh, don't you?"

"D'you see his eyes when he watched you? Did you see the smile that he was swallerin' while you puffed and talked like a fool about how mighty well you knew him? Why, I seen they was something on his mind right from the first! And why shouldn't Destry come this way?"

"Why should he, ma?" asked Pop, still staggered and hurt, but fighting to save himself from this new suggestion.

"Wouldn't this be his straightest line between the capital and Wham, if he went back that way?"

"He wouldn't go back that way," said Pop. "He's through with Wham. He'd be driftin' around the country, pickin' off the jurymen. Everybody knows what he'd do!"

"He'd go back to Wham," insisted the wife. "And ain't he ridin' a tall bay mare?"

"A skinny, long-legged thing," interjected Willie. "He said himself that she was so tired that she was plumb bogged down!"

"Gimme that lantern off the wall and we'll go

see," said she. "You Willie—you Pop, you never neither of you never had no eye for a hoss! But my old man raised 'em!"

She led the way with rapid steps, which her two men imitated poorly, as they followed stumbling in her rear; and through the darkness, Willie again and again turned his head and stared wistfully, with a sick heart, toward his father. He had been in doubt about this man many a time before, but now he feared that doubt would become crushing certainty.

They entered the barn, passed by a pair of mustangs which were in stalls there, and came to the place of the bay mare. She started as she heard them, and, lifting her fine head, turned it full towards the lantern light which the woman had raised high.

She did not go closer.

"Thoroughbred!" she said. "That's all that mare is."

Pop and Willie did not answer. There was no need, for the truth which they had overlooked now seemed to be stamped in letters a foot high upon the forehead of Fiddle.

"It's Fiddle," said Willie slowly. "And him—he was Destry."

His mother suddenly put an arm around Willie's shoulder and drew him close to her.

"Don't you bother none about this, son," said she. "Men are mostly like this. You hear about 'em and away off in the distance they look as big and blue and grand as mountains. But bring 'em up close and they ain't no more than runts and dwarfs!"

They left the barn, Pop recovering a second wind as soon as they were under the stars again.

"As if I didn't know!" said Pop. "Why, what was I doin' all of the time but praisin' Destry right to his face? What was I doin' but makin' him feel good? You'd think that I was a fool, the way that you carry on. But I know what's what. I know how to handle things. I was just soft-soapin' Destry a little and——"

"Leave off! Leave off!" said the wife. "It ain't that I mind for myself. But Willie—give him a chance to respect you a little, will you?"

Willie, however, had gone rapidly ahead and was now out of sight. It was for him the crashing of a world about his ears. He had not been able to avoid seeing the truth about many phases of his father's idleness and shiftlessness, but, no matter what else he might be, for these years he had loomed in the mind of Willie as a great man, because he was the companion of Destry, the famous. A hundred stories he had told Willie of adventures with that celebrated man, and now the stories had to be relegated to the sphere of the fairy tale!

So Willie ran forward around the corner of the house and up the road with a breaking heart, not knowing or caring where he was bound so long as it was away from the persistent misery of the pain in his heart. He went blindly, and as he hurried up the trail he found himself suddenly caught by both shoulders.

"Who are you, kid?" asked a gruff voice.

Willie looked up to the face of a big man who held him, and behind him appeared eight or nine others, looming more or less vaguely through the dark of the night. It was more mysterious, even, than any of the stories that his father had told him. For every one of these men carried rifles and revolvers, and every one of them was on foot! Here, where men walked two miles in order to catch a horse and ride one, here was a whole troop coming softly down the road with weapons in their hands. The unreality of it made Willie's head spin, as though he were plunged from the actual world into a dream.

"I b'long here," said he.

"He b'longs here, he says," repeated his captor.

"Lemme see him," said another.

They talked very quietly, guarding their voices. The second spokesman now approached him, took him with a jerk from the hands of the first, and shook him so that his head teetered back and forth dizzily.

"You lie!" said the second man. "You been sent up the road with word to somebody. Don't lie to me, or I'll jerk you out of your skin! Who sent you, and where?"

"Nobody sent me no place," said Willie, anger growing greater than his fear. "And you let go your hold on me, will you? I b'long here, I tell you, and I gotta right to walk up the road."

He who was now holding him chuckled a little.

"Listen to the kid chirp up and talk," said he. "He's a game cock, this kid is. You belong back there in that house?"

"Yeah."

"That's the new hotel, ain't it?"

"Yeah."

"Tell me something."

"Yeah."

"Did Destry come by your place last evenin'?"

"Destry?" echoed the boy.

"Don't stop to think up a lie. Did Destry come by your place?"

"Yes," said Willie.

"Did he stop?"

"Yeah. He stopped for chow."

"What did he eat? Answer up quick, now, and don't you try to lie to me."

"He had ham and eggs and cold 'pone, and coffee, and condensed milk in it. He said it was the out-beatin'est coffee that he ever drunk."

"Because it was good or bad?"

"Good, I reckon. He didn't say. Why you askin' me about Destry?"

The other hesitated.

"Because we're friends of his," said he. "There ain't a one of us but has a lot of interest in meetin' up with Destry. We like him a lot, and we sure yearn to find him! That's why we're all here!"

"Well," said Willie, "you're headin' exact the wrong way."

"Which way should we go?"

"Slantin' up the hills, there, to the right side of the pass."

"To the right side of the Cumber Pass?"

"That's it."

"Doggone me," said one, "I wouldn't aim to guess that he would go that far out of his way even if he knowed we was waitin' in the pass for him!"

"The pen has made him careful," said another. "We better turn back and cut through the pass agin and nab him when he comes down the far side. Did he saw where he was gunna go, kid?"

"He didn't say," replied Willie, "but he talked some about Wham."

"He talked about Wham, did he? And what did he say?"

"Why, nothin' much, except that he was needed powerful bad, back there."

They consulted in murmurs.

"He said he was needed powerful bad in Wham. I reckon he ain't needed so powerful as all of that!"

"No," uttered another, "I reckon that Wham could get along tolerable without him!"

He who had first seized Willie said suddenly: "Suppose the kid's lyin'!"

"He wouldn't dare to lie. What would he lie for, besides?"

"Because Destry's always a hero to the kids! They like the idea of the one man agin the many. They always have and they always will—the kids and the women. Maybe Destry's right back there in the house, this minute!"

"We'll go look!"

"It's no good doin' that," said Willie, "because Destry ain't there."

"Ain't he?"

"Besides, ma is down with the scarlet fever, and pa has got a terrible rash——"

"The kid's lyin' like a tickin' clock," said one of the men. "Take him by the neck, and we'll go back and look at all these here fever patients. Take my word—Destry's in that house!"

Chapter Nineteen

"Sam," asked one of the men, "shall we all go in?"

"I'll go in with a coupla you boys," replied Sam, the leader. "The rest of you scatter around the house. I wish that we had riot guns with us. But whatever you're in doubt about, use a cartridge on it. There won't be any harm in that! If Destry smells trouble, he's gunna be off like a shot. But if we have a fair chance, maybe we'll get him. I'll go in and talk to the folks!"

So he took Willie, still held by the nape of the neck, into the house and found his father and mother in the kitchen, still wrangling, though with voices subdued by the greatness of their guest.

"Hey!" said Pop, "if it ain't Sam Warren!"

"Yes, it's me," said Warren. "I hear that you're all busted out into a rash, and your wife clean down with scarlet fever."

"Is that Willie's talk?" asked Pop, glaring severely toward the boy.

But even in reproof, he was not quite able to meet Willie's eye, and the latter knew, with contempt and disgust, that he had taken the measure of his father forever.

He was more interested in looking up at the man who held him and who led the night party. It was a name which had acquired a sudden fame, along with the rest of that unlucky jury which had condemned Harry Destry to the penitentiary. He had been, only a few months before, a fairly obscure cowpuncher, rather well considered for his speed and accuracy with guns, but now he was celebrated as a marked man.

He was a very tall man, being upwards of six feet, and both his face and his body were unusual. His shoulders and hips were narrow, his body almost emaciated, and the arms and legs very long. Hair grew on the back of his hands, which were long fingered and suggested a strength uncanny in a body so slight. His face was almost handsome, up to the eyes, but these popped out with an expression of continual anger beneath a perpetually frowning brow. The forehead rose high above, swelling out almost grotesquely at the top.

When Willie had marked down the features of this man, he listened again to the conversation.

"Now, Pop," said Sam Warren, "you know why I'm here?"

"Why, I couldn't guess," said Pop.

Sam Warren loosed his hold upon the neck of the boy in order to lay his hand upon the shoulder of Pop.

"You better think it over, Pop," said he. "Mind you, I'm your friend, if you gimme a chance, and so are all of these here boys along with me. But we ain't gunna stand for no foolishness. Is Destry here?"

"Destry?" said Pop blankly.

And suddenly the very heart of Willie turned to water, for he knew that his father would betray the sleeping guest.

He worked, in the meantime, slowly toward the door, and heard Warren saying:

"If we have to search the house for him, he'll hear us and get away; and if we find out, we'll make things hot for you! But if you'll show us where he is—"

"He ain't here at all," declared Pop.

"You lie," said Warren with a calm brutality, and Pop shrank under that verbal stroke.

"Now talk up," said Warren. "I've wasted enough time. Likely he's in the next room, listenin' all of this while."

Here Willie gained the door and stepped back into the shadow. He hardly could believe, for an instant, that these keen manhunters actually had let him go, but expected a long arm to reach out after him.

Yet it was true!

He slid down the narrow hall, pulled the shoes from his feet, and then ran noiselessly to the top of the stairs. He found the door of Destry's room at once, and tapped softly, calling in a whisper through the crack of the door.

There was an answer immediately, the guarded voice of Destry calling: "What's up? And who's there?"

"Sam Warren's downstairs. He's huntin' for you!"

"For me?"

"Yeah. For you. For Harry Destry!"

The door opened.

Willie found himself drawn hastily into the presence of the great man.

"How many are there, Willie?"

"About nine, countin' 'em all. Three downstairs, and the rest circlin' around the house, ready to shoot at anything at all!"

"Warren? You're sure of him?"

"I'm dead sure of him. He's wearin' a pretty nigh snow white sombrero same as he always does; and you can't forget his face, once that you've seen it!"

"Warren," said Destry thoughtfully, "is a mighty

rash and pushin' man. Now, look here, kid. You see if you can get down to the stable and snake out the mare for me, will you?"

"I'll try!"

"Throw the saddle on her. Mind you watch her, because she snaps like a wolf at strangers. Hurry, Willie, and I'll give you something to remember me by——"

He was working busily in the dark of the room, as he spoke, gathering his pack together, and Willie waited for no more, but slipped from the room and hastened in his bare feet down the upper corridor, down the narrow, twisting rear steps, and so to the ground below.

He issued from a window to get to it, and flattened himself out like a snake in the dust. There was need of such caution, for hardly an instant later a form strode through the darkness, and the fall of a foot puffed the watery dust into his face. It filled his eyes, his nostrils, his lungs.

He lay quietly writhing in an ecstasy of strangulation and the overmastering desire to sneeze. It was terrible seconds before that paroxysm ended, and during it, he told himself that he was sure to die, so great was the pressure of blood in his head.

Gradually he could breathe again, and now he made slowly forward. He knew the back yard of the house as intimately as he knew the palm of his own hand, and so he was able to keep up his snake-like progress from one depression to another.

Near the barn, he looked back, and he was just in time to see a dark form slip out from the window of Destry's room. There it hung for an instant, dangling, helpless in this posture, while half a dozen guns began to roar at the same instant.

Never had Willie heard such a bellowing, crashing

noise. Men were shouting as the guns were fired, and yet for a long moment that swaying form remained there—surely with the life torn out of it long before—hanging so, merely by the convulsive grip of the hands, no doubt!

Or could it be that the darkness of the night was so great and the excitement of the hunters so intense that they were missing even at this short range?

Willie, his heart cold with anguish, stared dimly at that shadowy and pendulous form, while he heard the excited forms around him, and finally one loud voice that yelled: "I'll get him, damn him, even if he gets me!"

A man rushed foward, rifle at shoulder, shooting, advancing, shooting again.

Then:

"It's a fake! It ain't Destry! It's a dummy he's hung out for us! A fake! A fake! Scatter and look for him somewhere else, or he's sure gone from us! He's snaked himself out the far side of the house, I reckon!"

They did not wait for further consultation, but splitting apart, one to one side and one to the other, they rushed to block any further possible flight of the fugitive.

Willie, however, remained for one moment longer, for he was so overwhelmed with relief at the saving of his hero that he was incapable of movement; so it was he and he alone who saw another form slide out over the sill of Destry's window.

This time it did not hang foolishly by the hands, but flicked like a shadow down the side of the house—a shadow such as a fire casts up and down a wall, sending it flickering from the height to the bottom, all in an instant.

Willie saw no more.

He turned madly and plunged into the barn, tortured by the thought that he had betrayed his own trust by not obeying the orders of Destry long before.

Now he rushed for the stall of the tall mare, and whipped into it—to find himself embraced in long, powerful arms.

"It's the kid, is it?" said the voice of Sam Warren. "It's the scarlet fever kid, is it? And where's the rash breakin' out now? Where's Destry now?"

His hard tipped fingers sank into the flesh of the boy as he spoke. And Willie could not stir.

He could only gasp: "Destry's dead! They've murdered him."

"You lie," said tall Sam Warren. "And here I got you on my hands——"

He found a short way out of that difficulty by rapping the youngster across the head with the barrel of his Colt. It was a crushing blow, but though it felled Willie in a heap, it did not altogether stun him, for through a mist he could see a form leap into the entrance of the barn. Then desperation gave Willie voice to yell: "Look out! Warren's here!"

He heard Warren curse through gritted teeth; he saw the form that had darted through the barn door swerve to the side just as the revolver above him thundered and thrust out a darting tongue of fire.

It was answered swifter than its own echo by a leap of flame from the hand of Destry, and Willie saw the tall man stride over him, picking up his feet in a foolish, sprawling way. As Warren stepped forward, he sent in a steady fire, but Willie knew that the shots were wild. He heard one crashing through the shakes that covered the roof of the shed; he heard another smash a lantern so that there was a jingle of wires and a fall of glass.

Then Destry fired again, and Warren toppled stiffly forward, for all the world like a man tipping off a platform for a high dive. His long body struck the ground with an audible thud, but did not move again. From the dark waters into which Sam Warren had fallen, Willie knew that he never would arise.

But he had no time for reflection. There was work to do, and he sprang up with tigerish eagerness in spite of his reeling head. From the peg he jerked the saddle. He had it over the back of the mare as a pantherlike shadow went by him, flirting the bridle over the head of Fiddle. Quick hands dashed those of the boy aside and jerked the cinches up, as voices bawled from the direction of the house: "What's goin' on back in the barn? Hey—Pat and Bill, come along with me!"

Destry was already out the rear door of the barn, and there he took the head of Willie between his hands—and felt the sticky, hot blood that streamed down one side of his face, for the sight of the revolver had torn his scalp!

Chapter Twenty

"Did Warren do that? He did!" said Destry.

"Go on—doncha wait here!" pleaded Willie. "I'm all right. He had to whang me to keep me quiet, only he didn't whang hard enough. Go on, Destry. They're comin'!"

"You done this for me," said Destry. "May I die tomorrow if I ever forget."

"I only wanta say one thing—Dad was only pretendin'—he knew you all the time—he wouldn't be such a doggone fool——"

"You Pop's all right," said Destry. "He's your father. That's the main thing that's right in him. Willie, so long. I'm comin' back to see you. We're gunna be partners!"

He flashed into the saddle. To the bewildered and admiring eyes of the boy it seemed as though no bird with an airy flirt of the wings ever could have moved more swiftly and lightly. Then the tall mare swept into her long canter that flicked her off around a corner of the barn and instantly out of sight and hearing. At that very moment, there was a jumbled outcry from the men within the barn as they stumbled over the limp body of Warren, and then a yell of fear and of fury as they discovered who it was that lay there.

They would not remain long on the ground after that, the boy guessed, and in fact, there was an instant flight for horse and saddle where they had left their ponies up the road and among the trees.

Still Willie remained, as one entranced, behind the barn, looking in that direction where the darkness had swallowed the great Destry. At last he heard the voices of his mother and father entering the barn; the swinging light of the lantern which one of them carried set the cracks flushing and dimming as it rose and ebbed.

"A fine thing you've done, sicking murderers onto one of your guests!" said the woman.

"I was helpless; they was too many for me!" said he. "Besides, he's a bad one. The law's after him!"

"The law ain't after that fox. A wise hoss that has tasted rope-fire don't never pull agin the lariat again! Neither will Destry. He's got his lesson! They didn't do nothin' in the name of the law, but all in the name of this here Sam Warren that feared for his own hide—and lost his scalp tryin' to save it! Look at him lyin' there! He comes with his eight or nine men, and Destry, he sees him, and finishes him, and then fades out! But if I was——"

Willie heard no more. He had faded off among the brush nearby, for all at once the voices of these people made him sick at heart. He had looked on a hero; he had seen a hero in action; upon his head the hands of the great man had been placed.

So, like a prince anointed for the throne, he turned his back upon the facts of life and wandered off into the woods to commune with his swelling heart, and with the future.

The hands of Sheriff Ding Slater were crammed with news of this affair as he walked down the street to the gate of his garden in Wham. He had telephone messages transcribed among the package of papers in his hand, and he had moreover notes upon verbal reports which had been made to him at his office. And yet the affair of the Cumber Pass and the death of Warren did not occupy a great portion of his thoughts. It was something else that bowed his head as he slammed the gate behind him.

"Hey, Ding!" called his wife from a front window.

He was silent; having closed the gate with much force, he remained there, glaring up and down the street.

"Hey, Ding, what's the matter?"

"Aw, nothin', except that after weedin' the crooks out of Wham, they've come crowdin' all back in on me to bother my old age."

"What's happened?"

"Why, an hour ago a gent with a mask on walked into the Fitzgerald store, stuck up young Fitzgerald, and walked off with the money. Not much. Three hundred. He takes that and says it's enough, and walks out again by the back way. Fitzgerald grabs a gun and tears after him, but there ain't anybody climbing the frame of a hoss in the back yard. Whoever it is must of just gone right on around the corner of the house, takin' off his mask as he went, and walked into the crowd on the corner! Cool as ice! Fitzgerald tears into that crowd, but nobody had seen nothing, because they'd been watchin' down the street! There you are! A package of trouble. Open light of the day. And nobody has no clue. Why, that's enough to start a whole crowd of daylight robberies, ain't it?"

"It's gunna work out all right!" said the wife. "Come on in. Here's somebody to see you!"

"I don't wanta see nobody," said the sheriff. "Send him away."

"It ain't a him," said the wife, "and she's waitin' here and noticin' the things that you say and the way that you carry on!"

"Is she?" said the sheriff.

He came stumping up the steps and flung open the door.

"Hey, Charlie," he called to the visitor. "Where'd you come from?"

"How are you, Uncle Ding?" said she.

"Got the rheumatism and the blues," said he, "and my liver's out of kilter. Otherwise, I'm pretty fit for fifty-five!"

"You oughta have a helper," said the girl. "You can't go on bein' the lead hoss and the wheeler and do the brain work and pull all the load, too!"

The sheriff threw his hat into a corner.

"Who'm I gunna get?" he asked. "I been lookin' all these years for a deputy that was worth his salt, but them that I've tried, they spend their time at home shinin' up their badge, and spend their time away from home showin' the badge off to the boys. It don't take much notice to spoil a man, these days. They're gettin' like girls; they like to be all ornamented. Set down, Charlie. I'm plumb glad to see you. We ain't gunna talk about my affairs no more. What about that Destry of yours, that's gone and got himself another man?"

"He ain't mine no more," said she, with a rather twisted smile. "But I'll tell you what, Uncle Ding. He'd make a deputy for you!"

"He? Him? Destry?" gasped Slater.

"I mean he, him, Destry," she answered.

"Why—honey, you mean it really? Destry's—he's—why, I never heard of such an idee."

"Think it over," she said. "Particular if that rheumatism is bad. He'll pull at the wheel for you, all right."

"What would bein' a deputy mean to him?" asked Slater.

"It would mean that the men who hate him wouldn't be so bold to attack him. It's one thing to go after a common man, but an officer of the law is different."

"I ain't noticed it much," said the sheriff. "However, you're right. But it ain't what he wants. It'd cramp his style, considerable, I reckon, seein' that he's doin' most of the lead-in', and the rest of 'em are just playin' on the tricks and followin' suit, most of the time."

"He might of had that idea yesterday, but not today," she replied. "They've hunted him pretty hard, and would of nailed him, too, if it hadn't been for a mite of a boy, people say. Well, that'll make him want to go slower!".

"Sure," agreed Slater. "Fire'll burn you before you boil, and I guess he's been singed a little. But he ain't left his street number with me. I dunno that I could pick the mountain top that he's settin' on now, gettin' ready to pounce like an owl on mice as soon as the evenin' comes."

"He's likely layin' up at Chester Bent's house right now," said the girl.

"What makes you think so?"

"Because Wham's the center, and the folks he's after are scattered all round it. He'll come back here, and he'll likely go to Chet's place."

The sheriff said not a word before he had gathered his hat off the floor, but before he left the room, he took Charlotte Dangerfield by the arm and asked her gravely: "How long'd it take you to work this out?"

"All night," she replied at once, and smiled at him.

"Ay," said the sheriff, "a house you once lived in is always partly home. So long, Charlie. This here may be an idea that I can use."

He went straight up the long street from his house, only pausing at the first corner to look back and see Charlotte saying good-by to Mrs. Slater at the gate. He could guess, by that, that she had made her call for one purpose only.

He continued his way until he came to the fir hedge that surrounded the house of Bent, and opening the gate in the middle of this, he left it swinging, with the latch clicking to and fro across the slot, while he marched up to the front door.

It was opened for him by Destry!

That worthy held out his wrists with a grin.

"I seen you comin'," said he, "and I thought I'd save you the bother of huntin' me up."

Ding Slater had recoiled a little from his unexpected appearance; then he brushed the extended hands aside.

"It ain't for Warren that I'm here," he said. "When a man tries murder, there ain't anything in the law that'll help him when he gets killed. Warren's dead, and Warren's been ripe for dyin' a long time, by my reckoning. I've come here on my own troubles, Harry. Go back in there and set down with me!"

They sat down in the parlor, hushed and dim. Only one shade was raised a few inches to admit the hot light of the middle day. This illumination was only sufficient to reveal them to each other in rough profile.

"Harry," said the sheriff, "sometimes a kid'll play in one back yard just because he don't know what it's like on the far side of the board fence. Maybe you're like that kid?"

"Maybe," said Destry, "I could agree, if I follered the drift."

"You been agin the law or outside of it since you

was a kid. Now you're playin' safe, but still you're agin the house. Suppose, Harry, that I offered to give you a pack to deal for me?"

Destry raised his eyebrows in surprise.

"I mean," said the sheriff, "that I need help, and you kind of need a roof over your head to keep the stones from fallin' on you. Suppose, then, that you was to put on a badge and call yourself my man for a while? Hired man, y'understand?"

Destry tapped the tips of his fingers together.

It's this here Fitzgerald business that bothers you some, I suppose?" he queried.

"I suppose that it does," said the sheriff.

"It'd give me a fine way of fadin' out of the picture for a few days," said Destry, thinking aloud. "It'd make my game easier and their game harder. Why, Ding, I dunno that I can afford to say no to you, no matter how low the wages might be!"

Chapter Twenty-one

The details of the Fitzgerald robbery were quickly told, and Destry considered them for a moment with the blank eye of a man in deep thought. At last he asked: "What's funny about this job, Ding?"

"What would you of done if you'd robbed a store?" asked Ding.

"Waited for dusk, when the till was fuller of money, and the lights was bad outside."

"What else?"

"Had a hoss handy and flopped onto it and rode off."

"But what did *he* do?"

"All different. He took three hundred. How much more was in that till?"

"Three times that much."

"He took a handful and ran?"

"That's it."

"He ran—" muttered Destry absently.

"Are you day dreamin', son?"

"I'm gunna slide away on Fiddle and try this job."

The sheriff pinned a badge inside his coat, saying: "Mind you, Harry, while you wear this, you don't belong to yourself; you're property of the law!"

"Sure," said Destry. "I follow that, all right. If there ain't anything more, I'll start movin'."

"That's what the cat said when she walked on the stove. Are they makin' it that hot for you?"

"They are," admitted Destry. "When they wake you up at night, nine strong, that's something, ain't it?"

"Ay," said the sheriff. "That'd make me take to an out-trail! I'd never come back, neither! This job is gunna rest your nerves considerable, Harry! Good luck to you. They's one last thing."

"And what's that?"

"It was Charlie Dangerfield that suggested where I'd find you, and that I get you for this job."

"She knew I was here?"

"Yeah. Or guessed it."

"She's mighty thoughtful," said Destry. "She reminds me of the gunmen of the early days, that never let a dead one go without a good funeral. It used to set some of 'em back a lot, buyin' coffins and hirin' hearses. And Charlie's that way. She takes care of you after she's done with you. So long, Ding!"

He departed in haste, heedless of the last anxious words which Slater was calling after him. Out to the barn went Destry, took the mare from her pasture, saddled and bridled her, and then chatted for a moment with Bent's hired man, who eyed him with equal awe and suspicion.

"They've done a lot of improvin' of the roads around here, Mack?" said he. "Since I was away, I mean?"

"They've done considerable," said Mack. "The old roads wouldn't satisfy people none. It wouldn't cost enough just to fix them up. They've even had to build a lot of new ones."

"Where to?"

"Why, up Amaritta way, for instance; and down through the Pike Pass."

"That's down towards the railroad, ain't it?"

"That's the way. They let the old trail go. But right now it's twenty mile shorter. You can see from the upper trail how it would be; you can look right down at it, snakin' along the river bed most of the way, travelin' around shorter curves."

"Why did they ever make a new one?"

"Because to widen the old one for freightin' meant blastin' out a lot of rock. But for hoss and saddle, it's still pretty good, except that it's overgrowed a lot! They was uneasy, though, until they found out this fine new way of spending their money! They had to go and get shut of a pile diggin' out the new road."

Destry departed with no further conversation, for he had learned what he wanted, and, turning up the main street, he jogged Fiddle out the road to Pike Pass. Presently he came to the fork, the new road taking the left, the old trail dipping down on the right, but Destry kept the lefthand way.

As the slope increased against him, he drew the mare down to a walk, but it was faster than a cowpony's gait, the long legs of Fiddle stepping out at a good four mile clip up grade and five down. For she walked as eagerly as she galloped, and kept turning her bright head from side to side to keep note of her master, and of all that lay around her.

As they climbed, the old trail was indeed visible, on the opposite side of the cañon, and far lower down. It was not smoothly graded, but jerked up and down according to the way the action of the water, ten thousand years before, had leveled the rocks.

After a few miles, Destry reached a little shack at the side of the way. Weather ages unpainted wood so rapidly that it was impossible from that clue to determine the age of the house, but the brush and the mesquite still grew up close to the door, and Destry could guess that the place had not been occupied very long. Otherwise this firewood would have been cut back to a far greater distance. A half-breed woman sat in the doorway, patting out tortillas from wet corn meal; she nodded in response to Destry's salutation.

"D'you move up here from the old trail?" he asked her.

"No," she replied. "We ain't been in these parts more'n six months. My man wishes he'd never seen the place, too! But cows is cows, I always say, and them that follers them is bound to live miserable. Too hot in summer, too cold in winter, bogged down in spring, and sold in the fall; that's the life of a cowman, God bring 'em help!"

"I thought that I'd seen you once on the old trail," said Destry.

"Never not me!"

"I reckon some still ride that way," he suggested.

"Some that are powerful hurried out of Wham," she replied. "And some I've seen that fair flew!"

"Not many no more?"

"No, not many. After the new trail was opened, they was still some that kept the old way, 'cause they found out that they might save time; but they used up the legs and feet of their hosses down there, so now pretty nigh everyone comes by my house. I pick up a good deal sellin' meals. You ain't hungry, are you?"

"No," said Destry.

She went on: "One come by there two hours back; not fast, though. Easin' his hoss around through the brush and actin' like he was enjoyin' himself on the ride."

"That so? From Wham?"

"I reckon from nobody else."

"I wonder who. Maybe Jimmy Pemberton. He was ridin' out into the pass today."

"Did he have a pinto?"

"Yeah. He did."

"Then that was Jimmy Pemberton that rode up

along the old trail, and you'll never catch up with him on this one!"

"I reckon I won't. I'll just leave him be."

He went on, but no sooner was he around the next hill-shoulder than he turned aside, and slid Fiddle down the slope to the bottom of the ravine.

Two hours would have made about the time that the fugitive from the Fitzgerald robbery would have been riding up this cañon if, as Destry suspected, he had been making for the railroad line; and he was willing to wager a fair sum that the rider of the pinto was the man the sheriff wanted. Therefore, in the name of the law and his new office, Destry sent Fiddle scampering up the old trail.

She went as a deer goes, lightly, gracefully, never fighting the steep places as most horses will do, never getting into a sweat of anxiety over sharp drops in the way, but studying out everything in detail and going nimbly about the solution in her own way. She was one of those rare animals that accept the purpose of the rider and then bend themselves intelligently to fulfill it, without starting and plunging at every unexpected obstacle along the way.

He helped her, too, in that perfect partnership. Often the old trail jumped up the almost sheer face of a rock, and then Destry leaped to the ground and worked his own way up, without giving her the pull of that extra burden. Or again, where it plunged sheer down, he was once more running beside her, and leaping into the saddle only where the ground became more favorable.

So they went on swiftly—an amazing speed, considering the nature of the way. But Fiddle could leap little gullies through which most cowponies would have to jog, staggering down one bank and laboring up the other. And she seemed to know, with that extra instinct which seems like eyes in the foot, exactly which stone would bear her weight, and which would roll and make her stumble.

However, no matter what speed they were making, Destry did not push her too hard, for he realized that a stern chase is a long one, and that the pinto had two hours' start on him. He worked rather to come up with the leader by the dusk of the day than to overtake him with one sustained effort.

So he checked Fiddle, rather than urged her forward.

It was bitterly hot in the ravine. Even when the sun made sufficient westing to fill the ravine with shadow, the heat which the rocks had been drinking all the day they now seemed to give up with one incredible outpouring of locked up energy. No wind could find its way down into the heart of the cañon; the air was close and dead. The mare was cloaked with dripping sweat that rubbed to foam where the reins chafed the sleek of her neck and shoulders. Destry himself was drenched, but he regarded his own comfort less than that of the mare. Four times he stopped to slush water over her, and four times she went on, refreshed, while the pass darkened, and the sky overhead began to grow brilliant with the sunset.

Then Destry called on her for the first time, and she responded with a gallant burst up the long last rise to the summit of the trail. That long mile she put swiftly behind her, and, as he came to the top of the rise, Destry saw before him a sea of broken ground on which the dim trail tossed like the wake of a ship on a choppy sea, swinging this side and that.

But all that he could see of the trail was empty;

then something loomed against the skyline—a pinto, surely——

No, it was only a hereford!

But a moment later, as he was digesting this first disappointment, he saw a broad sombrero with a lofty crown grow up against the sky, and a rider beneath it, sitting tall and straight in the saddle, and finally a pinto mustang; all three were only two swales away from him; and, seeing the pinto stumble with weariness, and sag as a tired horse will do, he knew that man, whoever he might be, was within striking distance!

Chapter Twenty-two

A wind blew across that height and cut against the face of Destry, whipping the dust from his lungs, the weariness from his heart. Across the rise and fall of the hills, he saw the dirty smudge which was the desert atmosphere; behind him the mountains rose up, splitting apart at the pass through which he had just ridden. He gave it one glance, and then made up his mind. The wind came from the left; it was to the right that he sent Fiddle, down into the hollows, so that the wind's own voice might help to stifle the sound of her hoofbeats. Cat claws tore at them as they whipped through, and the mesquite rose up around them like a dusky mist, rolling back on either hand, as he kept Fiddle at full gallop for two miles at least, jockeying her forward with his weight shifted toward the withers.

Then he pulled her up onto the trail, the old trail in the red of the sunset, and, leaping down, threw the reins. She was breathing hard, but cleanly.

He hurried to the crest of the swale before him, and, glancing cautiously over, he saw the pinto and its rider jogging through the hollow beneath, straight into his hands.

He looked back over his shoulder. Fiddle already was cropping grass at the side of the road, and far off he saw a slowly moving cloud of smoke in the lowlands. It might have been dust raised by a whirlwind, but it leaned back too far for that, and he knew it was a train. From this same rise the fugitive—if fugitive he were—would sight his open door to flight.

The thought pleased Destry and all the iron in his heart!

He crouched in a nest of stones and waited. He stayed there until he saw the sombrero grow up on the other side of the rise, then the nodding head of the mustang—and the face of the rider.

It was Lefty Turnbull! It was Lefty, who, during the trial six years before, of all the twelve jurors, alone had sat from first to last with a fixed sneer of hostility on his lips.

It seemed to the startled and vengeful eyes of Destry that the same smile was now on the lips of this man, and it transported Destry back to the courtroom, to the spiderweb in the corner of the ceiling, to the slant shaft of the sunlight that streamed through the window, to the barking voice of the district attorney— and again to this sneering smile of Turnbull!

Or was it merely weariness, the grin of long labor, which will make men seem to smile?

"Hey—!" cried out Lefty softly, and reined in his horse as he saw the mare before him.

"Fill your hand, Lefty," cried Destry, from the side. "Fill your hand." Then, remembering on what commission he rode, he added loudly: "In the name of the law!"

There was an old saying among those who knew that there was enough of the cat in Lefty Turnbull to land him on his feet from any height. Or, hold him by hands and feet a foot from the floor, like a cat he would land on all fours when dropped. Moreover, he was an old and experienced fighter, polished by a trip to the Klondike, and hardened by a few winters in the Canada woods.

To all that was said of him he lived up now.

For at the sound of Destry's voice, instead of

drawing a gun and shooting to the side from which the threat came, Lefty flung himself out of the saddle, and, as he dropped past the belly line of the pinto, he was shooting.

The first bullet might well have ended the fight, for it struck a boulder inches from Destry's head and cast a burning spray of rock splinters into his face. Had they volleyed into his eyes, that would have proved the finish! But luck saved him. His own first shot went wide to the right. He knew he had pulled it even as he compressed the trigger.

The second would split the forehead of Turnbull as a knife splits the brittle rind of a squash, yet there was somewhere a hundredth part of a second which Destry could devote to thought, and in that whiplash instant he remembered his word to the sheriff.

He was not his own man, now; he was the servant of the law and, being that, as Harry Destry he did not exist, nor were the quarrels and the feuds of that man of any importance to him. He was not even sure that this was the criminal for whom he had been sent!

So he turned his aim a little to the right, and literally saw the impact of the big slug jerk at the body of Turnbull. The Colt exploded in Lefty's hand; but dropped as it was fired, and rattled down the face of a rock.

Still, disarmed as he was, there was no thought of surrender in the man. He was lying sprawled on the ground, in the perfect position for accurate shooting, when the bullet of Destry plunged through his left shoulder and ruined his shooting hand. Yet he lurched up now to his feet and ran forward to scoop up the weapon with his other hand.

Never was there such fiercely sweet temptation in

Destry's soul as when he saw the full target arise before him. The buttons of the coat seemed to glimmer like stars, inviting the attention of the marksman, and the broad forehead seemed unmissable.

Yet he did not fire!

He belonged to the law. He was only a tool in the hands of the sheriff, and bitterly he told himself that Ding Slater well knew the identity of the criminal, and had despatched Destry merely to torment him.

"I ain't doin' murder today," said Destry. "Leave your gun be!"

Lefty Turnbull hesitated, his right hand reaching for the weapon. He was, like most left-handed people, quite hopeless on the other side. He knew that he had no ghost of a chance to manage the Colt successfully under the very nose of Destry's gun, but still the fighting fury ruled him for a breathing space. Then it passed and left him cold, very cold—trembling with the chill of realization that had struck through his mind.

He stood up, his empty hands dangling uselessly at his sides, his gaunt face as fixed as stone.

"It ain't murder," he said with perfect self-control. "It's your right. But tell 'em, when the time comes for the talkin', that I didn't go at you two for one, like the Ogdens, and that I didn't run, like Wendell, nor play the sneak, like Clyde Orrin, nor come at you in the dark, like Sam Warren. Do me right, Harry. Now turn loose and be damned to you!"

"If you was to of been told by me, you wouldn't of said more that I'd like to say myself," declared Destry. "But I ain't playin' my own game, or you'd be lookin' at the sky now, old son, and not seein' the pretty sunset Stand still. I'm gunna have to tie up that—did it nick you deep?"

"Through the shoulder—that's all," said Lefty.

"Lemme see."

Lefty sat on a rock, while his conqueror, in the ruddy but uncertain light of the sunset, sliced away the sleeve of his coat and examined the wound.

"It went clean through," said he. "Feel as though the bone was smashed, Lefty?"

"There ain't no feelin'."

"Try this!"

He grasped the dangling arm and slowly worked it around, listening closely for the grinding of the broken edges of bone, while Lefty cursed steadily through his teeth, but endured.

"The bone's safe," said Destry. "I'm glad of that. I'll save you whole and sound for——"

He stopped the sentence in its midst.

"For the next time?" completed Lefty. "I'm ready for you any day or time, young feller. I would of got you plenty today, only you had the break of takin' me unexpected from the side. Which I don't mind telling you that I nigh dusted you that time, Harry!"

The familiar sneer of ferocity and contempt was on his face as he spoke.

"You talk fine; you talk like a teacher," said Destry. "Now shut up while I work on you."

With dust he clotted the blood; with strips of his own under and outer shirt, he bound up the wound and fastened the arm tight, from shoulder to elbow, against the side of his victim. All of this, Lefty endured in perfect silence, though the sweat dripped steadily from his chin.

It was utterly dark when the last knot was tied.

"Now," said Destry, "you ornery, low-lifed son of mis'ry, did you rob the Fitzgerald store?"

"Are you doin' errand boy work for the sheriff?"

"Which I ask you a question, which you ask me another. Does that make sense?"

"They's a wallet in my coat," said the prisoner. "You can look in that."

"They is striped skunks and spotted polecats," said Destry, "and you're both if you think that I handle another gent's private wallet."

"The mail—that's different, eh?"

"You fool," said Destry, "if you'd had a right to run me up, d'you think that I'd ever be here on your trail this minute? D'you think I cant take my medicine as well as the next man? I ask you again: Did you grab the coin from Fitzgerald's store?"

"Suppose I did?"

"Then why didn't you clean out the till?"

"That's my business. I needed some change. I didn't want to harm Fitzgerald none. He's white."

"You lie!" persisted Destry. "You wanted a couple hundred so bad that it looked to you like a million. You grabbed what you needed and the rest didn't matter. You wasn't thinkin' about Fitzgerald, but about your own hide!"

"Go on," said the other. "You act like you know!"

"You was sneakin' out of town," said Destry quietly, "because you'd heard about Sam Warren's bad luck, and about me headin' back for Wham. And when you heard that, you figgered on the railroad. You were scared out of Wham, son, and it was me that scared you!"

"That's the grandpa of all lies I ever heard!"

"Lefty, it's the straight! By the look of the case I knew that him that grabbed that money was pretty much on the wing; I figgered that the railroad was where he was headin' for, with enough money to see him out. He only stopped at Fitzgerald's for a ticket, as you might say, and havin' that, he breezed along. Look me in the eye, Lefty, and—"

But though the darkness might have helped Lefty, for some reason he was unable to raise his head, which had fallen on his chest.

"A peer!" said Destry bitterly. "One of the twelve peers! Peer of a gray cat and a yaller hound! I was aimin' to be sorry for you, Lefty, and I was aimin' to figger a way to keep you out of jail, but there's where you b'long, and there's where I'm takin' you! Half of 'em are off the list. But it's still six to one, and I've an idea that the rest of 'em are gunna play their hand together, and close to the chest!"

Chapter Twenty-three

Slowly they worked back through the mountains. The way was long, and the wounded man had to have rest and sleep and food. Destry was guard, nurse, and cook for his companion, and silent in all three occupations; and sometimes as Lefty Turnbull lay in the shade, setting his teeth against the pain in his wound, he would feel a slight chill run through him, and then he dared not glance at Destry, for he knew that the latter would be watching him with cold, ominous eyes which it had grown impossible for Lefty to meet.

Savage hate, contempt, bitter disappointment were the iron in the heart of Destry now; and once Lefty strove to banter with him on the subject.

"Now, look here!" he said to his captor. "There's only two dead. There's Wendell scared stiff and driven away from home; there's Jud Ogden cripple, hut livin'; there's Clyde Orrin shamed in front of everybody, but livin' too. Why should you pick me out for a killin', Harry? Why should it bust your heart that I'm gunna be sent up to the pen for a dozen years, maybe? Ain't that enough?"

"Why, man," said Destry, "they's some folks that I'd hate to send behind the bars for a dozen days—if I could pick the dozen! But one like you—you'll be at home up yonder. They make trusties out of your kind of a man, and set 'em to spyin' and playin' stool-pidgeon. You might even get promoted to shine the warden's boots, or play catch with his little boy. Prison ain't gunna mean much to you, but the sheriff's tied my hands, and I've had to do his dirty work and leave my own work slip by!"

After that, Lefty did not pursue the subject for most obvious reasons, and so they worked gradually on their way, avoiding all traveled trails, until in the dusk of the next day they came out from the woods upon the shoulder of the mountain overhanging Wham.

There was still light to blink rosily on the windows toward the west, and to show the coiling arms of dust which enwrapped the town; to show also the trailing smoke that traveled up the opposite slopes towards the mines of the Crystal Range.

"You don't look happy," suggested Lefty, staring aside at his companion.

And Destry said gloomily: "They've got together by this time. They scattered when they heard of me comin' back; they joined again when they heard I was tame; they ran again when they seen I wasn't so safe. And now that I've worked down a few of 'em, they'll gather once more!"

"And you're scared, Harry?" asked the other, very curiously, as though he really felt that this was an emotion about which Destry could know nothing.

"Scared to death, pretty near," replied Destry sourly. "Who wouldn't be? What's the old yarn about the six sticks in one bundle, and apart? They're down there plannin' and workin' together. Six rats, cornered, back up agin the wall, poison as rattlesnakes, they're hatin' me so hard! And him— the one that's leadin'—he's the one that I'd like to find!"

"What one?" asked Lefty.

"Him that runs the party for the rest of you!" said Destry fiercely. "Who sent Jose Vedres with the letter to Orrin? That's what I wanta know! Lefty, if you'll tell me that, maybe I'll be able to wangle you away from the sheriff. I promised to turn you in to him as deputy. What hinders me tearin' the badge off right after and takin' you away agin?"

"For the name of who?" shouted Lefty, irritated by this hope, dangled under his nose. "Who is it?"

"You don't know?" asked Destry, more curious than before "Does he work in the dark even with you? No wonder that I can't find him out! I tell you, old son, that the thought of him scares me more and more. It wasn't either of the Ogdens, or Orrin, or Wendell, or you, or Warren. Who's left? There's little Clifton. Looks like his forehead is too narrow to hold such ideas. There's Henry Cleeves that knows more about machinery than men. Bud Williams would be fine if it was only fightin' with his hands that he had to do, and Bud Truckman and Bull Hewitt are both too slow to think twice standin' in the same place. They's Phil Barker left of the lot. It might be that they's somethin' more than his jokes about him, but I ain't so sure. Lefty, if I could lean on you for that information, I'd sure pay you back! I'd wipe out the score agin you, and be in your debt for the bullet that snagged you! Who's him that stands behind the show and tells the others what to do? I gotta get him, or I've got nothin'."

This speech he delivered in a murmuring voice, for he was thinking aloud, rather than addressing his companion, but when Lefty heard the gist of the words, he was forced to shake his head.

"I dunno who it could be—not nobody!" he said. "You been imaginin' all of this here direction and deep thinkin'!"

"Is rats hard to smell in an old house?" asked Destry.

"I reckon not!"

"I've smelled a rat, and a big one!" said Destry. "Now it's dark enough for us to get down the hill!"

They went down to the rear of the village, and there they moved cautiously, with Destry directing the way, until they came in behind the house of the sheriff.

They could look readily through the lighted kitchen window, and see fat Mrs. Slater washing supper dishes; rounding to the side, they observed Ding Slater himself sitting on the screen porch with his feet in carpet slippers, a newspaper spread out in his hands, and a pipe between his teeth.

"If the crooks hate him, why don't they come and murder him on a night like this?" suggested Destry.

"Because birds don't come nigh to snakes if they can help it," replied Lefty readily. "Harry—whatever I done—the minute you walk me onto that veranda, I'm in hell! I voted with the rest of 'em on that jury—"

"Are you gunna beg like a cur in the wind up?" he asked scornfully.

"No," said the other. "I'm damned if I will. Shall I walk first?"

"Yeah. Go in first."

Destry marched Lefty up the front steps in this fashion, and through the screened door until he was confronting the sheriff. Ding Slater folded the paper in his lap.

"Hello," said the sheriff. "You need a doctor, and not Ding Slater, Lefty. Who's that with you?"

"Me," said Destry.

At his voice, the sheriff leaped to his feet like a boy.

"It ain't Lefty that raked out the till for Fitzgerald!" he exclaimed. "Lefty ain't cut small enough to do that sort of a job!"

Destry threw a wallet on the table beside the sheriff's chair.

"He says the coin is in this. I dunno. I leave it to you to look for it. But here he is. Ding, you knew before I started out that he'd done that job!"

"Confound, you, Harry. How should I know?"

"You sent me out to keep me from drillin' him, which is what's comin' to him. Ding, you did that on purpose."

"If I'd knowed who done the job, would I of asked help from any man?" exclaimed the sheriff. "Harry, they's times when you talk like a young fool. But——"

"Take this," said Destry. "I've done enough dirty work for you. I've mopped up your floor once, and that's enough. It'll take me years to wear the stain off of my hands!"

He flung the badge of deputyship on the table and turned on his heel.

"But Harry—Harry!" called the sheriff.

Destry was already gone.

He passed back to the place where he had left the mare tethered and, taking her by the reins, led her slowly past the fence of the rear yards of Wham, until he came to the place of Chester Bent.

Once more he left the mare at a distance, and approaching the house with caution, he slipped around the side of it and came to the lighted front window. He caught the sill, and, drawing himself up, saw Bent himself inside his library, reading, or seeming to read; but every now and then the glance of Bent rose from the book and was fixed in solemn reflection upon the wall.

The front door was not far away, but Destry had several reasons, one better than another, for not going around to it. Instead, he swung himself up on his hands, sat on the sill, and turned into the room.

A quick side step removed him from the lighted square of the window and he stood against the wall rolling a cigarette.

All of this had been accomplished so softly that Bent had not lifted his eyes from the big book which was unfolded in his lap, and Destry waited before scratching his match, until he had made sure that his friend was not actually reading, but was immersed in his own thoughts. For though he fingered the edge of the page for some time, he never raised and turned it. At last, Destry struck the match. The explosion of the head sounded wonderfully loud in the room; it sent a shock through Bent like the explosion of a revolver.

But he did not leap up to his feet. Instead, instantly mastering himself, he leaned forward a little in his chair and turned his head toward the intruder.

Then: "Harry!" he said, and laughed with relief.

Destry went to the big library table and sat on the edge of it, swinging one slender foot while he eyed his companion.

"Why the window, Harry?" asked the other.

"A man ain't like a hoss," said Destry. "He gets mighty tired of walkin' through the same gate into the same pasture. So I come in tonight over the bars."

"Into the same old pasture, though. Eh, boy?"

"No," said Destry. "I've found somethin' new to think about. I've found it since I came in here!"

"What is it?"

"A thing I better not talk to you about," said Harry.

The other looked down at the floor, then tapped his fingers lightly on the face of his book. As he looked up once more, Destry said: "Them wrinkles in the back of your neck, and that sleekness all over you, Chet, is it fat or muscle?"

"Muscle? What do I do to get muscle?" asked Bent. "I'm no athlete, Harry. You know that."

"Some men are born strong and stay strong," said Destry. "But that ain't what I was thinkin' about."

"What was it, Harry?"

"I was rememberin' back to a time when a strange boy come to school. He was not very big, but he looked thick and strong and fast. I was scared of him from the first glance. And for a month I dodged him till one day as I went home after school I came up sudden behind him and seen his eyes open big as I went by. By that, I knew he was as scared of me as I was of him; and so we fought it out right pronto!"

"And you won, eh?"

"I disremember, but——"

"Am I afraid of you, Harry?"

The other thought, then shook his head.

"Of the whole bunch," said Destry slowly, "I reckon that you're the only man that ain't afraid of anything above the ground or under it!"

Chapter Twenty-four

It seemed that this compliment was not altogether pleasing to Bent, for he waved it hurriedly aside and said: "I'm pretty soft. I always was!"

"Some of the soft colts make the hard hosses," observed Destry. "You've growed up, old timer. But I was thinkin' as I stood agin the wall that you ain't everything that I thought you was."

"Maybe not, Harry. You've had pretty high ideas about me."

"Why the book, when you don't read it?" asked Destry.

At this, Bent took his eyes definitely from his own thoughts and stared fixedly at Destry. Then he pointed to the window shade behind his head.

"Fake?" said Destry, his lips compressing after he spoke.

"Fake," said Bent frankly.

"I'm mighty sorry to hear it."

"I knew you would be. But there's the truth. I can't lie to you, Harry."

The latter sighed.

"To make 'em think that you're in here studyin'?"

"Mostly that. I'm ambitious. I want the respect of other people. The fact is, Harry, that when I've finished a day at my office, I'm so fagged that I can't use my head for much else. I like to be alone and think things over. That's the way of it! Well, I got into the habit of sitting here; then I heard people talking about my late hours and all that sort of thing, so I rigged up the sham, and there you are!"

Destry nodded.

"I can follow that," he said. "But I'd rather——"
He paused.

"You'd rather that I'd rob a bank than do this?"

"Pretty near, I think!"

"You're right," answered the other. "Any crime's better if it takes courage to do it! You'll never think much of me after this, Harry!"

"I'll like you better, because you told me the straight of it. I suppose I'll like you better for this than if you was to lay down your life for me!"

He went suddenly to Bent and laid a hand on his shoulder.

"Sometimes," he said gravely, "I pretty nigh believe in a God. Things are so balanced! My friends turned out crooks and traitors to me; the woman I loved, she turned me down the first chance; but I've got one friend that balances everything. You, Chet."

He stopped abruptly and snapped his fingers.

"I'm going up to bed. It's my last night here, I reckon."

"Why the last night? Why d'you say that, old timer?"

"I can feel in my bones that they're close to me. Six of 'em are left."

"I thought it was seven?"

"I brought in Lefty, this evenin'. That's where I been, on his trail. Old Ding Slater put me on the job, and I had to bring him back and turn him over."

"Tell me about it! Lefty gone? He's worth two, to have out of the way!"

"I don't wanta talk. You'll hear people spin the yarn tomorrow. Good night, Chet."

"Good night, old man. Only—I should think that you'd feel safe now! In my own house!"

"Of course you'd think that. But you ain't got eyes for every door—or every window!"

He smiled and pointed at the one through which he had entered. Then he left the room.

The instant he was in the comparative dimness of the hallway, his manner changed to that of the hunted animal. Swiftly and lightly he walked, and paused now and again to listen, hearing the stir of voices at the rear of the house, and then the whir of the big clock which stood at the landing, followed by the single chime for the half hour.

Then he went up the stairs, treading close to the wall where the boards were less apt to creak under his weight. So he went up to the attic floor where his room was, but he did not turn in at the door. Instead, he paused there for a moment and listened intently.

There was not a sound from the interior.

Yet still he did not enter, but, turning the knob of the door by infinitesimally small degrees, he pushed it a fraction of an inch past the catch, then allowed the knob to turn back. He drew back, and a moment later a draft caused the freed door to sway open a few inches.

There was no movement within the bedroom. Yet still he lingered, until the current of air had pushed the door wide. Drawn far back into a corner of the corridor, he still waited with an inhuman patience. The dark was thick, yet he could make out the glimmering panel of the door's frame.

Finally, out of this issued a shadow, and another, and two more behind. They stood there for a moment, and then slipped down the hall. Close to Destry, the leader paused and held out his arms to stop the others.

"We're chucking a chance in a lifetime!" said he.

"I've had enough," replied another. "I can't stand

it. When the damn door opens itself—that's too ghostly for me!"

"It was only the wind, you fool!"

"I don't care what it was. I've got enough. I'm going to leave. The rest of you do what you want!"

"Bud, will you stay on with me?"

"Where?"

"Back in that room, of course! He's bound to come there. He seen the sheriff, and after that, he'll come here. Likely talkin' with Bent downstairs, right now!"

"I'll tell you," answered Bud, "I wouldn't mind waitin', but not in that room, after the ghost has got into it!"

"Ghost, you jackass!"

"You're tellin' me that the wind opened the door. Sure it did. And it blew the ghost in on us!"

"Bud, I don't believe you mean what you say. I won't believe that! Ghost talk out of you!"

"A wind," said Bud, "that's able to turn the knob of a door, can blow in a ghost, too!"

"You fool, of course the latch wasn't caught!"

"Anyway, I've had enough."

They went down the stairs. Noiselessly as Destry had ascended, so noiselessly did the four go down, and Destry gripped the naked revolver which he held, tempted to fire on them from behind. In spite of the darkness, he could not have missed them!

However, he let them go, still kneeling on the hall carpet and listening.

He thought he heard the opening of a window, but even this was managed so dexterously that he could not be sure. It was only after several moments that he was sure that the house no longer held that danger for him, and he started down to tell Chester Bent about what he had seen and heard.

However, after a moment of reflection he changed his mind. There was nothing that Bent could do except feel alarm and disgust at his inability to protect a guest. The men were gone; Bent could not overtake them in the dark; and since one attempt had been planned for this night, it was not likely that there would be another before morning.

So Destry went into the bedroom, threw himself wearily on the bed, and, without even taking off his clothes or locking the door, went instantly to sleep.

When he wakened, it was not yet dawn. He rose quickly, washed his face and hands, and, sitting down by lamplight at the table, he wrote hastily:

Dear Chet,

This is to say good-by for a time. I'm going to leave Wham, and even leave you.

I'm traveling light, and leave a good deal of stuff behind me. You might let it stay in this room. It will make other folks, probably, think that I'm coming back here. And the more I can confuse the others, the luckier it will be for me.

They're hot after me, Chet. There were four men waiting for me in my room, last night when I came upstairs. I managed to get them out without trouble, but the next time won't be so easy.

So long, old fellow. You certainly been the top of the world to me.

I'm not thanking you for what you've done. But I'll tell you that you're the man who makes life worth while for me.

HARRY.

This message he thrust under Bent's door, and hurried away into the dark of the morning.

Chapter Twenty-five

The emotions of Chester Bent were not at all what Destry would have imagined. For when the former rose in the morning and found the note which had been pushed under the edge of his door, his face puckered savagely, and one hand balled into a fist.

He dressed hurriedly and went to the house of James Clifton. It was a little shack that stood almost on the very street, built by the father, and now occupied by his talented son, who was a serious investigator of the mines and therefore, according to the public, a "lucky" investor.

Chester Bent walked swiftly enough to feel his leg muscles stretching, and every step he took restored his confidence, though it did not diminish his irritation. Early as it was, there were already people on the street, and, of the dozen he passed, he knew the face and name of every one. Moreover, each of them had a special smile, a special wave of the hand for him; each looked as though he gladly would pause for conversation. But Bent went quickly by. He knew his own power in that town, however, from the looks he had seen in the faces of the pedestrians, and he was smiling to himself when he came to Clifton's house.

He found the proprietor in his small kitchen, with the smoke from frying ham ascending into his face. Jimmy Clifton turned a face as yellow as a Chinaman's toward his guest. He was like a Chinaman in other ways, for he had a froglike face, with a little awkward body beneath it. Some said that Jimmy Clifton had been through the fire when he was an infant, thereby accounting for the quality and color of his skin, which looked like loosely stretched parchment over the bones.

In spite of his peculiarities, however, Clifton was not really an ugly man so much as a strange one. He had a cordial manner which made him many friends, and he showed it now as he advanced to meet Bent and shook him warmly by the hand, hoping that he would join him at a breakfast which was ample for two.

But Bent refused. His irritation increased and his good humor lessened as he accompanied his host into the next room, which served for dining room, guest room, and living room in the shack. There they sat down, and, as Clifton began to eat, Bent observed:

"Suppose that your father had been tangled up in a row like this? How long would he have hesitated? He would have stayed there in Destry's room until morning. For that matter, he would have stayed there alone, too, and waited until he was in bed!"

He pointed, as if for verification to a long string of grizzly claws which hung across the wall from one side to the other. Old Clifton had killed the animals whose claws were represented there, and Indianlike he had saved the mementoes. There was a tale that he actually had engaged one of the great brutes in a cave and had killed it with a knife thrust. Without imputations upon the courage of little Jimmy Clifton, it was plain that he was a lame descendant of such a hero.

That young man now regarded the sinister decoration on the wall as he tackled his breakfast. The greatest peculiarity of Jimmy Clifton was that he was never perturbed, by words or deeds.

Then he said in answer: "I don't know. The old man was a pretty tough fellow, but I don't know about him staying alone in the same room with

Destry. I'll tell you this, though. I tried to get the rest of 'em to stay with me!"

"Bah!" exploded Chester Bent. "Tell me the truth, Jimmy! You were all of you in a blue funk!"

"I was scared, sure," said Clifton readily, "but not in a funk. I would have seen it through, but not alone. I wasn't up to that. You don't know what happened. The infernal latch of the door hadn't caught, and all at once a draft must have hit it, though there was no whistle of wind around the house. But suddenly the door sagged; then it opened, and a whisper of air fanned through the room. A pretty ghostly business!"

"What did you do? When was it that this happened?"

"About ten, I suppose!"

"I'll tell you who the ghost was! It was Destry. He went up to bed at exactly ten, I think!"

"Hello! You mean that he opened the door and stood there waiting for us?"

"Of course he was there in the hall, laughing at four scared heroes as they sneaked off. I was waiting downstairs, and waiting and waiting to hear gunshots. Then I thought that maybe you'd closed in on him and done it with knives. But I decided there wasn't enough blood in you all for that sort of work!"

"Did you?" asked the other blandly.

"I did! And now you've foozled the entire thing, and Destry's gone. He left me a note. Confound it, Jimmy, you've thrown away a golden opportunity!"

The other nodded.

"It was a great chance," he said. "Of course I didn't expect that the boys would get such a chill at the last minute. They were game enough for men, but not for ghosts, Chet. Not for that! They light-footed it out of the room, and they wouldn't come back. That's all there was to it."

"But to think!" groaned Bent. "Four of you—in the dark—and Destry in your hands!"

"Tell me," said Clifton. "What makes you hate Destry so like the devil?"

"I'll tell you, Jimmy, that you'd never understand why I hate him so completely. But let that go. The main point is that I see nothing will ever be done with him, no matter how many opportunities I give him, until I take up the work with my own hands!"

"Is it the girl?" asked Clifton. "Is she still fond of him? With Destry out of the way, d'you think that you could have her?"

"Jimmy," said the other darkly, "that's a confounded impertinence that I can't take even from you!"

The other waved his hand.

"Let it go. I'm sorry. Only, we know each other so well, old fellow, that I thought I could talk out to you!"

Bent shrugged his shoulders, but he added at once: "I'm sorry I lost my temper. You can see this is a blow to me. Now the bird's escaped out of my hand, and God knows how I'll get a string on him again! It's a blow to the rest of you, also! He's snagged six; the six who remain are apt to do a little sweating now!"

"I'm sweating, for one," said Clifton.

"Then we'll have to put our heads together and try again. There's another thing. When you got them into my house, you didn't have to let them guess that I was with you?"

"Not a bit," said Clifton. "The boys thought you'd be almost as dangerous to them as Destry!"

"I'm glad that you've kept me sheltered! A whisper of the truth would bring Destry down on me like seven devils!"

"Of course. No fear of that. I've kept a closed mouth about you. And Destry will never know! People are a little afraid to be too curious about you, anyway, Chet."

"Afraid? Of me? That's a joke!"

"Is it? I don't know," replied Clifton. "There are some who say that there's an iron fist under Bent's soft hand. I'm a little afraid of you myself, old son! Or else I'd have talked before about something that I want to know!"

"What's that?"

"The notes are due today, Chet."

"Hello! Those notes? But not the grace, Jimmy!"

"The grace, too! The time's up today."

"Forgot all about 'em," said Bent rising. "But I'll have the money for you in a day or two."

"Are you sure?"

"Of course I'm sure!"

"I need it, pretty badly," said Clifton.

"Are you pinched?"

"Yes."

"Drop over to my house this evening, will you, and I'll give you a check?"

"Thanks," said Clifton. "I'll do that!"

And Chester Bent departed with a little haste that was not thrown away on the observant eye of the smaller man.

Back in his office, Mr. Bent sat for a long time at his desk, considering ways and means. His secretary, after one wise and sour look at him, left him strictly alone.

It was not until the mid-morning that he ventured

out on the street. Then he went straight to the bank and found the president in, a rosy, plump man of fifty, whose refusals were always so masked and decorated beneath his smile that most of their sting was taken away.

He wanted to know what he could do for Bent, and the latter said instantly: "I have some deals coming up. I need twelve thousand. Can you let me have it?"

The president's eye grew rather blank in spite of his smile. Then he said with the Western frankness which invades even the banking world:

"Bent, this is one of the times that I'm stumped. Look here. You're a rising man in this town. You own property in mines. You own a good deal of real estate——a lot of it, in fact. You're what people consider a rich man. That's the opinion I have of you, myself."

"Thanks," said Bent, "but——?"

"There is another side to it, too. That's this. You're young. You've made a quick success, out of nothing, apparently. You've rolled a big load right up the hill. But one can't be so sure that you're at the top of it!"

"Go," encouraged Bent. "I like to have frankness, of course."

"You'll get that from me. On the one hand, I don't want to antagonize a man whose patronage will probably mean a lot to this bank. Personally I think you're all right. But a banker can't let personalities enter too far into his business dealings."

"I understand that. But even banking has to be a gamble."

"Yes. That's true, but with as narrow a margin of failure and chance as possible. Now, then, Bent, as I say, you seem to have gained almost the top of the hill, rolling up a big ball before you. How you made your start, I don't know. But six years ago you seemed suddenly to come into your own. You extended in all directions. You got your hands on property. Almost like a man who had come into a legacy—"

The glance of Bent strayed a little uneasily out the window.

"You've done wonderfully well, but suppose that several things happened. Most of your property you don't own outright. You have a lot of mortgages. Convenient things—they leave an operator with his hands free for more speculation. At the same time, they're dangerous poison. Here you are, in need of twelve thousand. On the face of it, it's not a large sum. But suppose, Bent, that Wham went bust? It's a quick boom town; it may be a skeleton in another year. There's a new town opening up on the other side of the Crystal Mountains. Seems to me to be better placed than this. Perhaps it'll kill us. That would wipe out your real estate holdings in Wham at a stroke and fill your hands with heavy cash debts—because you haven't bought in at the bottom of the market by any means! As a matter of fact, you've been pretty high in it! I suggest this to you, not because I haven't confidence in Wham, but because I'm trying to explain to you why I don't think it would be good banking to lend you twelve thousand dollars."

"Bad policy?"

"It might be the best policy in the world, Bent. It might secure your faith in us and we'd grow as you grow in the world. But on the other hand there's one chance in ten that you might break, and if you break it would be a serious loss for us. I don't want to take that ten per cent chance. I don't feel justified in doing so!"

"That's business luck," he said. "I don't blame you a bit. And I'll manage this all right. Only a temporary need, old man."

He went out onto the street, and walked down it, still smiling a little, and envious glances followed his contented face. But as he went on he was seeing such a picture as would not have pleased most men, and which did not please Bent himself—a dead man was stretched before him, and the dead man wore the face of Jimmy Clifton.

Chapter Twenty-six

Back at his office once more, his secretary, Sarah Gann, came in to tell him that a visitor was there for him.

"Send him away," said Bent irritably. "I don't wanta see him, no matter who it is."

"A boy," said Sarah Gann.

"Well, I've told you what to do with him."

"He's come for something about Destry," said she, looking back as she reached the door.

"Destry? Then send him in!"

A faint grimace that might have been triumph appeared on her lips as she went out, and presently at the door appeared as ragged a boy as Bent ever had seen. He had on a coat that reached to his knees, the two side pockets bulging. His feet were without shoes and apparently as hard as sole leather. All his clothing was that of a man, abbreviated and tattered. Yet he gave an impression of a swift, muscular young body beneath those drapings.

"You carrying bombs in those pockets?" asked Bent, leaning a little forward in his chair and resting his elbows on the edge of his desk.

For every man carries within himself a sympathy for free boyhood in which he can plunge and be lost; and Bent had reasons for wishing to be freed from the facts of the moment.

"I got pecan nuts in this pocket," said the youngster.

He was a little frightened, a little awestricken, but a fine straightness of regard was in his eyes.

"You like 'em?"

"They don't weigh much, and they last a long time," said the boy.

He took out a chamois bag and, opening it, revealed a quantity of kernels.

"The other pocket's pretty full, too, eh?"

"Toothbrush," said the boy, and, unconsciously smiling a little, Bent had a glimpse of snowy teeth. "Ma got me plumb in the habit," he apologized. "Then they's a change of socks, and a bandana, and a chunk of soap."

"You're fixed for traveling," declared Bent.

"Yeah. I done a hundred and ten mile."

"In how long?"

"Three days."

"Mountains?"

"Yeah."

"That's good time."

"My feet ain't weighed down with shoes, none."

"I don't see a hat, though."

A battered wisp of straw was produced from behind his back.

"It don't look very much," said the boy, "but it sure sheds rain pretty good, account of it havin' so much hog grease on it."

"Who are you, son?"

"Name of Willie Thornton, sir."

"And what brought you here?"

"Destry."

The man started from his leisurely posture, his leisurely thoughts.

"Destry! What's he to you?"

"He said he wanted to see me agin; so I come to him. Home didn't seem much after he been there.

Nobody knows where he is unless you can show me the way. They say you're his best friend."

"I'm his friend, Willie. Tell me. Are you the boy who stood by him when Sam Warren tackled him one night?"

"I was around," said Willie with diffidence.

"Is that where you got the bump on the side of your head?"

"It might of been. I got whacked that night," said Willie.

Bent suddenly realized that something was to be done. He left his chair with a start and held out his hand.

"I'm mighty glad to see you, mighty glad!" he said. "So will Destry be when you show up. He's talked a good deal about you. D'you want to start for him now?"

"I'd like that pretty well, sir."

"You go home to my house, first of all. You need a couple of good meals under your belt and a sleep in an honest bed. Where have you turned in the last few nights?"

"I found a farm once and made a bed of boughs the next night. It was tolerable cold, though."

"I'll bet it was. Ask your way to my house, up at the end of the street. Wait a moment. Take this!"

He scribbled a note on a piece of paper.

"Give that to any one at the house; they'll take care of you till I come home, and if they don't treat you right, you tell me about it, Willie."

Willie shifted from one foot to another.

"If I could find out the trail to Mr. Destry—" he began.

"You'll have that trail told you, Willie. There's no

hurry about that. In the meantime, I want to get to know you better. Remember that Destry's my best friend, and I want to know you for his sake. Run along, Willie; I'll be home before very long."

He took Willie to the door, patted his shoulder, and dismissed him; but the last upward flashes of Willie's keen gray eyes unsettled Bent a little. The wolf on the trail is a sleepy thing, and the wildcat is totally unobservant, compared with the eye of a young boy; and Bent knew that he had been searched to the soul and found not altogether such a person as the best friend of the great Destry should be.

Thinking of that, he turned back gloomily into his office. There appeared to be in Destry a force which frightened most people, but which attracted a few with an unexplainable power. Here was this lad, whose eyes grew larger and whose voice changed when he mentioned the great man; and there was Charlie Dangerfield who loved Destry still, as he very well knew. What was there lacking in himself that he failed to inspire such emotion in others? He had ten thousand acquaintances; but no man even called himself a near and dear friend to Chester Bent—no man except him whose death he desired above all things! The irony of this made Bent laugh a little, and the laughter restored his spirits.

So he went on to the end of the day, until the unwelcome time came when he must go home and there face Jimmy Clifton. But he put that time off, ate at a small restaurant across the street wedged in at a lunch counter between a pair of huge shouldered cowpunchers and finally, after dark, went home.

He found Jimmy Clifton in the library, deep in one of the books which he himself pretended to read, and the little man put it aside almost reluctantly, blinking his odd round, flat eyes as he did so.

"You're late, Chet," he observed, "but don't say you're sorry. I've had a good time. I brought the notes over with me. I'll cancel 'em for your check."

The ease with which the visitor got to the heart of the business upset Bent in spite of the fact that he was hardening himself for more or less such a scene. But the matter of fact swiftness of Clifton disturbed him. He looked at the little sheaf of papers in the hand of the smaller man and, with all his heart, hungrily, he wished to have them. Or to touch them with the flame of a match, and let the fire work for one second.

Instead, he had to say: "I want to talk to you a minute about those notes, Jimmy. Of course you can have the money, but as a matter of fact——"

Clifton shook his head.

"Don't start it, old son," he said. "Talk won't help. If you have the money in the bank, I'll take your check now. If you haven't money in the bank, I'll take it dated ahead. I don't want to be short, but I want to keep us from embarrassing one another."

"Of course," said Bent. "Of course."

But all of his wiles and his prepared persuasiveness shriveled up and became dead leaves in his hand. He could only say slowly: "It looks as if you think I'm not sound, Jimmy."

"Chet," said the other, "in a business way, it's pretty doggone hard, I think, to have to moralize about deals that have been made. When you wanted that money, I gave it to you, because I thought you were a good business man, not because you were my friend. Now the money's due with interest. I want it back, not because you're an enemy, but because the money's due!"

"But speaking only in a business sense——"

Bent paused for a reply and got one straight from the shoulder.

"In a business sense, then, I think that you've been flyin' a hawk with a hen's wings. Or to put it in another way, I think that you're too high up in the air, and that you're going to have a fall. Mind you, there's no reproach to you, Chet. I like you fine. But I think you've extended yourself too much. If Wham stopped booming tomorrow, I don't think you could pay sixty cents on the dollar the next day! That sounds hard, but I want to be straight and open with you. Sorry as the devil if I hurt your feelings. But I want my money now."

Bent hesitated a little longer. All day he had seen the necessity of the thing for which he was now nerving himself, but still he needed a breathing space.

"It hits me hard, Jimmy, as I don't mind letting you see. However, to take a weight off your mind, I can pay you in full at once. But I'm going to take a walk with you—it's too hot in the room here—and see if I can't think up some good business reason for you to change your mind."

"All right," said Clifton. "I've sounded pretty harsh, I know."

"Not a bit, I like to hear business from a business man."

He went to the door, saying that he would be back in a moment, and went up the stairs to Destry's vacant room.

This he entered, lighted the lamp, and closed the door.

A dozen articles that belonged to the other were scattered here and there—an old quirt, for instance, lay on the bureau, a battered hat hung in the closet, in the top bureau drawer there was a hunting knife in a rawhide case, rudely ornamented, in the Indian style of decoration.

This was what he wanted. He took it out, unsheathed it, and tried the edge with his thumb. As he had known beforehand, so it was—sharp as a razor. Of its own weight, well nigh, it would bury itself to the hilt in living flesh.

He put the knife in his pocket and was starting for the door when distinctly he heard something stir. He whirled and ran back into the room, the naked knife instantly in his hand, but as he turned he heard a sound again, of the shutter outside, moved by the wind, and told himself that this was the same.

Yet he was still not at ease as he went down the stairs, and still he felt a weight curiously cold in his heart, as though some human eye had observed him taking the knife of Destry from the drawer.

Chapter Twenty-seven

"We'll take the short cut home," said Clifton, as they walked out of the house together.

Bent lingered on the steps, as though enjoying the evening; for it was just between the last of the sunset and the total dark of the night when the shadows had blanketed up the glare and the dust of the day, when the ground had yielded up its first radiation of heat, and the night wind began to fan cool through the trees and enter windows that yawned for it. The stars were coming out dimly, twinkling, seeming to advance toward the earth. The very sounds of the day were altered. The wheels and wagon beds of huge freighters no longer rattled and groaned in the streets, with a jingling of chains and hoarse shouts from the teamsters. Hammers that had clanged in the smithies, and thudded in the houses which were building nearby, were now silenced, as was the long, mournful scream of the saws in the lumber yard. Instead, they could hear children playing in the streets, their joyful yells of laughter suddenly blotted out as they turned corners, and coming into ken again, musical with distance; choruses of dogs suddenly began and ended, except for one sullen guardian who barked on the edge of the horizon, a mere pulse of sound.

Now Bent stood on the front steps and seemed to drink in these sights and noises with a smile on his face, while Clifton said quietly, as though ashamed to break in on him:

"Hate to hurry you, old fellow, but I have a meeting with some people at my house, tonight, and I have some things to finish up before they come. If you don't mind, we'd better start on."

"Why the short cut?" asked Bent, stepping down beside the other.

"I don't show myself in the street more than I have to, these days. You can guess why."

"You mean Destry?"

"That's what I mean."

"I don't think he'd murder you, Jimmy. Not off hand like that!"

"Murder's not the worst thing. See what he did to Orrin!"

"Have you been dabbling in politics, too?"

"Not like Orrin, thanks. But as soon as I can wind up some affairs, I'm pulling out of this section of the country until things quiet down a little."

"Meaning by that, Destry?"

"Ay, somebody's sure to get him, just as he's gotten so many others. That's reasonable to expect. And I'm going to advise the rest of 'em to follow my example when I see them tonight."

"They're all coming—is that the meeting?"

"That's the meeting."

"You'll be giving them a dinner, I suppose?"

"Not me. You know the old saying. A filled belly makes a blunt wit. We'll need our wits tonight."

"You will," agreed the other. "So you all meet there and talk over Destry and what to do with him? I hope he doesn't come and listen in through the window."

Clifton stopped short and raised his hand.

"Let's not talk of that demi-devil any more," said he. "We'll chat about the notes, if you wish."

But the plan which already had been forming in the mind of Bent now took a definite shape; for they were walking along narrow alleys and winding paths where no eye observed them, as it seemed, and the secure shelter of high board fences housed them on either side a great part of the time.

"I don't know about that," said Bent. "Perhaps the best way is just to give you a check and finish the business."

"You can? I'm mighty glad that you're able to, Chet. That's the best way for me, and for you too, in the long run, I daresay. I'm glad that you have the money on hand. Matter of fact, I was afraid that you didn't!"

"Were you?" said Bent "Were you?"

He laughed, in such odd key that his companion looked quickly up into his face.

"I've got a reserve fund that I don't like to dip into. I'll use it now."

He grew bolder as the sinister irony of the statement came home to him.

"The last time I used it was six years ago! Well, here we are at your back gate, Jimmy!"

The latter raised the wire hoop and pushed the door open, as a dog rushed at them, barking furiously, but immediately began to whine and leap up at his master.

"They see with their noses, eh?" said Clifton, pushing the dog off, but with affectionate hands.

"Well," said Bent, "I don't know but that it's the better way to see. A lot of things aren't as they seem to the eye!"

"No," said Clifton, "of course they aren't. Come on in."

He pushed open the rear door, and they passed through the kitchen and living room, into Clifton's bedroom, which had a desk in one corner and was evidently his office as well.

He lighted a lamp and hung his hat on a peg in the wall.

"Sit down here, Chet," said he. "Here's a pen and ink, if you want to make out the check at once. It may be a while before the boys come in, but I'll have to hurry you a bit. Make yourself comfortable. I'll go and put the chairs around the table in the other room."

With that, he took a stool and a chair from the bedroom and carried them into the adjoining apartment, where he quickly arranged six chairs around the table.

Bent, in the meantime, took a check book from his pocket and wrote out a check for twelve thousand dollars with the greatest of care, forming the letters with a beautiful precision.

He had finished when his host returned.

The latter scanned the check, blotted it, and nodded.

"That's finished, and a good job," he said. "If I told you what a weight was off my mind, you'd be surprised. At the same time, now that the thing's ended and I know you could pay, I'm sorry that I pressed you so hard."

"Business is business," said Bent, and smiled in an odd way at the other. "You have to have what's coming to you."

"You're a lucky fellow to have a reserve fund out of which you can dip such a bucketful as this!"

Bent bit his lip. The thing for him to do, he understood, was to finish what he had in mind as quickly as possible; and yet all that was evil in him rose up from his heart to his brain and urged him to torture his victim before the stroke. So he lingered, the smile still on his lips.

Clifton smiled in turn, but hesitantly, as one not following the drift of his companion.

"You see how it is," said Bent. "A man needs to have something at his back?"

"Of course," said Jimmy Clifton. "A good reserve—generals plan on one in a battle, but it makes me feel that you're sounder than I thought, old man, when I hear you talk like this!"

"You thought I'm one of these fly by night investors, eh?"

"Not exactly that. I always credited you with insight and brains, but——"

"But what?"

"Caesar was ambitious," said Clifton, smiling at his own small jest.

There was a slight creaking sound, and Bent jerked about.

"What was that?" he asked. "Have they come? Have they come?"

Clifton was amazed at a sort of hard desperation that had crept into the voice of his friend.

"They? The five, you mean? No, they don't show up for a few minutes. But they'll come along. That was the wind handling the kitchen screen door, I suppose. It's in the right quarter for that, just now."

Bent turned back, with a great gasp of relief.

"Thank God!" said he.

"What's the matter, Chet?"

"I thought I was going to be interrupted," said Bent. "But now that I see I won't be, I wanted to ask you if you'd like to know the nature of my reserve?"

"Of course I would. Some good bonds, I suppose? Negotiable securities? Those are the things to have on hand!"

"Yes, but as a matter of fact my reserve is only re-lated second-hand to money."

"What in the world is it, then?"

"A good right hand!" said Bent, still smiling.

Clifton frowned, then started a little as a possible interpretation jumped into his mind, only to be dismissed at once as a total absurdity.

"A good right hand?" he echoed, in a rather worried manner.

"That's it. A good right hand."

"With what in it?"

"Not a pen, Jimmy."

"No."

"No, but a gun, or a knife!"

Clifton looked in the same puzzled manner at Bent, trying to push into his innermost thoughts, but it was impossible now to place any other than one construction upon the fixed and baleful stare of Bent.

The man seemed to grow taller, and stiffer in his attitude. His eyes glittered, and the smile froze on his lips into an archaic grimace, such as that with which the kings of Egypt look at their people in the tombs and on the pyramids.

Jimmy Clifton was not a coward. There was hardly a braver man in all of Wham, but he could not stir in his chair as he heard the other continue:

"For instance, six years ago it looked as though I'd be disgraced and found out as a *petty* thief, and therefore I determined to become a real one, and on a big scale. So I went out and held up the express— the job that poor Destry went to prison for."

Clifton smiled wanly.

"I'm trying to see the point of the joke," he said.

"It's not a joke. That's one reason that I hate Destry,

I suppose, because I've wronged him, as the poet says. Oh, no, I'm not here to tell jokes tonight, Jimmy."

"You're not?"

"No."

Clifton stood up from his chair slowly.

His eyes wandered instinctively toward the wall, from which hung weapons enough. And by that glance Bent knew that the man was helpless in his hands.

"Then what in the name of God *have* you come here for, Chet?"

"To cancel the notes, Jimmy, of course, but with a knife instead of a pen!"

Chapter Twenty-eight

It is necessary to return to young Willie Thornton as he approached the big house of Bent earlier in that day and stood at last before it quite overcome with awe. It was the largest and finest dwelling house he ever had seen. It even had little wooden towers at each of the corners that faced on the main street, and those towers, it seemed to Willie, would be marvelous places for princesses to inhabit by day, and ghosts and owls by night. When he had passed the front gate and it had clanked behind him, he made sure that he had taken the first step into a fairyland.

It was hard for him to strike with the knocker at the front door. He had to linger on the front steps and look up and down the street, where a cloud of dust was enveloping a train of burros which were waddling along under great packs. This dust cloud, the burros, and the signs of the shops looked so thoroughly familiar to Willie, and so like any other of a dozen Western towns he had seen, that he recovered somewhat from his awe and was able to use the knocker.

The door was presently opened by a scowling negress, who waved him away and assured him that no dirty little beggars were wanted there. He was so overwhelmed that he barely remembered the note he carried, and then only because he was gripping it in his hand.

This he now presented, and the effect of it was instant! He was not allowed in the front door with his dusty feet, to be sure, but the cook in person issued forth and escorted him around to the rear.

There he was made to visit a pump and wash basin, with soap and a towel, but after that trying ordeal, he found himself in a trice with his legs under a kitchen table and quantities of food appearing before him.

Such food and such quantities he never had known. Ham spiced with cloves, fragrant to the core, and corn bread made with eggs and brittle with shortening, and great glasses of rich milk. This was only the beginning, to be followed by an apple pie from which only one section had been removed.

He took one piece and hesitated.

"He'p yo'se'f," said the cook.

He helped himself. Assisted by another glass of milk, he gradually put himself outside that entire pie. He felt guilty, but he also felt happy; and what is more delicious than a guilty joy?

Immediately afterward, he was sleepy, and straightway his mentor led him up a winding back stair and into a little attic room.

She shocked him into wakefulness for an instant by saying: "Right next, there, is where Mr. Destry lives, honey, if you ever heard tell of that man!"

Destry lived there!

"You lie down," he was commanded.

And the instant that he was stretched upon a bed of marvelous softness, his eyes began to close, as though they were mechanically weighted, like those of a doll. His heart beat fast with excitement and happiness at the thought of having his hero so near to him; but sleep was mightier than his joy.

The last he knew, as his head swam dizzily, was the voice of the cook saying: "Growin' tenderhearted—and to beggar boys! They ain't no tellin' how men'll change. Money to a man is like water to a desert, I declare. They begin to grow kinder!"

But the meaning of this did not enter the mind of the boy, for a great wave of sleep swept over him, and instantly he was unconscious. It was dusk when he wakened.

As he lifted his head, he saw the red rim of the horizon sketched roughly across the window, and by degrees he remembered where he was. His stomach was no longer tight; his head was clear; he was refreshed as a grown man could not have been by sleeping the clock around.

Yet his feet were on the floor and he was stretching himself myscle by muscle before he remembered that the cook had said Destry lived next door. At that, excitement made him instantly wide awake.

He slipped into the dusky corridor and tapped at the door of the adjoining room, tapped three times, with growing force, and with respectful intervals between. But there was no answer.

At last, he tried the knob, found that the door opened readily, and entered.

"Mister Destry!" he called faintly.

He had no answer.

But when he scratched a match and looked around him, the sight of battered boots and a quirt, and a rifle in a corner suddenly re-created Destry, as though the great man was there in the body.

Willie was happy and comforted.

He could have sat among those relics with a swelling heart of pride in his acquaintance with that man of destiny!

Then a qualm struck him, as he wondered whether or not the hero would care to remember him. There is nothing in the living world so proudly sensitive as a boy, but when he recalled the manner of Destry on that night of battle he was reassured. There could be nothing but honesty in such a man as that!

So thought Willie and pursued his investigations, lighting match after match. He even opened the bureau drawers. It was not that he wished to spy on the secrets of Destry, but that every sight of the possessions of that wanderer filled him with pleasure. There in the top drawer, standing tiptoe, he found the hunting knife, and took it out. There were legends about this knife, as well as the gun of Destry. Had not Pop said that Destry could throw a knife accurately a hundred feet?

Pop lied, perhaps. Alas, he had lied in other matters dealing with Destry, and perhaps about this, also. But at least, this was the hero's knife, with a small "D" cut accurately into the base of the handle.

He put it back reverently, in exactly the position he had found it; he had not dared to bare the bright blade.

He had barely pushed the drawer in when he heard a step in the hall and terror mastered him. Suppose that it was Destry, coming to his room, and suppose that a thief or a spy was found therein?

He slid into the closet and hid behind a long slicker, leaving the door a little ajar just as it had been. There he was hidden when Chester Bent entered and lighted the lamp. He saw the investigations of Bent with wonder, and with a growing fear, for there is something in the manner of a vicious man that betrays him as clearly as the manner of a stalking cat. So did that gliding furtiveness of Bent, in spite of himself, cast a light on him.

And the boy, watching, knew by an instinct that all was not well. He saw the knife taken, and, in his excitement, he stirred, and the buckle of his belt scratched against the wall behind him.

The whirl of Bent was like the turning of a tiger, as he ran back into the room, the knife now naked in his hand. For a moment he glared about him, then the shutter moved in the wind and he seemed satisfied that all was well. Still grudgingly he left that room, and the boy remained for a long moment trembling in the closet, surrounded by utter darkness.

However much he was devoted to Destry, his affection for that man was nothing compared with the terror he felt for Chester Bent! When at last he summoned the courage to leave the room, he glided down the stairs intent on only one thing—and that was to escape from this house of guessed-at horrors as quickly as possible.

He left by neither the front door, nor the back, but slid through an open window and dropped from the sill to the ground. The garden mold received the impression of his bare feet up to the ankles, and, stepping back onto the graveled path, he smoothed out the deep imprints which he had made.

He hurried on, now, crouching a little as if to make himself smaller, after the ancient instinct of the hunted, and so he came to the front corner of the house just in time to hear the voice of Bent speaking from the steps of the house.

A moment later, he saw the man he dreaded going down the front path with a smaller companion. And Willie looked after them, breathing deep and thanking God that he did not have to accompany that man of mysterious fear.

Yet it is by the perversity of our emotions that we

are governed, as much as by the legitimate warnings which our instincts give us. The horse he fears is the horse the rider mounts. The man she does not understand is married by the girl. The dog who growls at him, the boy tries to pet.

And the instant that Willie told himself he must not remain near Bent, that moment he felt an inescapable longing to lurk near the man. It was something like the horrible fascination of a great height, tempting him to let go his hold and jump. He sweated in the grip of it; but as the gate clanged behind the two, Willie was down the path in pursuit.

The moment he was in action, the fear almost disappeared, and it was sheer delight, merely seasoned with danger, as he followed the two on their way. All the old joy of the hunter was running like quicksilver in the young veins of the boy, and he slipped from shrub to shrub, from tree to tree, from fence to gateway, always keeping his soundless feet on the search for twigs or dry leaves that might be in the path.

He kept step with the two he followed, so that the impact of their heavy heels might drown any sound made by his naked feet, and he could congratulate himself that they suspected nothing as they went in the back way to the house of Clifton.

He had gone far enough in his little scouting expedition, but still he was not content. Success, even in this small way, had mounted to his head, and he was keen as a hound to continue the trail, for he knew that in the pocket of Bent rested Destry's knife, as yet unused!

He determined to go on, but the dog, which had followed the master to the door of the house, bounding and whining with pleasure, now turned back, and made an additional danger. Boldness, he decided, was the better way. So he opened the gate boldly and walked straight up the rear path. His way was blocked instantly by the dog. He was a big yellow and black mongrel with a head like a mastiff's, less squarely made than the model. He came at Willie with a rush, crouching low, but as the bare feet swung steadily forward, the monster slouched guiltily, suspiciously to the side—and the road was open to the spy!

Chapter Twenty-nine

The bravado which had carried the boy past the dog endured until he had reached the kitchen door, with the cold nose of the animal sniffing at his fragile heels; even there it did not desert him, but, hearing voices inside, and seeing the darkness within, he wondered if he could not slip in farther and come closer to the words.

He actually had drawn the door open when he remembered what he was doing—entering a trap quite ready to close on him and hold him for disastrous punishment of which he could not even dream. In that moment, it seemed to the boy that the roar of the river, strongly with melted snow water from the mountains, sang suddenly louder, and in a more personal note warned him away.

He let the door close quickly, not enough to make it slam, but so that the rusted hinges groaned faintly. That sound made him turn to flee, but a sudden weakness unnerved him at the knees. He sank down by the wall of the house, panting. Before him came the dog, growling faintly deep in its throat, the hair lifting along the back of its neck; but a so much greater terror was in the heart of Willie that he did not regard this close danger.

He waited through the eternity of a dozen heartbeats, but no swift step came toward him through the house.

He was spared again!

And, as the heart of a boy will do, now that of Willie leaped up from utter consternation to overbearing presumption. If there was anything worth hearing in that conversation between the knife bearer and the smaller man, he intended to hear it. The opportunity was not far away. Lamplight streamed through another window at the rear of the house, and Willie started up and went toward it.

For the dog he had developed a quick contempt, the fruit of reaction from his greater fear, and he cuffed the brute in the ribs with his bare foot; the cur snapped, but at the empty air, and slunk away mastered.

If anything could have raised the spirits of Willie higher, this was the final touch. He had been the cowering hare the instant before; he was the brave and cunning fox, now.

Through the lighted window came the voices which he sought, but indistinctly at times, so that he could not follow the trend of the conversation; and that made Willie climb up on the base board that encircled the bottom of the cheap little house.

Gripping the corner of the sill, where it jutted out on the side, he was in a difficult position, but one from which it was possible for him to hear every word and, if he dared, look in on the actors. He barely reached that place of vantage when he heard Bent saying in a voice which he hardly could recognize:

"To cancel the notes, Jimmy, of course, but with a knife instead of a pen!"

The voice ended, and there was a breath of silence that stabbed Willie to the heart, like the stroke of a knife. Irresistible instinct made him look, and he saw Clifton just arisen, still partly crouched, from the chair.

He could not watch the face of the victim, but he could see Bent's clearly, and the murder in it.

All that wild action of the night of Warren's death now seemed as nothing compared with the horror of the silence in which Bent looked down at the smaller man.

Willie could not endure it. Choked and faint, he looked away, ready to step down, but fearing to move lest he should fall and the noise attract the attention of the monster in the room, three short steps from him.

He looked away, therefore, trying to steady himself for flight and he saw the dark, dim rows of the greens in the vegetable garden, the vague outline of the dog not far away, standing remorsefully on guard, with less courage than suspicion. More than that, he heard again the distinct roar of the Cumber River as it hurried through its shallow gorge at Wham; and in some house nearby people were talking—women's voices, rapid, beating one on top of the other, filled with exclamations and laughter that tumbled together like the gamboling of puppies.

Even in that moment, the lip of Willie curled a little, and into his troubled brain flowed other sounds, and above all, that of a mandolin far off. He could hear only the jangle of the strings that kept the tune, and the pulse of a soft singing rather than the actual timbre.

So that moment was filled for the boy, when he heard Clifton saying:

"It's hard to look at you, Chet, you're acting the part so well. I'd almost think, to hear you, that you *would* murder me!"

And he laughed. So rich and so real was his laughter that the boy looked back with a sudden great hope. It was, after all, only a practical jest!

But no! The instant he saw the face of Bent he

knew, as he had known before, that murder was in the air!

And Clifton knew it, also. His laughter died away with a break. One hand was behind him, hard gripped, and again the dreadful silence went on, heartbeat by heartbeat.

Then Bent said through his teeth, "You're not a fool, Jimmy. You know that if I let Destry go to prison in my place a thing such as wiping you off the ledger with blood won't stop me for a moment!"

"You know that you'll infallibly hang!" said Clifton, in a shaken tone.

"Don't be a fool," said Bent. "Don't comfort yourself with that, Jimmy! Destry is my professional buffer state. The knife that I stab you with will be found in your body, and there is a clever 'D' cut into the handle of it. I suppose that a hundred people will be able to identify that knife as Destry's. He's been proud of his work with it, you know. He can hit things at twenty paces—sink the knife half the length of its blade into green wood, and that sort of thing. No, no, Jimmy! This will be laid on Destry's shoulders!"

"Then Destry will have you by the throat for it!"

"Have me? He'll never suspect! Destry's one of those clever, cunning people who prefer to keep a blind side for their friends. He has a blind side for me. He knows a dozen of my faults, has seen them, listed them, acknowledged them, but still he can't add up the total and see what I am. Destry's not a fool; he's only a fool about his friend, Chester Bent. The point will be that the cunning assassin of poor Jimmy Clifton stole the knife from Destry's room in my house in order to throw the blame on him! You see? But the rest of the world will have a fine reason for hanging Destry by the neck!"

He, in his turn, laughed a little, and did not finish his mirth in a hurry. Rather he seemed to be tasting and retasting it, and he was still laughing in that almost silent way when Clifton spoke again. His courage was going; with horrible clarity. Willie knew that, and saw a brave man turning into a dog before his eyes.

"D'you hear me—will you hear me, Chet?" he gasped.

"Of course. I want to hear you. I want to see you, too! I want to see you whine, you fool!"

"Chet," said the other, "I've never had anything against you, or you against me!"

"Except the notes, my boy!"

"They're yours! Look! Take and tear 'em up, and tear up your check, besides!"

"Are you a total ass, Jimmy? Tear the things up, but leave in Wham a man who knows all about me—and my reserve fund?"

"I'll forget it, Chet. Good God, man, I'll forget all about it. I tell you what—I'm going to leave Wham. You know that. I'll swear never to come back—"

"You don't have to. A letter to the sheriff would be enough."

"Man, I'll give you my sacred word of honor. The thing's ended with me. I'll say no more. It's finished. Every word you've spoken, and every act I've seen—which isn't much—I'll tear them out of the book of my brain and burn the leaves!"

Bent, listening, smiled with a peculiar gratification, as though the terror of the other were feeding him with a more than physical food.

This smile was accepted by Clifton, rightly as a refusal, and suddenly he slumped to his knees upon the floor.

Bent stepped back, in loathing, and yet in animal-like pleasure at this horror, and Clifton followed on his knees, reaching out his thick, yellow, trembling hands. His head was thrown back. His voice choked in his throat.

"Chet, you and me—for God's sake!—always friends—school together—"

A scream came up in the throat of Willie and stuck there like a bone.

"Stand up, and face it like a man!" commanded Bent.

"Chet, Chet, I've always respected you, liked you, loved you, d'you hear? Old friends! Chet, I'm young, I'm gunna get married—"

"You lie! Get up, or I'll lift you up by the hair of the head, you cur!"

"I swear it's true. Gunna marry Jenny Cleaver. She's to meet me in Denver—young, Chet—life before me—friends——"

Then the monster moved. He did not seem to hurry. It was like the action of the wasp in stinging the spider already paralyzed with horror. So Bent leaned and actually grasped Clifton by the hair of the head and jerked the head far back.

Willie saw the hands of the man stiffen as they clutched at the air, saw his mouth drawn open, and yet he did not scream for help.

Then Bent struck.

Straight through the base of the throat he drove the long knife, and left it sticking in the wound, then stepped back with blood running down his right hand.

Clifton fell on the floor, writhed his legs together,

then turned on his back and lay motionless. He was dead! Already the boy had seen a death, but it had seemed to him then the most magnificent thing he ever had witnessed—a strong man rushing into battle against equal odds, and beaten, broken with bullets, snuffed out like a light. It had left glory for the victor, but this was a thing that words could not be used upon!

His long held breath now failed him, and he gasped. It was only a faint sound, but it was enough.

He saw the eyes of Bent roll up and fix steadily upon him, and he knew that the shadows had not screened him. That keen glance had gone out with the lamplight into the dark beyond the window and clearly discerned the face of the witness!

Chapter Thirty

The spell that held Willie Thornton endured until Bent made a move, and then he dropped like a plummet from the windowsill and began to run.

He wanted his best speed to get to the rear gate of the garden and so dodge right or left into the obscurity of the safe night, but his knees were numb, and his breath was gone. He stumbled straightway into a wire erected to support tomato vines and tumbled head over heels. As he came to his feet again, he saw Chester Bent flinging himself through the window with the agility of an athlete, and straightway he knew that the slowness which he had hoped for in that sleek appearing man would never appear.

He reached the gate, snatched off the wire hoop, and whipped through, yet delaying a fraction of a second to jam the loop back in place. Then he headed like the wind straight down the path toward the shrubbery, with the roaring of the river flinging up louder and louder from the very ground on which he trod, as it seemed.

He turned his head and glanced over his shoulder in time to see Chester Bent take the gate in his stride, like a hurdler, with the shadowy form of the dog flying over after him.

Dog and man together against him, Willie felt very much smaller than ever before; but in a sense he was less frightened than he had been when he stood at the window and looked in on the murder.

That had been too horrible for the imagination, but his present case was perfectly clear and exact. If

Bent caught him, youth would make no difference. He would be killed!

Once he tipped up his face to scream for help—the thing which he had wondered that poor Clifton did not do—but he knew that as he cried out, his feet would be trailing and stumbling, and he dared not slow up, he dared not lose one breath of wind!

So he went on vigorously, probing at the dark of the winding pathway, making his legs work with all the muscle they had gained from trudging over mountain trails. A sharp stone cut his foot, but it only made his tread the lighter. He fairly flew, leaning aslant at the curves, but he knew that Bent was gaining rapidly!

The river roared nearer before his face, and suddenly he wondered that he could have been such a fool as to run in this direction! For the river was the very place which Bent would have chosen. Its rapid waters would be certain to cover a dead body quickly! Whereas if he had run toward the street, a single shout would have brought people around him!

The sense of his failure and folly made the boy weak. And then the mongrel ran up beside him, snapping and snarling, but not yet with quite the courage to bite; behind came the greater shadow of the man. His footfall sounded like a heavy pulse in the brain of Willie; and the boy could hear his gasping breath.

He swerved from under the very hand of Bent into the brush which rattled and cracked deafening him. A cat's claw gripped him and spun him around as he lurched away from it, but he darted on, and a moment later, with his lungs bursting and his eyes thrusting from their sockets, he threw himself flat on the ground beneath a bush and waited.

Desperately he strove to control the noise of his breathing; then told himself that the louder voice of the river probably would cover such a small thing as his breathing. So he lay trembling with exertion, hopeful that his hiding place would be overlooked, and at any rate thankful for this moment of rest.

He could hear Bent moving through the bush, cursing the thorns; then he saw the shadow of the man against the stars, moving past him.

He was safe!

Then a growl came at his very ear! It was the mongrel, which had followed the trail with a sense truer than the eyes in this dark of the night. Still the dog remembered the heel which had thumped his ribs, and though he snapped it was only at the air; then he backed up and began to bay the game!

There was no sense in waiting. Willie lurched to his feet, gathering up a broken section of a branch that lay on the ground beside him. With this he struck true and hard between the eyes of the brute. It yowled with pain and fear and fled, but yonder came the silhouette of Bent, rushing straight at his quarry.

There seemed no place to flee, now. The brush had proved a useless screen, and the danger was impending over him. But he sprinted desperately, with renewed wind, straight for the noise of the creek. He could not run as fast as his pursuer, but he had the advantage of being able to dodge more swiftly among the reaching branches of the shrubs.

The trees along the river bank gave him a hope, but when he reached them the hand of Bent was again stretched for him. He dodged, pushing his hands against a tree trunk, and barely escaped into the open.

There that hand gripped the shoulder of his coat!

He was lost, then. But where another boy would have surrendered, Willie Thornton still fought like a cornered rat against fate. The second strong hand of the man gripped him. He whirled, and the loose, over-size coat gave from his shoulders and left him suddenly free!

Bent, lurching back, sprang forward again with wonderful adroitness. There was no chance for the boy to dodge and run again. There was only one verge of the creek bank and the voice of the rushing Cumber beneath.

He did not hesitate. Even a river in flood was preferable to death by the hands of the monster! So he ran straight forward and leaped out into air.

He saw beneath him the glistening face of the water, streaked white by its speed against the rocks— white like a wolfs teeth, he thought, as he leaped into the thin hands of the wind. Then down he went as a rock goes. He smote the water with stunning force, but the cold of it kept his senses alert.

He knew that he was being whirled around and around as he was carried down the stream, and he gripped at the first object that he saw. It looked a soft shadow; it proved to be a sleek rock that sprang up from a root in the bed of the stream.

His grip held, though the current drew him out powerfully, like a banner flapping in a strong wind. He lay on his back, only his nose and lips above the surface, and, looking at the bank, he saw Chester Bent moving along the edge of the water.

Opposite the point where Willie lay shivering with the penetrating cold of the melted snow, Bent paused for a long moment He crouched upon his heels, the better to study the surface of the stream.

Then the lofty shadow stepped out upon a rock straight toward the place where Willie lay!

He was lost, he told himself, and prepared to loose his hold and try to swim down the stream to safety, well assured that if he did so one of the sharp teeth in that wolf's mouth would spear him to the life.

But Bent remained only an instant on that rock, then he stepped back to the shore. The old coat he tossed into the stream, and climbed back to the upper edge of the bank. There he loitered an instant and faded away into the trees.

Chapter Thirty-one

Five men had gathered, by this time, in the house of Jimmy Clifton, and Henry Cleeves took charge of the assembly. He came first, and had called for little Clifton, their host, who did not appear; then he had glanced into the bedroom and seen the lighted lamp, the bed with no sleeper on it, the chair in front of the desk quite empty.

He didn't examine the room further, but went back to join the others as they gathered. They came in not in pairs, but singly, each stepping with an odd haste through the front door and moving quickly inside of it, so that he would not remain silhouetted against the lamplight to any observer on the street

Having made this somewhat guilty entrance, each tried to assume a cheerful air, which was promptly discountenanced by their self-appointed chairman, for Cleeves was invincibly grave this evening.

Phil Barker, celebrated for his practical jokes, until that stinging jest of Destry's had altered his habits, was the first to enter, taking off his sombrero and looking cautiously about him as though he feared lest even Cleeves might have something up his sleeve.

Immediately afterward came Bull Hewitt and tall Bud Truckman, so close together that it was plain Bull had dogged Bud down the street, though he would not walk beside the other.

The last to come was Williams, the strong man, who gripped his hat so hard in his powerful hand that he soon reduced it to a ball; at the expense of his hat, he was able to maintain a fair calm of countenance.

Then Cleeves pointed to the chairs and bade them be seated, while he drew down the shades of the windows and closed the front door. He explained that their host apparently had stepped out, but must be back in a short time. They could sit down and open their minds to one another in the meanwhile.

So they sat down around the table and each man looked upon the other as though he never had seen him before and was ashamed to be seen by him, in turn. Only Cleeves kept his mind clear for the business before them.

He said: "We know why we've met here, but I'll say it over again to bring things to a head. Then, if we get any conclusions, we'll tell them to Jimmy when he shows up. He's stepped out for just a moment; there's still a lamp burning in his bedroom. In the first place, Destry is living up to the promise he made to us that day in the courtroom. We've scattered and tried to get away from him; still he hunted us down. Warren and Clarence Ogden are dead. Jud Ogden is worse than dead—crippled forever. Lefty Turnbull's in jail and will soon be in the pen for a long time. Orrin is hiding no man knows where; he'll be tried for graft when found and in the meantime he's looked on as a yellow dog. Jerry Wendell has been hounded out of Wham; his heart's broken. And that leaves six of us. If we can't run away from him, we'll have to bunch together and fight him. We're here to discuss ways and means. As for the money end of it, if that enters, I suppose I can begin by saying that any of us will pay anything up to life to keep life. If I'm wrong, speak up!"

They did not answer. They listened with their eyes on the table, not the speaker.

"I'm right, then," went on Cleeves. "Now, then,

we're ready for the ways of disposing of Destry, alive or dead."

"Alive, he'll never stop," said Barker.

"Dead, then. We've got that far. He has to be killed! How?"

No one spoke, until Bull Hewitt lifted his stupid face and said sullenly:

"You gents all know I never was agin Harry so much. I wouldn't of voted him guilty at the trial, if you hadn't crowded me agin the wall, all talkin' together. But now that it comes to the pinch, I say that Destry's gotta die, because I wanta live. There's just a few ways of killin' a man—rope, knife, gun, poison. But hit on one of 'em quick."

After this, there was a bit of a silence, until Phil Barker struck the table with his fist.

"Poison! It works secret and secret ways are the only ones that'll ever catch Destry. We've tried the other kind and they're no good!"

"Ay, poison. But how?" asked Hewitt.

Cleeves took charge again.

"We've all agreed, then, that we'll use anything from a knife to poison on Destry?"

He took the silence for agreement, and then he went on: "The first great problem is how to get in touch with him. We'll need Jimmy Clifton's good head to help on that. I wonder where he's keeping himself so long?"

They waited, looking at one another.

Cleeves, making a cigarette, scratched a match, and they all saw his big, bony hands trembling as he strove to light the smoke. At last, he snapped the match away, and struck another, looking around the table with a swift, guilty glance.

They avoided meeting it. Then Barker broke out, quickly and softly: "We're all thinkin' of just one thing. Is Destry the reason that Jimmy ain't showed up?"

No one answered, till Cleeves cried: "Ay, and is Destry curled up somewhere, now, and listening to all that we have to say?"

"Or," suggested Bull Hewitt, "is Destry about to slip in with a pair of guns ready to work? He's got us all here in one pen!"

It was at this very crucial moment that they all heard, distinctly, the sound of the kitchen screen moaning on its hinges, and they stood up as though at a command.

The kitchen door yawned slowly open. Cleeves had a gun in his hand. Barker was reaching for a weapon, when they saw in the dark doorway the smiling face of Chester Bent. It was at least less unwelcome than that of Destry, and there was a faint general sigh of relief. But Bent, standing in the doorway, ran his eyes carefully across their faces.

"Friends," said he, "you're sitting here planning how to kill Harry Destry, and I've come to help you plan!"

Cleeves exclaimed angrily: "Bent, we know that you're his best friend! D'you think that you can come here and listen to us under such a shallow pretext as that?"

"Am I his best friend?" asked Bent.

Then he laughed a little, adding: "Jimmy Clifton can tell you how much of a friend I am to Destry. Where's Jimmy now? I thought that all six of you would be here!"

"You knew about this?"

"Of course. Jimmy told me and asked me to come here; because I have the only scheme that will kill Destry!"

They watched him in suspicion and in amazement. Yet what he had said carried with it a certain portion of self-proof. For if he knew of the meeting, it seemed logical that he must have learned from one of the six, and who would have been mad enough to tell him without good reason?

"Go on, man," said Cleeves. "God knows we *hope* that this is true, because I don't know a stronger hand or head to have us! *You* want Harry Destry's death?"

"More," said Bent fervidly, "than any of you! And more tonight than ever before!"

As he thought of Willie Thornton, and of that lad's knowledge, and of the uncertainty of his death, such a world of sincerity gleamed in the eyes and roughened in the voice of Bent that to see with a single glance was to believe him. There was not only real firmness of will, but a ravening hate which made their own fear-inspired hearts seem bloodless things.

He added quietly:

"You know what was attempted in my house the other night against Destry. Do you think that Clifton would have tried that without my permission and my help?"

It was the final proof and convinced them all. They looked at Bent with wonder, but they also looked at him with a growing hope.

"Where's Clifton now?" asked the new recruit peevishly. "We must have Clifton. He's the one of you who understands my position and can tell you whether or not I'm really with you. Isn't he in his room?"

He pushed the door open as he spoke.

"He's not there," said Cleeves, "I looked a while ago and there was no——"

"Great God!" cried Bent, and rushed into the room as though from the door he had seen something horrible that called him forward.

Cleeves followed him; the others flocked behind; and they gathered about the prostrate body of Clifton, dead, with the knife fixed to the hilt in his throat.

"Dead!" said Bent. "But—how long have you been here? Who was here first? What——"

Cleeves grew pale.

"Are you pointing at me, Bent?" he demanded hotly. "I was here first, if that's what you want to know!"

Williams was leaning above the dead man.

"The knife!" he said. "The knife! Will ya look at it, all of you? Will ya see the 'D' carved into the butt of it? Destry! Destry was here before us! I've seen this here knife in the old days. I've seen him throw it at a mark! I'd swear it was Destry's, even without the letter made onto it!"

Cleeves was drawing down the shade across the window.

He came back to the frightened circle and said firmly: "He's been here. There's his hand on the floor. Now what will we do?"

He turned to Bent.

"You wouldn't be here without an idea, Bent. *He* thinks you're still his friend?"

"Yes."

"Can you draw him back to your house?"

"Not since Clifton made his try there. He won't come back."

"Is there any other way?"

"There's one other way. There's one house that he'd go to, if a message was sent to him."

"Charlie Dangerfield?"

Bull Hewitt cried out in a choked voice: "You mean to use her for bait, to draw Destry into a trap?"

"Look!" said Cleeves, pointing to the floor.

And Hewitt, staring at the dead body and the blank, smiling face of Clifton, turned back abruptly, his argument crushed.

"Can you get a message to him, Chet?"

"I know how to get to him. I'll do it tomorrow afternoon. I'll have to do a bit of arranging, in the first place. I'll have to see Charlie Dangerfield. I'll have to have her written invitation to him. I'll have to get that and bring it out to him. I'll have to do everything, boys. And your only job will be to lie close and get him when he comes. But I'll arrange the details. You'll know everything! Only—what if this thing should happen, and she knew who had led Destry down into the trap?"

They nodded at one another, for they saw the point. If there was one fact in his life which Bent had taken no trouble to hide, it was that he worshiped Charlotte Dangerfield.

"Chet," said Cleeves, "if you can do this for us, you don't have to doubt! The rest of us would kill the man who talked! Great heavens, man, who would be fool enough to say that he took a hand in the killing of Destry?"

"Get Ding Slater, somebody!" said Bent.

He waved to the door.

"Some of you better leave, too, before Slater comes. You stay on, Cleeves. And here's an old friend of Clifton—Barker. You and Barker. The rest of us will start. Move the chairs away from that table. Get the blinds up. And don't touch the dead body. Don't move a thing in this room—not a chair or a rug. Don't touch a thing, so that Ding can use his gigantic intelligence on the spot and try to make out what the 'D' on the knife may mean!"

He sneered as he spoke, and, hurrying to the door, waved his hand at them and was gone.

"I wonder," said Cleeves slowly, as their new confederate disappeared, "who would win the fight if those two were thrown down hand to hand? That wild cat Destry, or this sleek bull terrier, Bent!"

Chapter Thirty-two

The next morning, Bent rode out to the Dangerfield place dressed like a puncher of the range, not because he wanted to play that part, but because the cowpuncher's costume is the only perfect one for rough riding across the brush-laced country of the Western range. His tall hat turns the heat of the sun or the downpour of the rain. It is hat, parasol, and umbrella all in one. His bandana keeps dust from falling down his neck, keeps off the hot rays of the sun where they are apt to fall with most force—the back of the neck—and in time of need is the sieve through which his breath can be drawn and the dust kept from his lungs. His leather chaps turn the needle points of the thorns. His high heeled, narrow toed boots, foolish for walking, are ideal for a man who is half standing in the stirrups on a long ride and does not wish his foot to be too deeply engaged in case of a fall.

Bent was dressed in this fashion, and he was well accustomed to it. He took a strong, fast horse from his barn and went on a line as straight as a bird's flight from his house to the Dangerfield place. He found "The Colonel" on the front veranda smoking a long cigar.

"Hello," said Dangerfield. "Are you masqueradin' as a workin' man, Chet?"

"I'm a working man every day," said Bent with a smile, as he threw the reins over the post of the hitching rack and came up to the steps. "I have to sit and grind, while you're here in the cool of the wind."

"There ain't any sitting work," declared the Colonel. "The curse of Adam was sweat of the brow, not sweat of the brain."

Bent stood with a hand against one of the narrow wooden pillars of the veranda and smiled down at the rancher.

"What about the worry of the poor devils in the offices?" said he. "Worry and trouble all day long!"

"What do kids do when they sit in the shade?" asked the Colonel.

"Day dream, I suppose."

"A gent that lives on his brain is simply turning day dreams into money."

"He has no pain, then?"

"Not a mite," said the other. "But he knows that he's makin' a living, and that starts him pityin' himself. Most men don't complain of work till they get married, and then it's only to impress the wife. Because he finds out pretty pronto that he's gotta be the comforter if he don't ask to be comforted. But toilin' with your hands, that's different. Seein' the sun stick in one place in the sky for a coupla dozen hours—that's pain, with payday always about a week away."

"I think that I have pain enough," said Bent.

"You got it in your imagination," said Dangerfield. "And there ain't any larger or more tenderer place to have a pain than in the imagination. Women folks used to have that kind; men *always* have 'em, unless they're laborin', and then they don't need any imagination at all. But I've set here on this porch a good many years and never seen much trouble, except thinkin' of the first of the month, now and then. But it wasn't anything serious!"

"Have you lived such a happy life, then?"

"Sure," said Dangerfield. "By not workin' I kept

ready for the luck, and when the luck came, I grabbed it and took off its scalp."

He added: "I expect you didn't sashay all the ways out here to talk to me, but if you came to see Charlie, I'll tell you that she ain't good company lately."

"I've never found Charlie dull," said Bent.

"Mostly," said Dangerfield, "young men don't know nothin' about girls. It ain't that girls wanta lie and be deceivin' but they just nacherally can't be themselves when a gent is around. They gotta put the best foot forward. I tell you what, Chet, Sunday's been a mighty miserable day around this place for years and years, with Charlie usin' up a whole week of good spirits on Saturday night. But now she ain't dull; she's just mean."

"Mean?" said Bent. "Charlie mean?"

"A surprisin' thing to you, I reckon. She's so mean that she won't talk to nobody, except a word or two to the niggers. The rest of the time she spends wranglin' mustangs. And the wear that she gives a cayuse in two days is enough to keep him thin the rest of his life. I says to her: 'Charlie, when you break a hoss, aim to save the pieces, will you?' "

"I didn't know that Charlie went in for rough riding."

"Sure you didn't. But she's gotta have some way of lettin' off the steam, I reckon. It ain't the hosses she's mad at."

"What is it, then?"

"Herself. Because she once had that crazy, fast flyin' snipe, Destry, tied to a string, and now she's gone and cut the cord. Where's he now?"

"I wanted to talk to her about that," said Bent.

"Then she'll listen," said Dangerfield, "if you keep close onto that track."

"Where is she now?"

"Anywhere from hell to breakfast—from that broken headed mesa yonder to the corrals."

At the corrals, Bent found her. She had just turned loose a sweating mustang, chafed with white foam and froth about the shoulders; the tired horse merely jogged wearily away. In the meantime, Charlie Dangerfield leaned against the corral fence and criticized the handling of the next candidate for her attention. This was a bald faced chestnut with a Roman nose and the eye of a snake, which was trying to tear the snubbing post out of the ground, and bite, kick, or strike the two men who were working on it. The double purpose kept it from succeeding in either hope.

"Hello, Charlie," said Bent. "That's a pretty picture you're going to fit yourself into, it looks to me."

She waved her hand to him briefly, and hardly gave him a glance.

"Sweet boy, isn't he?" said she. "Look at the iron hook in his nose and the hunch in his back. Up on that back, you'll feel as if you're sitting on Mt. McKinley and looking down at the birds. Hey, Jerry, sink your knee in his ribs and give those cinches another haul, will you? You've got his wind inside that!"

Jerry obeyed, and finally the gelding was prepared for riding. Bent, in the meantime, was looking over the girl quietly, and found her much changed. She was thinner, he thought, and the shadow about her eyes made them look darker. She might have been an older sister of the girl he had known.

"Charlie," he said, "you come away and listen to me. I want to talk to you about Harry Destry."

"Do you?" she replied. "Who's Harry nicked lately?"

The hardness and casual quality of her voice did not deceive Bent.

"Little Jimmy Clifton," he answered gravely.

"Jimmy? What was Jimmy's shameful secret?"

"I don't know. No one ever will know—if there was one—because it died with him, it appears."

Still she would not turn her head, but he well knew that her pretended interest in the mustang had disappeared.

"Died?" she said.

"Yes," answered Bent.

She turned slowly and faced him. He saw she was white.

"What made *that* a fair fight?" she asked. "Did Jimmy have a crowd with him?"

Bent looked down at the ground and seemed to study it before he answered; in reality he was concealing his exultation.

"Of course Jimmy must have had help or Harry never would have tackled him. But—no one knows who was with Clifton. He was found with the knife—er—in his throat, Charlie!"

She threw out her hands as though she were casting away a disgusting thought.

"Not a knife!"

"Yes. It's the worst business of all."

"Stabbed Jimmy Clifton? Jimmy? I don't believe it!"

"I don't either," said Bent hastily. "Only—the knife was there! The 'D' carved on it, and everything!"

"If he'd done such a thing, he wouldn't be fool enough to leave the knife in the wound—not a knife that could be identified. Somebody stole that knife and murdered Clifton!"

Protest, Bent had been prepared for, but not the naked truth so suddenly thrown in his face.

He was saved the necessity of finding words by the girl herself.

"Jerry," she called faintly, "you take that red-eyed devil, will you? I'm afraid of him!"

She put her hand on Bent's arm.

"Start me walking, and keep right on," she said. "I'm mighty dizzy! Stabbed Jimmy? Stabbed him and left the knife in the wound and——"

"Forget that, will you?" asked Bent. "I didn't come to talk about it!"

She stopped short, and her hand gripped his arm fiercely.

"Why should I care a rap about him? Thief, gunman, professional fighter, lazy, shiftless—and now a murderer! Why should I care a rap about him? I'm a fool! I'm a fool!" cried Charlie Dangerfield. "I don't want to talk about him any longer!"

Bent looked hard at her, and then he answered: "If I thought I could believe you, Charlie, I'd lose my heart about saying what I intend to say—what I came here to say. But I don't believe you. Should I?"

"You came out to talk about this killing. You came out to explain it away, I suppose? God knows how Harry can deserve such a friend as you are!"

"What of you, Charlie?"

"Ah, he found me when I was young—I was a baby, only. And he took my heart in his hands with such a grip, Chester, that I've never been able to take it back. What with loving him, pitying him, being shamed for him, fearing him, and then losing him! Why, the thought of Harry's all around me, just as the hills and the mesas are all around this ranch. But what keeps you true to him? That's what I don't understand!"

"Because, Charlie, I don't care to analyze my best friend."

She watched him for a moment, and then he saw her glance melting.

"Dear old Chet!" said she. "One man like you puts all the rest of us in our places! You're true blue! Tell me what I'm to do, and I'll do it!"

"Is there a quiet place, a secluded place near the house, Charlie?"

"What d'you mean?"

"Some shack, say?"

"There's the house by the old well."

"The one that went dry?"

"Yes."

"That would do, perfectly. You're to be there tonight."

"Am I?"

"Yes."

"Night, did you say?"

"Yes. You can't expect him to ride about the country during the day, can you?"

"Harry? Is he to come there?"

Bent set his teeth for an instant—such a joy came up in her eyes, and flushed in her brown face, that bitter envy burned him up. This for Harry Destry, even when she thought that his hands were red with the murder of a helpless man!

"He's to come there, I trust. If I can persuade him, at least."

"And then?"

"And then you're to start persuading where I left off!"

"Persuading him to do what? Am I to reform him? Is that the little thing you expect of me?"

"I expect that you can do anything with him, if you have a chance. If you're not proud with him, I should say! Because there's enough iron in him to resent pride."

"Proud?" said she. "Oh, I'll not be proud! But what would I say?"

"You'd ask him to leave five of the twelve men untouched, and go away with you!"

She considered the idea, trembling.

Then, in a rapid murmur so that he hardly heard the words: "He wouldn't listen, of course. I've failed him when he needed me—when he pretended to need me. I'm dead to him, now!"

"You're not. I don't think so, at least. At any rate, will you make the experiment, Charlie?"

"Ask drowning men if they'll catch at straws!" said she.

Chapter Thirty-three

A happy glow of achievement already possessed the body and the soul of Bent as he returned to Wham. For if he had not actually fulfilled all his purpose, the first part was done, and the remainder seemed easily at hand.

It was not possible that a guilty conscience could move him. Too much is made of guilty consciences. They generally begin to work on criminals after the stern hand of the law has grasped them by the nape of the neck. They prepare for a holy death to make up for a bad life, only after the hangman is assured. So Bent was unencumbered with remorse of any kind.

What fascinated him was the intricacy of his plan, the width of the end which he aimed at, the skill with which his purposes were so dovetailed together that where the one plan ended and the other began would have been hard to tell.

On the whole, everything that he did seemed based upon the putting down of Destry. To the imprisonment of Destry he owed his own safety from prosecution for the train robbery in the beginning of his prosperity. Again, to the cruel fame of Destry he owed it that he had been able to strike down a creditor and cancel that debt. Yet again, the very act which would kill Destry would be interpreted by Charlie Dangerfield as an accident which had taken place through the malice of others, and in spite of the guarding care of the real contriver. She would credit him with having tried to save Destry from any calamity; the very death of Destry he would so arrange that she must feel Bent was least concerned in it.

The death of Clifton had removed the last danger to his fortune. The end of Destry would clear his way to the hand of Charlotte Dangerfield. And as an extra profit, he would receive the undying gratitude of five men whom he had shown a way to rid themselves of a mortal danger.

He knew that his way was not yet clear, but out of the darkness he saw light and was well content. Indeed, as he rode down the street of Wham he was hardly sure that he would have been pleased to gain all his ends by legitimate means; crime, which had been a tool, now was becoming an end, desirable for its excitement.

He drew up at the shop of Cleeves, who came out to him with the soot of the forge on his face, and black streaks of grease on his hairy arms.

"You know the old dry well on the Dangerfield place?" he demanded without prelude.

"I reckon I do."

"Be out there tonight and have the rest of the boys handy. There's plenty of chaparral growing right up to the door where the rest of 'em can hide. But you, Cleeves, you're a shot-gun expert."

"I can handle a shot gun."

"You've got a sawed off gun?"

"I have one."

"You get out there well before dark. Get up into the attic and lie there. Mind you that nobody sees you on the way. You're out to shoot doves, if anybody in the shop asks you when you start. Lie up there in the attic and wait for Destry to come. The girl will be there first. Lie still as a mouse till Destry comes. The fact is, I don't depend on the other four; I depend on you, Cleeves!"

The other nodded. "If I miss that close up," he said, "I'm a fool and I'll never shoot again!"

"If you miss, you'll never shoot again," said Bent. "You're right about that. If you miss, you'll be a dead man, old fellow! But you're not going to miss. What's happened in town today?"

"The merchants have got together and offered a reward for Destry. The coroner has hung the killing of Clifton on him. It's clear sailing in that direction."

"What about old Ding Slater? What's he done?"

"Nothing—as usual. He'll never hold a job in this town when his term's up this time. They're tired of him."

"What happened when Slater got to the house the other night?"

"Nothin' happened. You can't get fresh sense out of a dry brain! He just looked around and clucked like an old hen. After a while, he stood in the doorway and asked if any of the furniture had been moved, and I told him it hadn't. Then Ding says he don't see how Bent could of seen the dead body from the door, or something like that. The old man's pretty far gone!"

This observation made Bent sit a little straighter, but he said nothing. To him, the observation of the sheriff seemed to prove that Slater's was far from a dry brain! However, the news about the reward was far the more important tidings, he judged.

He left Cleeves at once, and riding down the street he straightway encountered the sheriff and dismounted to say to him anxiously: "Ding, it doesn't seem possible that Harry Destry could have stabbed Clifton!"

"He didn't," said the sheriff.

"Didn't he? Then what's all the talk about?"

"I dunno. Some mighty ornery sneak got into the house and stole that knife; or else it's an old knife that Harry give away a long time ago. Anyway, Destry never done the job."

"I knew he didn't have that sort of work in him!"

"You knew right, Chet. They's more knowledge of people in friendship than there is in the law! A mighty lot!"

"But who could have done the job?"

"They're in town—plenty that hate Destry and would be glad to knife Clifton if they could do it so safe!"

With that uncomforting knowledge in his mind, Bent rode on from the town. Yet however keen the old sheriff might be on the trail, it was patent that he did not suspect Chester Bent of the crime, otherwise he would not have spoken so freely. But close trailing of the crime might reveal the real criminal. There was no doubt of that, and, though Bent could not see where he had left incriminating evidence behind him, still he knew that a clever hand and a sharp eye can unravel nearly any crime, no matter how well covered the traces of it may be.

He was reasonably confident, but he knew that his safety was not yet built upon bed rock.

There remained the problem of the boy, as well. If he was alive, then nothing but ruin hung over Bent's head. But there was hardly a chance that the youngster had not been torn to death among the sharp rocks of the Cumber Creek.

With that comfort, with no sureties, but with many excellent high hopes for the future, Bent rode out of Wham and took the old trail toward Pike Pass.

He rode on through the heat of the afternoon, with the rocks burning about him and smoking with heat waves, until the mesquite thinned out, and then the dauntless lodgepole pines, which seem able to live in a furnace or an icebox, began to cluster on the hills.

He had turned a sharp corner of the trail when the voice of Destry called suddenly behind him. He whirled about, his hand instinctively flying to his gun, and there was Destry in the middle of the trail with Fiddle sticking her head out from the trees close by. The man was greatly changed. Continued exposure to wind and sun had browned his face, and as he took off his hat and waved it, Bent saw that the hair of Destry was growing long. The clipped skull had made him seem a criminal by right and profession; now he appeared a typical wild man of the mountains.

"I wanted to see if you'd lost some of the edge of your eye, Chet," he called, "and here you been and let me stalk you like a blind man!"

Bent came back to him, smiling and holding out a hand which was received with a quick grip, like a clutch of iron, a familiar grip to Bent. And every time he felt it, he wondered how his own might of arm would match against that of Destry!

"I was hoping to be stalked," said he, "not dodging it. Harry, I've brought you news. They've put a price on you, for Clifton!"

"For Clifton? What about him?"

"D'you ask me that?" said Bent slowly.

"I do."

"*He* was found dead last night, and with a knife of yours in his throat!"

"That leaves five," was the first response of Destry.

He added: "How come a knife of mine? I wasn't near the town!"

"I'm going to believe you, Harry. Then what scoundrel could have done it?"

"I dunno," said Destry. He asked curiously: "They've put a price on me?"

"Twenty-five hundred, and it'll soon go up."

"How did you know the knife was mine?"

"By a 'D' carved in the butt of it."

"I left a knife like that in your house, Chet. They've stolen it."

"Who would have dared——"

"Why, one of the five, d'you see? To throw the blame on me and bring the law onto their side of this business. When you can't win your own fight, call in a dog to help you! What does Ding say?"

"He's for you. Three people in the world stick to you, Harry. I'm one. And the third is what I've come to talk about. Charlie wants to see you."

"Charlie's kind," said Destry drily.

"Are you going to take it like this?"

"How should I take it?"

"Man, man, she talked to me with tears in her eyes, and she's not a soft headed type, as you ought to know."

"Then what does she want?"

"She wants you."

"Now that I'm a murderer, too?"

"What does she care? She wants you. She's ready to pack up and leave with you. She'll do anything. But she begs you to come down to see her at the old house by the dry well."

"I know the place."

Bent laid a hand on the shoulder of his companion. "You're arming yourself with indifference, Harry," said he, "but the fact is that you know you love her still!"

"I've taken her out of my mind," said Destry firmly.

"You think you have. She's at the door now. Can you keep her out, Harry?"

Destry drew a great breath.

Then he said thoughtfully: "If they's more than you two that know of the meeting place, I'm no better than a dead man, Chet, when I start down there. You realize that?"

"Who else *could* know?"

"True," said Destry. "They wasn't pity or conscience in what she said, man? She wanted to see me?"

"I give you my word."

Destry threw up his hand. "Look!" said he.

"At what, Harry?"

"My good resolutions. There they go like smoke! And I'll be riding down there this same evenin'; but I reckon that I'll need my guns before that ride is over!"

Chapter Thirty-four

Out of Cumber River, Willie Thornton had crawled at last like one half drowned; and so exhausted was he that, when he reached the shore, instead of shaking himself like a dog, as most boys would have done, and then taking off and wringing his soaked clothing, he merely sank down on the rocks to rest.

An increasing wretchedness possessed the boy. Not only was he exhausted, but the wind which came down the valley clipped him to the bone with its cold tooth, and his breathing began to send a pain through his chest.

He remained on the rocks in a stupor, for a time, and when he recovered enough to stand up, he knew that he was sick. For his head was heavy, his eyes were dull, and his lips felt numb.

He walked forward without a purpose or a goal, except that he guessed it would be death to remain wet and exposed much longer. When he came to the bank, his legs collapsed, and he had to scramble up slowly, using hands and feet and knees.

At the top, some of the dizziness left him. He kept shaking his head like a stunned prizefighter, to drive that confusion from his brain, but now the dark woods were around him, and with them came the thought of Bent like a prowling panther.

That cleared his brain like a breath of open air after a close room. His very muscles grew stronger, as it seemed, and he went forward cautiously, every now and again pausing to stare about him. And it seemed to the boy that the breathing of the wind was that of Bent, hurrying up behind him, and when a branch caught at him, it was the hand of the murderer on his shoulder once more!

These fancies grew a little less strong as he wandered on through the trees, until at last he came from among them and saw before him the shattered rays of a lamp's light that shone in the distance.

He made straight toward it. Dipping into a sharp sided draw, the light disappeared. The loss of it discouraged him mightily. The old bewilderment returned, but a curious bulldog instinct, such as keeps an army on the go during a forced march, carried him straight ahead, laboring shakily up the opposite bank until he came out in view of the light once more.

It was much nearer, now. He was able to distinguish that it came from a small shack with sage brush growing about it—he knew that by the smell of the bushes when he struck against them in floundering forward. Behind the house there was a stack of hay or straw, and toward this he headed.

Sleep was the panacea which always had cured his ills, and he intended to burrow his way into cover and there close his eyes. He felt guilty over his decision. In his confused mind there was a voice which told him that he must not stop, but must go on and on in the cause of Destry.

What he could accomplish, or what he should try to do, he did not know, but loyal service to a friend seemed to demand an unfailing effort on his part.

However, he surrendered to the necessity for rest and was through the bars of the corral when a voice called loudly behind him: "Who's there? Stop!"

Bent?

The terror of the thought made him suddenly strong to flee. He raced across the corral, vaguely conscious that he was again pursued; but as he strove to slide through the bars on the opposite side of the enclosure, strong hands gathered him up lightly, easily.

He expected that grip to shift to his throat, but his hands lacked strength to struggle.

"A kid, eh?" said the voice of the man. "Come to fetch yourself a coupla chickens, have you? I'm gunna take the hide off you so's you can go back and show the brats in Wham what happens when they come sneakin' out here again!"

He bore Willie back into the path of the lamplight, calling: "I got one of 'em, Jack! I got one sure! We'll make a doggone bright example of this one. Must of fallen into the trough; he's wet as a rat!"

Willie was brought into a region of what seemed to him supernal brightness and before him appeared the face of another man; or did he have two faces?

Curious dimness beset the eyes of Willie; he forgot whatever danger he might stand in and squinted at the face of the second man.

"Hold his hands!" said the captor. "Hold him while I make him dance, the chicken stealin' little son of a gun!"

The hands of Willie were firmly held, but still he squinted up at the face of his jailer, amazed at the manner in which it receded into the distance, and then swept close, as out of a cloud—an unshaven, sun reddened face.

Then a whip lash struck a line of fiery pain across his shoulders. But the pain seemed detached from the brain of the boy. It was as though his body belonged to an impersonal set of nerves. Again it descended——

"Quit it, Pete!" shouted Jack suddenly. "A doggone

good plucked one as ever I seen! Clean gritty. He ain't winked an eye. Leave the whip be! Who are you, kid?"

"Willie," said he.

"Willie who?"

"I dunno. Thornton, I guess."

"He ain't very sure of his name!"

"Hold on. The kid talks kind of loony. D'you fall into the trough, Willie?"

"I fell into the river," said the boy. "Destry——"

His mind had snapped back to that controlling thought, but with the name his voice stopped. His throat was oddly dry and hot.

"He's shakin' all over," said Jack. "What's the matter with him?"

A hand was pressed against the forehead of Willie Thornton, and immediately the harsh voice of Pete softened.

"The kid's sick. He's got fever," said he. "And I've put a whip on him! Damn my heart!"

"Look at him shake—he's sick, right enough. How d'you feel, Willie?"

"Kind of like the way a calf looks—wobbly," said Willie.

He heard them laugh. The sound came to him from a distance in booming waves that flooded upon the drums of his ears and ebbed vibrantly away.

"Get him to bed," said Jack. "I'll fix up some quinine and whiskey. There ain't anything better'n quinine and hot whiskey, I reckon."

Then rapid, powerful hands removed Willie's clothes. He tried to help, but his fingers were numbed. He tried to walk, but his knees sagged. He only knew that he was profoundly eager to lie down. The very word "bed" was like a promise of heaven to him.

He was picked up.

"Gimme one of your flannel shirts, Jack. That'll do him for a nightgown. Gimme a towel first, and I'll dry him off. Skinny little rat, ain't he!"

"Look where you put your marks on his back, Pete."

"I'd rather have 'em laid across my own. I done what I thought was right, though. He run when I called!"

A rough towel burnished Willie dry, almost rubbing away his skin. And his brain spun more and more.

"Destry—" he gasped.

"He's got Destry in his head," said Jack. "Has Destry been after you, son?"

"Yes—no—I mean Destry——"

"He thinks Destry's been after him!" said the other. "Go down to Wham and get some milk for him. He's gunna need milk. Find out who Willie Thornton is. I never heard of no Thorntons around here before!"

Willie was laid between blankets that had a smell of horse-sweat about them; but it was fragrance to Willie, so profound was his weariness.

He closed his eyes in an instant torpor, from which he was roused to have a stinging potion of hot whiskey, bitter with quinine, poured down his throat.

It half choked him with pungency and with its horrible taste. But he hardly had lain back, gasping for breath, when sleep rushed over him like a dark flight of crows. He heard the rushing of their wings—or was it the noise of the pulse in his temple?

And then he slept.

When he wakened, he was wet with sweat, he was weak, but his brain was much clearer. He lifted his brown hand from the blanket and wondered at it, for it hardly seemed to belong to him, though he recognized the down-curved nail which had grown to replace the one that was broken off in his fall of the year before.

He turned his head toward the roar of the kitchen stove, freshly crammed with fuel, and smoking and trembling with the force of the fluttering flames.

There stood Jack of the night before, turning a dream into a fact.

He came and stood over the boy.

"You feelin' better, kid?"

"Yeah. A lot, thanks."

"You got scared out of your wits about Destry. And there ain't no wonder. Destry's killed another, and this time it's murder. The worst kind of murder. With a knife!"

"Destry didn't—" began Willie.

"He did, though. Clifton's dead, stuck like a pig for the autumn slaughter. And Clifton was one of the jury. Here, you, lay back and take it easy."

"I gotta get up," said the boy. "I gotta tell——"

"You lay back. You're still pretty woozy; and you lay back and take it easy. You look pretty done up, I guess. Thought Destry was chasin' you into the river, did you?"

He laughed, but added at once: "It's all right, kid. I seen you show your game, and it was first class. You can have my hide whenever you say the word, I'll tell you! That Destry that you're scared of, he's a gone goose now! I always used to think he'd oughta have a better chance, but there ain't a man in Wham that wouldn't take a shot at him now, if he could, excepting Bent. And maybe even Bent has had enough of the murderin' devil by this time!"

"Bent?" said the boy.

And he closed his eyes, bewildered and half sick by the memory of the face of Bent, as the murderer had stood above the dead body of Clifton.

"You're still mighty done up," declared Jack. "Lay still. Don't you trouble yourself, none. Unless you could tell us where you come from, because nobody in town seems to know."

"I'm out of the Cumber Pass. Destry——"

He wanted desperately to explain, but the other broke in before he could speak.

"It's all right, son. Destry'll never bother you none. There ain't a man in town that would have a word for that red-handed skunk. Nor no woman, neither, exceptin' Charlotte Dangerfield. But a woman'll always stick to a lost cause like a skipper to a sinkin' ship!"

The name thrust deep in the mind of Willie and gave him a sudden determination. Destry had one friend; therefore, to the girl he must go to carry his tidings about the truth of the Clifton murder. No other person would listen. Had not Jack said so, almost in so many words?

Chapter Thirty-five

When at last Destry saw Bent turn back down the trail, he grew heavy of heart, for this man meant to him more than the rest of the world.

He took from his pockets the last things that Bent had brought. There was a steel backed and rimmed pocket mirror; a good strong knife; a quarter pound of Bull Durham and a supply of wheat-straw papers, some matches; some oiled silk, invaluable to keep small necessaries dry; and above all, there was the last strong grip of the hand, and the straight, steady look of Bent's farewell.

And Destry felt that he himself had failed miserably, for he should have been able to find thanks— not eloquent ones, perhaps, because eloquence was not necessary—but a few words to show something of the gratitude that he felt. But how infinitely he valued not the gifts but the thought behind them, he could not begin to express. He could only trust that something of his feeling might have been conveyed by his own silent handshake.

Over three hills he watched the rider appear and disappear, finally dwindling away. Then he turned away with a sigh and mounted Fiddle, who had come out in the trail as though made curious by his movelessness.

He rode her at a walk up the first slope and paused her on a bald headed hill to look over the sun bathed mountains. Naked and grim enough they appeared to the casual eye, but Destry loved them because he knew them. That apparent nakedness did not deceive him. The shadow on the side of Mount Scare Crow was really a wood in which fat deer were grazing; on the flats between he did not need to waste ammunition to make his bag of rabbit, when he cared for that meat—a few simple snares would do instead. Between the Scare Crow and Timber Peak the sage hens were always plump and their flesh more delicately flavored than in any other part of the range, and along the sides of Timber Peak itself the squirrels lived by thousands among the trees. And whose palate grows tired of squirrels, toasted brown above wood coals? Off the side of Chisholm Mountain leaped a brook where the trout were silver flashes in the water; and at its base the elk came down to the salt lick. Bears, too, were everywhere, not to be hunted except with fatigue, but bagged readily enough by those who were content to wait for opportunity to come their way.

So all this rough-headed sea of mountains was really a gigantic preserve for Destry, and the harsh face of it pleased him more than ever did the barbed wire fence of a landowner who wishes to guard his game. Moreover, there was such beauty here as soft green hills, and pleasant meadows, and ploughed fields never could afford; for all about him the giants stood up in glistening armor against the pale blue sky and raised his heart and his thoughts with them.

So Destry felt as he stared about him at the highlands. But yonder in the mist which covered the lower region of Wham and its surrounding valley were many men, danger, deceit, struggle, doubt of one another.

There was also behind that veil Charlie Dangerfield, and the thought of her came home to him with a heady sweetness, like wine. That evening he would leave the mountains and ride down to her, and let tomorrow bring what it might!

The wind had paused with the mare, and stood still. Now it sprang up gently and carried with it a subdued thrumming sound. Destry listened to it with instant curiosity, wondering how the waterfalls on the side of Cringle Peak could send the rhythm of their beat so far as this.

Then he jerked up his canted head with a start, suddenly realizing the thing was impossible. The noise could not blow as far as where he sat the saddle.

The mystery was not a thing to be left uninvestigated. To him, as to a wild animal, every unexplained fact was a possibly potent danger. He turned the mare to the farther side of the crest, and looking down into the shallow valley, he saw the cause of the noise.

Five riders were pushing their horses at a steady trot up the gentle slope. They saw him at once, apparently, and the trot became a swinging gallop. It was Destry they wanted, evidently. Destry, and the price on his head.

And as he sat in the saddle, with the wind pressing against his face and the sun hot on his back, a fierce resentment surged up in him. If he got into the nest of rocks on the side of the mountain and opened fire with the Winchester, how long would that gallant charge persist?

However, it was not for him to resist with guns. If, in fact, Clifton had fallen at his hand, he knew grimly and certainly that fresh victims would be added on this day to his list; but the very knowledge of his innocence handicapped him in the fight.

He swung the mare about, therefore, and crossed

the mountain top to the farther side—and saw struggling through the brush three riders—their faint yells as they spotted him came tingling through the tin air to his ears.

Down the hill, then, to leave them soon far behind!

But as he started down the slope, out of the trees not a quarter of a mile away came a rush of three more mounted men! They fired as they came, trusting to a lucky shot, hardly bringing the rifles to the shoulder. And yet one of the bullets sang perilously close to Destry.

Up the grade he went, therefore, keeping the mare just under full speed, for he could tell that she would need her strength later on.

They had not come with single mounts, these eleven, but behind the last group of riders came two more, each leading a cluster of horses naked of the saddle. They were the relief mounts to be used when the first lot were exhausted. And by their action, Destry guessed the whole troop to be chosen animals.

He was glad of the rough ground. It was through such broken rocks that Fiddle made ordinary horses appear to be tied to the ground, and a mile straight up hill soon worked havoc with the horses behind.

It had taken a great deal from the good mare, also. She had traveled far enough for a day's work already, since sunup, and that hot mile started her lungs laboring like bellows. However, those behind had their heads bobbing hopelessly, and Destry grunted with complacent understanding of what that meant. At his last look, he saw the posse changing saddles, then he entered high brush that cut off his view.

He had three choices—to keep straight on, or to

turn to either side. To keep straight on would be a
sheer test of horse power, and he doubted the advis-
ability of that when Fiddle was already so tired. To
the left lay comparatively smooth going, where her
long stride would tell. To the right was a veritable
jungle, in which she would shine because of her
deerlike surety and activity of foot. He chose to turn
to the right; furthermore, it led him in the distant direction of the Dangerfield place!

He had a good hour of labor without sight of open
country. The lodgepole pines stood thick in his path
and gave him only the sky overhead, and occasional
glimpses of hollow valleys or sheer rocky slopes on
either hand.

When he came into the open, he was at the head
of O'Mara valley, and there was no sight or sound of
the enemy. The sun was dropping already behind a
Western peak; far beneath he saw a squatter's shack,
and the translucent twist of smoke that curled above
it. They were quietly cooking supper in that place,
cutting bacon, working up the fire, relaxing with the
cool of the evening, and the sweet sense of a night of
perfect rest before them. He, too, could relax now,
and let the mare rest!

He dismounted at once, slackened the girths, and
walked on with the tired Fiddle stepping behind
him, lagging more than was her wont. And then,
well out from the trees, he heard a roar like the beating of surf, and saw eleven horsemen in close for-
mation charging down upon him along the valley.

He could understand what had happened! Reaching the close covert of the trees, his pursuers had
turned the chances over in their minds. They could
go straight on, or else gamble that the fugitive would
turn to one side or the other; and they had taken the

long chance, had swung to the correct side, and here they were! Only by a little had they overshot their mark, but they had the double advantage of second mounts, and horses, moreover, which had been taken straight across open country instead of through the heat and the twisting ways of the woods!

But, though he could understand it, Destry was too stunned by the sense of disaster to move at once. Then, with an oath, he jerked up the cinches, sprang into the saddle, and gave the mare her head.

There was no dodging, now. He was too far out in the valley to venture a cut back on either side, for those behind would be sure to gain ground and fill the mare and her rider with bullets.

No, there was nothing for it except a straight pull down the valley, and a blind trust in the long stride of Fiddle.

He jockeyed her as well as he could. She, with a great heart, sprang out against the bit, ready to win her race or die, but he restrained her with his hand, and with a gently reassuring voice which will give a wise horse confidence up to the very gate of defeat.

Over his shoulder he looked back and watched and waited. They came fast. They came pouring in a rush, with heads straight out, and tails snapping in the wind of their gallop. He had to extend Fiddle more and more. She seemed to be flying now at full speed, but still she did not gain, and in her strong gallop there came a trifling heaviness which only her master could have recognized. Yet he felt a blind faith, a superstitious confidence. All the good that had come his way, in more than six years, had been through Chester Bent. Was not this animal his gift, and could she fail her rider?

Still the long beat of her stride continued. It is

marvelous that the pursuers could maintain the pace against her, fresh though they might be.

And now, as he looked back under the red of the sunset, he saw that they actually were failing. Back they fell, raggedly. Yonder a man had pulled up and was now standing beside his mustang, which stood with legs braced far apart, dead beat.

But two riders broke out of the pack, like thoroughbreds from among cold blooded stock. They, unfalteringly, clung to the race. They did not lose ground. Gradually they gained.

Destry called to the good mare. He felt the lurch of her muscles as she responded, but almost instantly she was back in her former gait.

He understood, then. She would maintain that gait until she died, but not even in her great spirit was there the power to do more!

He leaned a little aside.

Her head was stretched out true and straight. But he could see the red stain of exhaustion in her bulging eyes; and her red rimmed nostrils flared in a vain effort to drink in more of the life giving air. Froth dripped from her mouth, flecked her throat and shoulders. She still ran as only a great horse can run; but, with the suddenness of a bullet striking home, Destry knew that she was beaten!

Chapter Thirty-six

It was not that her stride was shorter or more labored, or less swift, but through her body, through the long rhythm of her gallop, it seemed to him that he could discern the slightest faltering, the slightest wavering from side to side. And he knew that she was gone, beaten, broken, perhaps ruined from that moment, perhaps doomed to die, even if he reined her in now!

Of the posse, there was not a man in sight except the two who rode the fine horses. Durable as iron they seemed, and though they could not gain on Fiddle, at least they were holding her even.

Destry turned down the first short valley on the left, and wound up it to a rough tableland above, in the hope that this might make the two realize that they were hunting dangerous quarry alone. And he even turned and tried his rifle at them, shooting perilously close. But still they kept pounding on! They began to shoot random shots, in return, but the most of their energy was given to driving the horses ahead.

Even looking back from the highlands, Destry could not see the rest of the posse and he guessed that they had been so hopelessly distanced that even the sound of firing probably would not bring them up. No doubt they were telling one another, as they rested far away, that the two lucky fellows who had such horses beneath them might let their nags take them up with the quarry—and then what?

Then what, indeed!

He needed only to pull the mare into the first clump of trees, and, leaping down, open fire with his Winchester. If he could not bag two birds as large as these, and so close, then his hand and eye had lost all skill.

But he knew that he could not shoot them. If only he really had had murder charged against him, then simple, simple to add another two to the list. One cannot be hung more than once, even for a thousand crimes!

But he could not fight them off, and close shooting would never do to frighten these fellows. By something in the swing of their shoulders, by something in the slant of their bodies as they came around curves, he knew that they were young boys, and he knew that they were ready to die for glory. It was no thought of the reward that drove them on, he could swear, but a resistless impulse toward great deeds!

He smiled as he thought of that, but the smile was sour. A bullet sang by his ear; he drew on the reins, called to Fiddle, and pitched himself forward along her neck!

She came rapidly to a halt. As she paused, he felt her trembling, her knees sagging and straightening beneath the pressure of his weight, almost as though the swing of the gallop had been easier for her to endure than to stand still, here, oppressed by her own weight and by that of her rider! Then he heard the pounding of swift hoofs behind him, and a pair of whooping Indian cries of exultation.

"*I* nailed him!" said one. "I got him clean through and through."

"Ay, it was you, Chip. But go mighty soft and slow, now, because he might be playin' possum."

"I'm gunna sink another slug into him and make sure."

"Doncha do it, Chip. He's never shot no helpless people himself, no matter what else he done."

"You're right," said Chip. "I didn't really mean it, anyway. Is he clean dead? Why don't he drop?"

"Because he happened to fall straight, forkin' the hoss. We'd better go slow, though, because you never can tell. These old timers are mighty foxy."

"Sure they are, but I got this old timer covered so doggone tight that he couldn't be got out of this here fix with a can opener! Step up slow. Doncha go forgettin' that this is Destry himself that we got under our hand!"

"Am I likely to be forgettin' that? Folks are gunna remember us for this day's work, if we never don't do nothin' else afterwards, as long as we live!"

"It was me that shot him. Doncha forget that!"

"I'll remember that, all right, Chip. I ain't gunna steal any of your glory from you—only, it was a kind of a lucky shot, I reckon. Keep him covered, will you, while I dismount?"

From the corner of the eye Destry saw the lad dismount. He was a tall, magnificent youngster, with a fine, brown face, and the clearest and most cheerful of eyes. His companion, Chip, was as brown as his companion, but he was prematurely old, with a sallow look and a sneer already forming on his lips.

He kept his rifle at the ready, but yet not completely at the ready, for the muzzle was turned a trifle away from the target, so that the stock of the weapon turned somewhat broadside on to Destry's eye.

He, watching with the most covert care, wondered if with a snap shot he could strike the stock of that gun and knock the weapon out of the hands of the marksman? If he missed the stock, he was reasonably sure to drive the bullet through the side of the boy; and that would be death for the youngster, a thing which Destry mortally shrank from dealing out.

"Go take that Fiddle by the head," the rider was directing. He appeared to have taken command and direction of the operations from his taller and handsomer companion. "She's sure done run a mighty fine race today. I'm gunna match you to see which one of us had oughta have her!"

"Would she come to one of us?"

"Sure she would! I'll wrastle you for her, Skinny."

"*You'll* wrastle me for her?" said the tall fellow, stopping short in his advance towards the mare. "Why, you sawed off runt, what chance would you have if I laid a hand on you?"

"The bigger they are, the quicker that I cut 'em down to my size," declared Chip.

"You talk like a fool!" declared the other boy. "You happened to get in a lucky shot, and now to hear you a gent would think that you was Kit Carson!"

"You'd think that I was before ever I got through with you, young feller!"

"I'm young, am I? Chip, you oughta listen to yourself and get ashamed. Which I never heard nobody talk so ornery and mean as you're doin'."

"Didn't you?"

"No!"

'Are you aimin' at trouble, Skinny?"

"I told you once that I'd lick you, if you didn't stop callin' me Skinny."

"You did. What you say don't make no difference to me. If I can't handle you with hands, I can do it with guns!"

"Hey, Chip, you don't mean that? You don't mean that you'd shoot me?"

"Like a skunk. Why not?"

"I pretty nigh believe that you would!"

"You believe right! I don't care nothin' about you, Skinny, or what you think, or what you want! I'm gunna have Fiddle, because I oughta have her. You can get half of the money, but I'll take Fiddle——"

"You be damned! You take *all* the money, and I'll have the hoss!"

"So's you can ride up and down through Wham and tell folks that you're the one that really beat Destry, and the proof is that you got his mare between your knees, right that minute?"

Destry had heard enough, and had made all of his preparations. He had been able to steal back his right hand and draw out a revolver; now Chip was turned almost at right angles to him, making the shot he wished to attempt twice as simple as it had been before.

Yet still it was difficult, for he knew that he would have to make the first bullet a snap shot, and a snap shot at any distance at such a thing as the stock of a rifle is a hazardous matter. If he failed in the first shot, the second would have to be for the life of Chip, the third for that of Skinny!

Twice he flexed his fingers on the handles of the Colt, then he flicked it across the hanging neck of Fiddle and fired.

He saw the rifle explode in the hands of Chip as it jerked sidewise and fell to the ground, while Chip, with a yell of pain, caught his right hand in his left.

The revolver bullet, striking the hard wood of the stock, had slithered down it, and thrust a great splinter into the hand of Chip.

Destry sat erect in the saddle, now. The gun in his left hand covered Chip, and the revolver in his right covered young "Skinny," whose own weapon was half drawn.

"We don't oughta have no luck," said Skinny with a wonderful calmness. "We was countin' chickens! Destry, you sure done us fine!"

"I wanted to put a slug through him and make sure of him!" wailed Chip. "Damn me if I ever go even huntin' chipmunks with a fool like you, agin, Skinny!"

"Young feller," cautioned Destry, "if it wasn't that I hadn't wanted to murder the pair of you, I'd of ducked into a grove and picked the two of you out of the saddle. Don't talk killin', Chip. You can shoot pretty straight, but you see you didn't get me today. You didn't even nick me! Killin' talk generally gets them done up that does the talkin', and that's a fact for certain sure! Unbuckle that gun belt and let her drop, if you don't mind. That's it. Now you slide down off'n your hoss—this side, please. You, Skinny, back up the road, and keep on backin' up till you hear from me to stop. That's better. Boys, I gotta borrow your hosses, because my Fiddle is plumb fagged. I've gotta ask you one question, though, before I start. How did you get onto my trail?"

"Why, there ain't any secret about that. Some of the old heads figgered that Bent would be tryin' to see you and let you know how things stood, after the killin' of Clifton. We laid guard watchin', and when Bent left in this here direction, we sure come along his trail on the lookout. That's all that they is to it!"

"That's enough. Boys, keep your hands up, and keep on backin'. That'll do, thanks! Who was leadin' you?"

"It was——" began Chip.

"Shut up, you fool!" barked Skinny. "You wanta get somebody in trouble, do you?"

"Skinny," called Destry, "you're all right, son. I leave your gun belt here for you, hopin' that you sure won't try to snag me while I'm ridin' off. Chip, you need a little agin' in the wood, but you're sure plumb poisonous just now. Don't you go to eatin' iron till you know that your stomach will up and stand that kind of a diet!"

Of the two horses, he selected a tough appearing buckskin for his mount, and swung into the saddle.

"Good luck to you on my hoss!" called Skinny. "You might of dropped us both, Destry, and I'm sure thankin' you."

Destry waved his hand, and glancing back, he saw that Chip was still scowling with furious hate.

Of such were murderers made, he was sure!

Chapter Thirty-seven

That morning, Willie Thornton slept; they roused him at noon only to have him stare sleepily at them, and turn his head away from the proffered food. They did not try to force him to eat. It was Pete who declared that sleep was better for him than nourishment, and so the boy was allowed to fall into a profound slumber.

He wakened, with a tremor and a shock, late in the afternoon. The blood gushed audibly in his temples, from the force of his frightened heartbeat, and he was oppressed with a cold sense of guilt.

It was Destry. He should have done something long before this to save the great man from danger, and now he sat up suddenly in his bunk. The movement made his head spin. He gritted his teeth and forced down deep breaths until his brain cleared, then took stock of the room which hitherto he had seen only as in a dream: the stove, the rusted pipe, the pans, the homemade broom, the cluttered corners, filled with old clothes, boots, traps, guns, fishing tackle, saddlery, harness. It was a junk shop, odds and ends invading the center of the floor.

Near the head of the bunk, depending from nails, were his ragged clothes. These he pulled down and began to dress. It was not easy. When he leaned, dimness rushed over his eyes, and a pain throbbed at the back of his skull. Weakness was in him a physical thing, like a thin tide of water ebbing and flowing in his veins. Sometimes it washed as low as his knees and made them shake. Sometimes it surged up to his armpits and made his arms shudder. It reached his head, and covered his eyes with a film of darkness.

Yet he persisted until he was dressed, and went to the doorway, feeling his way along the wall. The strong blast of the westering sun struck him like a hot hand in the face, and, piercing his shirt, it scorched his body.

He had to blink his eyes against that brilliance, but yet the force of the sun drove strength into his body, and the air seemed to fill him with more life.

He smiled at the weakness which he left behind him!

An old horse was grazing in the corral, wandering around the edges of the fence and reaching under for the grass that grew outside. It was a lump of a creature with a shapeless head and thick legs, but Willie guessed that there might still be too much life in it for him to handle in his present condition. However, he dragged out a battered range saddle, from which most of the leather had been worn away, or rat-eaten. It was a struggle for him to manage the clumsy weight of it. The effort sent sweat rushing out all over his body; his mouth twitched as though an electric spasm controlled the muscles.

Yet those who have known the pain of labor are schooled in endurance. So the boy endured.

When he got a rope from the shed, he had to follow the old mustang patiently for half an hour. Sometimes it would allow him to put his hand upon the mane, before it whirled away and darted off, throwing its heels into the air. He forced himself to be patient, setting his teeth hard, telling himself that this waste of his strength would not exhaust him too much for the work that lay ahead—if only the devil of a horse could be caught.

Snared at last it was, and then came reluctantly on the rope toward the fence, halting, jerking back, thrusting out its long, stiff upper lip with a foolish expression unmatchable except in the face of a horse.

Willie Thornton endured, snubbed the rope around a post, and so at last worked on the saddle with a mighty heave, then struggled until his head swam to force the bit into the stubborn mouth of the brute. At last that work was ended, but he had to sit down on a bar of the gate to steady himself before he could mount. This he only managed by climbing up on the fence and scrambling into the cup of the saddle from a height.

The mustang went off with a rush, rearing, pitching, while Willie reeled from side to side, his lips grinned back with the agony of effort to keep a grip with his short legs upon the barrel ribs of the horse. The kinks were soon out of the veteran mustang, however, and it developed a rocking lope which surprised Willie with its softness.

Once on the road, he looked back toward the shack with a touch of shame to think of what would fill the minds of Pete and Jack when they considered that their good Samaritanship had been repaid by the theft of a horse. But the future would have to be trusted to put all of that straight!

He came into Wham as wild a little figure as ever appeared in even that town, with his hair on end, clotted with dust, his face pale, his cheeks hollow, his eyes staring with the fever that burned him and froze him in turns.

At the blacksmith shop he asked the way to the Dangerfield place, and the smith came out to stare at him and point out the correct trail.

"You look kind of done up, kid," said he. "Better

get down and rest yourself a mite. Ain't that Jack Loughran's hoss that you're on?"

"I'm goin' on an errand for Jack," said Willie, and thumped the big ribs of the horse with his bare heels.

He rode into a queer fairyland, for it was the golden time of the afternoon, and hills and trees to the fevered eyes of the boy were enwrapped with mists of rich fire, shot with rose. The dust that puffed up under the hoofs of the horse rose as a magic vapor; the wind struck it away, or tossed it high and thin in weird shapes. The world was possessed of motion—the hills rolled in waves, the trees swayed, the road itself heaved and fell gently before him.

Willie began to laugh at the strangeness of this universe, and then found himself listening for another voice—so far away and elfishly thin did that laughter sound upon his ear.

Then he discovered that the rolling might not be of the landscape around him, but his own uncertain undulation in the saddle. When he tried to grip with his knees, they gave way from the hips, weakly. He could not control himself; the very reins shook in his hand.

Now it appeared to him, as the mustang seemed pausing between steps, that he was a fool to have come out from the town. The blacksmith, for instance, had had an honest face and might have believed the truth of what he said concerning the murder of Clifton. As it was, he probably would fall from the back of the horse long before it reached the house of the Dangerfields!

All was now so dim before his eyes that it was as though he rode through a storm, and when the sun sank, he was in dread lest he should be lost in the utter dark.

Then a great whirling seized his brain and he felt his senses sinking, as a boat whirls and sinks in the grip of a vortex.

When he recovered, he was sprawled forward across the pommel of the saddle and the neck of the horse, his head hanging down and the blood heavy as lead in it.

The mustang was contentedly grazing at the side of the road!

Pushing himself back into the saddle with both shaking arms, the boy looked desperately around him into thick darkness on every hand, a wall of impenetrable black. He was lost—he would die he knew, if help did not come to him, since he could not find his way to it! But his own death seemed a small thing to Willie. It was the great man, the hero of whom he thought most, Destry!

Now as he concentrated his thought upon that glorious image of Destry, the blackness that had covered his eyes lifted wonderfully. He saw that it was not thick night, but only the time of old gold and tarnished russet, faintly streaked along the horizon. The trees looked as huge as houses; he had to tell himself that the black outline he wanted to find would be marked by a few lights. Then he hammered weakly against the sides of the horse, and it went on, tossing its head until the bridle jingled, stepping out long and free as a horse will do when it feels that the end of the day's work must be near.

He dared not put the animal to a jog or a lope, because he knew that the swift motion would roll him promptly from the saddle, and, once out of it, he doubted his ability to so much as crawl. So greatly had the weakness increased upon him.

Then, with a turn of the road, he saw before him

the shining of a lamp through an open window, its rays fanning out in brilliant, trembling clusters. Toward that light he went, when a form seemed to rise before him out of the ground.

It was a man who was saying: "Hullo, kid! Where you from?"

"I'm lookin' for the Dangerfield place."

"Here's the house. Whacha want?"

"I wanta see Miss Dangerfield!"

"Come on in, then. She'll be back, soon."

"I wanta see her real bad," muttered Willie.

"Well, then, you traipse on across the field, yonder, and likely you'll find her. She went out walkin' toward the old shack. You can see the roof of it there between the trees—no, not that way. Look there! Can't you see?"

"I got dust in my eyes," said Willie.

His voice was uncertain.

"Whacha been cryin' about?" asked the gruff voice of the man. "Whacha cryin' about now? You're a mighty lot too big a kid to be cryin'. Y'oughter be ashamed of yourself!"

Willie did not answer.

He knew that the quaver in his voice was weakness, not tears, but the hot shame he felt at the reproof flushed him with a new strength. It cleared his eyes, and enabled him to see the pointed roof of the old shack between the trees, in the dusk before him. Toward it he aimed the horse.

The bushes washed about him; they scratched his bare knees cruelly, but he was glad of the pain, because it helped to rouse him for the words which he must speak when he found the girl.

If he found her!

The thought of failing made the frantic panic leap

straightway into his brain. He fought it back. But another thought now beset him. Friend to Destry though she was, still what could a woman do in such an affair as this? He should have found a man. He should have told his story to Pete and Jack. They were too kind to be dishonest. They would have believed——

So he rode on in a torment, and saw the trees and the bushes divide before him. The old house lay just before him, with the front door open, hanging from one hinge.

Above the door, one deep, empty attic window looked out at him like an eyehole from a skull. There was no life about the place.

"Miss Dangerfield!" he called.

It seemed to Willie that he heard an echo pick up the name and whisper it; or was that a stir in the bushes around him?

"Miss Dangerfield!" he called again.

A quiet voice spoke to him; he saw a woman come around the corner of the building, and slipping out of the saddle, he tried to go to her, only to have his knees buckle beneath the impact of his weight.

Chapter Thirty-eight

Now his body was hardly more than a bundle of limp string, but his brain remained clear enough. The girl ran to him, caught him beneath the shoulder, her fingers gripping the flaccid flesh with the strength of a man's hand.

But as for that, he remembered, she was the woman who loved Destry—not to be expected like other women! His faith in what she might accomplish soared suddenly.

"Who are you, son?" she asked. "And what d'you want of me. Why, you're sick! You're hot as fire with fever!"

"I gotta say something!" said Willie Thornton. "Will ya listen?"

"I'll listen! Poor youngster!"

She kneeled on the ground by him, supporting him still beneath the shoulders. Neither she nor the boy was conscious of the form that stepped silently from the shrubbery and loomed beside them, listening.

"You're Charlie Dangerfield?"

"Yes."

"You b'long to Destry?"

She hesitated not an instant.

"I b'long to Harry Destry," she admitted. "Why?"

"You swear you'll b'lieve what I'm gunna tell you?"

"I'll believe!"

"Destry didn't kill Clifton!"

"Ah, ah!" he heard her gasp. "Thank God!"

He raised a hand and gripped weakly on her arm. His head fell back with mortal weakness, but she passed a hand beneath it and held him close to her like a helpless child. He would have resented that support fiercely at any other time, but now he was glad of it, for out of her cool hands strength flowed into him, greater than the strength which pure air gives; and he breathed a delicate scent of lavender, held close against her breast.

"He didn't kill Clifton. I seen. I was in Bent's house. I seen Bent steal the knife from Destry's room."

He could make his lips move, but suddenly his voice failed him; his eyes closed.

"Make your strength hold out one minute," he heard the girl appealing to him.

Her face pressed close to his.

"Try to tell me the rest!"

"I follered Bent and Clifton out of Bent's house. I was scared, but I follered. There was murder 'n the air! I come to Clifton's house behind 'em—garden gate—dog——"

His voice trailed off.

"Try, honey, try!" she whispered eagerly.

"I got up to the window. I seen Bent talk to Clifton. I heard him say something about money he owned Clifton. I seen Clifton beg for his life, mighty horrible. I seen him crawl like a dog. I seen—I seen——"

"One more word—then I'll take care of you. I'll make you well again, poor boy!"

"I seen Bent grab him by the hair——"

"Clifton?"

"Ay, I seen him grab Clifton by the hair and yank back his head, and stab him in the hollow of the throat, and I heard Clifton gag, like a stuck pig, and fall, and twist his legs on the floor and——"

The life went out of Willie Thornton suddenly. He hung limp in the arms of the girl, breathing so faintly that she scarcely felt the stir of it against her cheek.

And now, as she looked up from him, ready to call for help to carry him to the house, she saw the silhouette of the second listener beside her.

"Harry?" she gasped.

"It's me," said Destry.

"Did you hear?"

"I heard."

"Is it true, Harry? Could Chet have done such a thing?"

"I'm plumb turned to stone," said Destry. "But the kid wouldn't lie. He's give my life to me once; tonight he's give it to me agin! It's Willie Thornton."

The voice of the boy began again in a fluttering gasp:

"He seen me at the window and hunted me through the dark. Him and the dog. Jumped—the water was mighty cold. But Jack and Pete they caught me—go on, old hoss, because I ain't gunna fall!"

"He's out of his head, poor kid!" said the girl. "He's tremblin' with the fever, Harry. God keep him from no harm out of this!"

"Give him to me," said Destry. "I'll carry him into the house. You go fetch over some blankets and more help, then we'll pack him over there!"

The voice muttered softly, barely audible to them both:

"You b'longin' to Destry, I didn't dare to tell nobody but you. It was a long way, between dyin' and livin'. One side of the road dyin', one side livin'— the old hoss kep' movin'—which I didn't fall——"

Destry stood up, with the youngster in his arms, holding him gently, holding him close.

"He's out of his head," said the girl.

"Quick!" said Destry, and she turned and ran swiftly from the shack, through the brush, and toward the house of her father.

Destry went on into the cabin where he managed to support the boy with one arm while he took out a match with the free hand and prepared to scratch it.

As he did so, something of an incredible lightness touched his face, like a spider's web, but falling toward the floor. He looked up, bewildered, and again there were several light touches against his skin.

"You're mighty strong," said the boy. "You're the one for Destry. You go tell the judge; you swear what I said was true. Them that are dyin' don't lie, which Pop always said in the old days. Me dyin', I'm tellin' the truth. I seen it. I seen him kill Clifton—not Destry—he ain't no murderer——"

"Son," said Destry, "it ain't Charlie that's holdin' you here. It's Destry. I——"

He felt the slim body stiffen.

"Hey! Is it you, Harry?"

"It's me, old timer! You ain't dyin'. Charlie'll get you well."

"Why, I wouldn't care much," said Willie, "me bein' tolerable sleepy, right now. Lemme get down, Destry. I can stand pretty good, I reckon—only bein' a mite sleepy——"

Destry struck a light, and looked down at a face white as the death of which Willie had spoken, and wildly staring eyes, rimmed with black; and pale lips, purple gray, as though they were coated with dust.

Such a horror struck through the man at the sight of this, that he jerked his head up, and saw, as the match flame spurted wide, the thin gleam of a fleck of straw falling from the ceiling above him.

But straw does not sift through cracks in an old

ceiling unless it is disturbed. By wind, perhaps. But there was not a mortal touch of wind in the air, this evening! What else was above them in the attic?

He dashed the match to the floor and leaped to the side. That moment, from the trap door, the sawed-off shot gun of Cleeves roared like thunder and lightning.

The flare of the double discharge showed the whole shack lighted, and, behind the leveled barrels of the gun, the contorted face of the marksman.

Destry, springing aside, had snatched his Colt out; now he fired at the point where the pale face had glimmered in the dark of the attic above him, and next stood still.

The boy had fainted. His legs and head dragged down feebly, loosely, but as Destry held the small body close, he felt the uncertain, slow flutter of the heart. Fortune and his own quick foot had enabled him to side step the double charge even at this close range. Too close, perhaps, for the purpose of the sawed-off gun; five feet farther away the charge would have spread out inescapably wide!

What was the marksman above them doing now? Destry poised his gun to shoot a second time, but he feared that the flash of his weapon would illumine him as a target for another shot; furthermore, if he strove to glide back through the doorway, he would similarly be placing himself against a light, no matter how dim a one it seemed. So he stepped back against the wall and waited through a long moment, lifting the head of Willie Thornton until it rested comfortably against his shoulder.

Now he heard, at first too softly to be sure of it, but presently distinctly, a sound which might have been the soft and regular movement of someone crossing the floor, or the creaking of the ladder as someone cautiously descended it, lowering himself softly from rung to rung.

There was this peculiarity about the sound, that it was quite regular, and yet that it seemed to come from different parts of the room, sometimes from the window, or again from the door, or rising out of the very floor, as it were.

The nerves of Destry were firm enough—none firmer in all of the world, perhaps—and yet they began to shudder a bit under this suspense.

He could not stand still. Moreover, there must be something done for the boy, who hung limply in his arms. This might be no fainting spell, but death itself, for he no longer felt the beating of the feeble heart against his breast!

So Destry started moving toward the doorway, and as he did so, a warm drop struck the back of the hand with which he held his Colt ready for a second shot. He stopped with a leap of nerves. Then, passing his hand over the same place, again the warm drop fell upon it.

And then he knew!

His first shot had gone home, and Hank Cleeves lay dead in the attic, whose loosened straw had sifted down and betrayed the presence of something living within the house. Cleeves lay dead. That was the reason there had been no stir of the man as he reloaded his double-barreled weapon. That was the reason that there had been no second shot, and the first spurt of blood, soaking through the crack in the floor, had made that singular tapping sound which had almost frightened Destry forth from the shack.

He shook his head to drive away the concern from

his mind. As he did so, he heard a stifled voice just outside the door exclaiming: "Hank! Hank!"

There was a pause, and then the voice repeated: "Hank, did you get him?"

And Destry grinned in the darkness and felt the hot blood thrill along his veins. More than Hank had come to make this trap and more than Hank might pay for its catch!

Chapter Thirty-nine

Somewhere yonder in the darkness, Fiddle waited for him; somewhere away from him, Charlie Dangerfield was calling together her men who were to carry poor little Willie Thornton to the house. But there was another danger close at hand. He heard voices at the door and a little outside it.

"Hank doesn't answer."

"Call again, then."

"Hey, Hank!"

Louder they called: "Hello, Hank!"

There was no answer from Cleeves. He never again would answer any man. His lips were cold. Until Judgment Day, a thousand trumpets might blow, and Hank never would reply. He whom a hundred thousand eyes had seen now had vanished. He was gone. He was away. Deeper than the seas he was buried, and deeper than the mountains could hide him. The impalpable spirit was gone, and only the living blood remained to tell of him, dripping down into the silence of the old shack, drop by drop, softly spattering, like footsteps wonderfully light and wonderfully clear. Hank Cleeves was ended, and his long fingers and his hairy hands would never again do wonders with hammer and chisel, with saw, and wrench. The boys would no longer stand around and admire the mechanic. They would no longer yearn to grow up to such a man. The chips would no longer fly, nor the nails sink home for Hank Cleeves, nor the rafters ring under his hammer.

He was gone. Yonder lay his body, perhaps with the heavy forty-five calibre slug of lead smashed through the breast and into the vitals. Perhaps the bullet had beaten through brain and brainpan, and so the body lay lifeless. But he was ended; that cunning machine could function no more; that ineffable spark was extinguished.

And Destry stood below in the darkness, still between life and death, with the limp body of the boy in his arms.

He heard from the lips of Willie the faintest of sighs, and it made his breast lift, as the breast of a mother stirs when the infant moves beside her, at night. He felt all of paternity, all of motherhood, also, since both qualities lie mysteriously buried in the heart of man; since he strives to be himself, and also to reproduce physically what cannot physically be born to the world. His ideas, his spirit, his heart and soul he would put into flesh, but they must remain forever unfleshed, ideal, impalpable, here glimpsed at with paint, here staring out of stone, here charmed into words, but always hints, glimpses, and nothing to fill the material arms as a child fills the arms of its mother.

So these mysteries softly thronged down on the sad soul of Destry, and he touched them in their flight as a child might hold up its hands and touch moths flying in the night, without comprehension, with only vague desires and emotions.

But one thing he could know, in the feeble rationalization of all men, with which they strive to reduce the eternal emotions to concrete "yes" and "no," that this boy had once almost died for him, and now actually might be dying for him in very fact. He knew it, and wonder filled him. He became to himself something more than a mere name and a vague thing; he for the first time visualized "Destry" as that man appeared before the eyes of others, striking terror, striking wonder, filling at least the eyes of a child with an ideal!

Knowing this, he felt a sudden scorn for the baser parts that were in him, the idler, the scoffer at others, the disdainful mocker at the labors of life. He wished to be simple, real, quiet, able to command the affection of his peers.

It seemed to Destry that, through the boy, for the first time he could realize the meaning of the word "peer." Equal. For all men are equal. Not as he blindly had taken the word in the courtroom, with wrath and with contempt. Not equal in strength of hand, in talent, in craft, in speed of foot or in leap of mind, but equal in mystery, in the identity of the race which breathes through all men, out of the soil, and out of the heavens.

So it was that hatred for his enemies left him.

In another day, he had derided them, he had contested with them, he had conquered them; for those defeats they had avenged themselves by confining him for six years for an offense of which he was innocent; but, at the same time, of another offense he had preeminently been guilty, for he had looked down upon them, and from a tower of self-content, he had laughed at them.

Why?

Because they were less swift in unsheathing a six-shooter!

Because they stuck less firmly on the back of a horse!

Because there was more weak flesh and less leather in them!

Because they faltered in the climb, weakened under the weight, staggered in the crisis, looked for help where no help could come! So he also had faltered, had weakened, had staggered, had looked about him in the prison.

They were not different. They were made of one flesh and spirit and therefore they were his equals, his "peers." To them the world in which he had been free was to them, in a sense, a prison.

These understandings, rushed suddenly upon him, made him slip back closer against the wall, and hold the limp form of the boy more tenderly in his arms. He, too, had been a child; so were they all, men, and women, children also, needing help, protection, cherishing, but capable now and then and here and there of great deeds inspired by love and high aspiration. It was such a power that had come upon little Willie Thornton. He with his small hand had snatched a life from the shadow of the law and thrown another man in the peril of the gibbet!

So Destry stood close by the door and waited, more stirred with sudden, deep striking thoughts than in all his life before; so that it seemed to him there was a pure, thin light of beauty falling upon the world and upon all of the men in the world, except only Chester Bent. He, like a shadow, lay athwart the life of Destry, and there arose in the latter no boyish and irresponsible hate, no transient hunger for vengeance, but a vast and all possessing disdain and disgust.

With it came a fear, also. For if Bent had deceived him, then he knew that Bent was such a power as he never before had tried his strength of mind and hand against.

He heard the voices continue, close beside him.

"There ain't any answer."

"He's there."

"He couldn't of missed."

"I seen that gun loaded myself with two charges of buckshot. Extra big. It would of blowed the side out of a house."

"I think I heard them shot strike wood, though! They rattled!"

"Sure, but some of them hit Destry."

"I heard him fall!"

"What about the kid?"

"He's scared sick, somewheres in there."

"Maybe the slugs hit him."

"A kid like that ain't much loss."

"Why don't Hank answer?"

"Because he's gloatin'. He ain't a talker, anyways!"

"Go on in, Bud."

"I'm with you, Phil, but I ain't gunna go in first!"

"Come on, all of us!"

"We'll all go in, or Hank'll say we was scared!"

Suddenly four men slid through the doorway, closely packed, one behind the other.

"Hey, Hank!" called one of the voices softly.

There was no answer from Hank Cleeves.

"Hello, Hank, where are you?"

Destry stepped into the doorway, and then outside into the open, pure, safe air of the night, and no eye noted him against the stars beyond the door. Certainly he heard no voice call out after him!

But within the house, he heard a voice insistently repeat: "Hello, there, Cleeves! Where are you?"

And then a faintly groaning throat replied, above them: "Dead, dead, and God forgive me!"

Destry paused, with an odd thrill running through his body, for he remembered Hank Cleeves of old, tall, wiry, pale, thoughtful, an ironic and caustic boy, walking apart from the rest, acclaimed as a genius by boys with lesser talents for the making of sleighs, and toys of all sorts.

Now Hank lay dying in the attic, and his friends were climbing up the ladder toward him, and Destry was filled with a sense of desolation because he was the slayer, and not among the rescuers!

The hot, long school afternoons poured back upon his mind, the races to the swimming pool, and flash of naked bodies from the old log into the water, and Hank Cleeves treading water and throwing back his long hair from his eyes with both hands—a bold, strong, fearless, reckless leader among boys, until Destry adroitly had pushed him to one side. For that very reason, he knew in his heart, Cleeves now lay dying in the attic of the shanty!

But he stepped around the corner of the cabin, hearing the half-suppressed, excited voices behind him in the house, and passed through the thicket to the place where he had left Fiddle tethered. Here he mounted, and leaning from the saddle, he picked up the still senseless body of Willie Thornton, and rode back with him toward the Dangerfield place.

As he went he heard a sudden snorting of horses, a trampling of hoofs, rushing off violently, as if under the thrust of the spur, and a crackling of the brush as the mustangs were forced furiously through it.

The four who remained were in full flight, the four left of the twelve men he had selected as his enemies. Perhaps they feared that he might be rushing on their trail, ready to pick them off, one by one, for he could hear them scattering to either side, and fanning out to make his way behind them yet more difficult.

They were not in his mind, except with pity.

He went on toward the Dangerfield house, and on

the way, he met three men and Charlie Dangerfield herself, coming in haste with a litter borne among them, to carry Willie Thornton back to the house.

He gave the child down into their hands. He saw Charlie Dangerfield cherishing his face between her hands, by the starlight.

She paid no more attention to Destry than if he had been a spirit rather than a mounted man. So he turned the fine head of Fiddle toward Wham and rode straight toward it across country, going as the bird flies, regardless of fences and ditches in his way.

Chapter Forty

The sheriff was not on his veranda, neither was he in his bedroom, but in his small office, adjoining the jail cells, Destry found him bent over a desk which was piled high with papers, photographs, and such encumbrances. Through the window Destry watched him for a moment; then shrank down into the shadows as a noisy group of miners went down the board walk, chattering and shouting in their eagerness to spend a month's pay.

In the dark, Destry considered, but finally he went around to the door of the jail and rapped on it; the jailer opened to him with a growl that turned into a groan of terror when he saw the face of his visitor. He staggered back with his arms high in the air.

"I never was none of 'em!" he gasped. "I never had a hand again you, Harry!"

"I don't want to bother you none," Destry explained. "Turn your back a minute, Tom."

Tom obeyed willingly, and when the click of a door sounded, he looked over his shoulder in fear. But Destry was out of sight!

He stood now before Ding Slater without a gun in his hand.

"You come to give yourself up?" asked Ding quietly.

"I ain't pullin' a gun on you, Slater," said the other. "I reckon that speaks for itself!"

"Of course it does," said the sheriff.

"You'll be pretty set to hang me," suggested Destry.

"For what?" asked Ding Slater.

"For Clifton?"

"I been a long time sheriffing," said Slater, "but I never took no pleasure in the hangin' of a man for a thing he didn't do!"

"Hold on," broke in Destry. "There was my knife in his throat!"

"Sure there was," replied Slater, "but there wasn't your hand hitched on to it."

Destry stared.

"Besides," went on Slater, "I never heard of a Destry bein' so plumb careless as to leave a knife stickin' in the throat of a dead man!"

"Who did it, then?"

"Somebody that if I was to tell you who it was, you would almost of rather that you'd done it yourself."

"That's a lot to say, old timer."

"Ay," nodded Slater. "It's a lot to say. What's really brought you in here, son?"

"I wanted to ask you to come along with me and watch me shoot up a gent, Ding."

"Go on. I'm ready for the joke."

"I'm plumb serious."

"What man?"

"I'm going to kill Chester Bent, or be done in by him."

"Bent?" cried Slater, rising to his feet.

"Ay."

"You know about him, then?"

"I know everything!"

"About the old robbery, too?"

Destry hung on the verge of the next prepared sentence which he had been about to speak and looked at the sheriff with amazement. "What robbery?" he managed to gasp.

"The express! The express six years ago!" said Slater impatiently. "The train you were supposed to rob! The robbery that put you in prison—the robbery that's killed or ruined eight of the twelve men who put you there."

"Hold on, Ding," urged Destry. "Don't run away with this here race all by yourself!"

"It was about then that Bent got rich, all at once. Begun to buy and speculate. How? Stolen money, I say! Stolen money, and the man that he was befriendin' so's the ladies cried over him about it, that was the man that had gone to prison in his place. No wonder that he was kind to you, Harry!"

Destry, like a bewildered child, held out one hand and curled up the fingers of it as he counted over the points of the case:

"Chet grabs the money—he plants the package of coin on me—why, I even remember talkin' to him that day on the street, when he gave me the hundred!—he skids me to prison, sittin' by my side in the courtroom—he takes me into his house after I get out, and tries to have my throat cut for me so's he can take in Charlie Dangerfield——"

Truth, at which he had guessed, suddenly was revealed to him with a naked face, and Destry groaned in his anger.

The sheriff finished: "And finally, he murders a man to put the curse of the law on Destry. Harry, I dunno that I got a right to interfere with the right workin' of the law, but I'm gunna go down with you and let you arrest Bent. If you miss him, which ain't likely, I'll pull my own gun on him! Come along. Start movin' to cool off, because you look pretty much on fire!"

They hurried from the jail and down the street,

the jailer aghast at the sight of the two men, shoulder to shoulder, and Destry not in irons! In front of the jail they took their horses, and the first fear struck at Destry.

"S'pose that he's guessed something and skinned out of town?"

"It ain't half likely. He's got his whole stake here. There's the light in his library window."

They left the two horses at the corner of the hedge and went on toward the gate; from a house down the street they could hear an old man's voice singing one of the monotonous songs with which a night herder keeps the cows bedded down with comfortable minds. The sticky new sprouts of the fir touched their clothes and hands. Acrid dust they breathed still hanging in the air from the last riders who had galloped down the street.

But all was peace, and the bright mountain stars watching them, as they cautiously drew the gate ajar and slipped through. From the lighted window they looked in on Bent, and the first glance was enough.

He was not busied now with his pretense of study. Instead, he was emptying a saddle bag onto the face of the center table, and out of the bag tumbled packages of green and yellow backs, neatly held together by elastics. There was a little chamois sack, moreover, the mouth of which Bent undid and poured out as a sample of the contents a handful of jewels which he shifted back and forth so that the lamplight sparkled on them before he restored them to the sack.

There was no doubt about it. Bent was about to take wing! He wore not his office clothes but a full cow-puncher's outfit. There was even the cartridge belt about his hips and a holstered Colt low down on his thigh. He was ready to take wing, and with him he was to bear away this nest egg from which he might build up a fortune in another place.

Destry and the sheriff drew back from the window, and inside the coat of the former, Ding Slater pinned the priceless badge.

"The law's made you sweat, son," said Ding. "Now it's time for you to get some advantage out of it. Go in and get him, and bring him out to me! I wouldn't spoil this party for you."

Destry gripped the hand of Slater and without a word glided up the front steps of the house. The door was not locked. It opened silently upon its well-oiled hinges, and Destry passed into the darkness of the hall. The first door to the right was faintly sketched by the light of the lamp, leaking through the crack around it.

He found the knob, turned it softly, and pushed the door wide—then stepped in to find Bent turned toward him with a leveled revolver!

He nodded toward Bent with a smile and closed the door behind him, only noticing for the rest that the money had been swept from the table and restored to the fat saddle bag that lay on a nearby chair.

"You?" said Bent.

And he let the muzzle of his revolver slowly tip down. Not a sudden motion of friendship, but a gradual decline of the gun, while his eyes still glittered coldly at the intruder. Plainly he was asking himself if it would not be worth while to finish off Destry this instant. But his glance flashed toward the window, and he seemed to decide that the noise was more than he cared to risk.

"It's me," said Destry. "Did I scare you, Chet, comin' in like this, soft-foot?"

"You gave me a start," said Bent, and he put up the gun, but still reluctantly.

"I've been out at the ranch," he added, indicating his outfit. "And now, old son, how are things with you? Did you go down to see Charlie?"

Destry had prepared his answer to this question, but he noticed that as Bent asked it, he looked down toward the floor and seemed tensely expectant. Something was known by Bent. How much, he could not say. Therefore Destry changed his mind. He had intended to say that he had not been near the Dangerfield place, but now he said: "Yes, I was there! And half an inch from bein' trapped, Chet."

"How come."

"The skunks had word about what I was gunna do, or else they'd been trailin' me pretty close."

"Trailin' you?"

"When I got there to the old shack, they was outside and inside."

He hesitated.

"What happened?" asked Bent, his voice guarded and husky.

"There was a slip of a kid that came in, Chet. He had something to tell me, he said. I'd barely started talkin' with Charlie when he arrived and the first thing that happened, this kid come sashayin' up. The one that had helped me up in the Cumber Pass. Sick with fever—mighty dizzy—he staggered into the shack——"

"And what did he say?" asked Bent in a snarl.

"Why, I didn't have no good way of findin' out, because the minute that he was startin' to talk, a double-barrel shotgun went off from the attic of the shack, and I seen the face of Cleeves behind the flash of it! I took a snap shot that finished Cleeves, but the buckshot pretty nigh tore the boy in two!"

A glare of the most ferocious joy appeared in the eyes of Bent.

"Killed him, Harry?" he asked, and came toward the other.

"Killed him dead," said Destry, "the poor little devil! And the same minute, the gents outside—for there was the rest of 'em ready—made a rush for the door, but a couple of bullets turned 'em back. And here I am. I come fast to you, Chet, wantin' to ask you what I'd better do next. Because Charlie and me had no chance to talk."

"Go back to her," said Bent. "Go back, and I'll ride along with you, Harry! I'll ride with you out to the place!"

Excess of relief overwhelmed him and he laughed a little, shakily.

Chapter Forty-one

He had learned, no doubt, of the appearance of the boy at the house of Jack and Pete, and again of his riding through Wham. That was the death blow to Bent's tower of ambition, for with ten words the youngster could destroy him utterly. He had made his preparations for departure rapidly. Another minute, probably, and Destry would have been too late to catch the fugitive.

But now Bent heard that his small enemy was dead, and life inside the law again became possible for him. For with Willie Thornton out of the way, Destry was the murderer of Clifton!

The relief spread over the face, the eyes of Bent; it appeared in the heartier voice of Bent as he spoke again.

"Harry, you've taken a long chance in coming into Wham. No matter what happened, you should have stayed out there to see Charlie. But I'll take you back. The poor kid was killed, eh?"

"He might have been," said Destry.

"Might?" said Bent.

His voice was almost a shout.

"Mighta been scared to death," said Destry. "But he had a chance to say a few words."

Fierce pleasure filled him as he saw the face of Bent whiten, and the green light of desperation come into his face.

"What did he say?"

"Raved a mite, Chet. Crazy talk. Something about you bein' the one that killed Clifton."

Bent laughed.

But suddenly he was aware that there was no answering smile on the face of his companion, but gravely, keenly, Destry was watching him. His laughter halted abruptly.

"And what about you, Harry?" he asked. "What *d'you* thing about the kid's story?"

Destry waved his hand.

"Kid's get a lot of fool ideas," he said. "I ain't so much interested in that, old son, as I am in the yarn that Slater's just been tellin' me about the job that you done on the express six years ago——"

It was a blow so sudden and crushing to Bent, and it came upon him so unexpectedly, that he went back a staggering pace and rested his hand against the wall.

Swiftly he rallied, and Destry covered the moment of confusion by saying: "And I've been admiring the way that you handled everything from that point on, Chet. The way that you passed me into the pen for six years, say, and the way that you pretty nigh cried with joy when I got out again! The way that you been befriendin' me ever since, too, is pretty touching. Traps in my room, guns in the dark, lies and sneak-in' treachery!"

His voice did not rise as he talked.

Bent, on the farther side of the room, looked like a half stunned fighter striving to regain full control of his wits.

At last he said: "I'll tell you, Harry, that you've been listening to a poor sick kid and to an old fool. You don't mean to tell me that you believe what either of them have been saying?"

"Not more'n I believe the Bible," said Destry.

"Harry, what's up?" asked Bent, his face shining with sweat.

"This!" said Destry.

He drew aside the flap of his coat, and exposed the badge of office which the sheriff had just pinned there.

"So?" said Bent.

He looked up at the ceiling, but Destry knew that the other's attention in spite of all seeming was constantly fixed upon him.

"Jail or guns, Chester," he suggested. "You can come along with me and be poisoned with the things that everybody's gunna say about you, or else you can take your chance right here and now with old Judge Colt, that don't never make no mistakes!"

Bent drew a quick, long breath and straightened.

"It's better this way," he said. "I've been a fool in leaving you to other hands. I should have known from the first that you're enough of a man to need my special personal attention, which I'm going to give you now, Harry!"

"You'll fight?"

"I'll kill you," said Bent, "with a good deal more pleasure than I ever did any act of my life. Before this, I've been held back by other considerations."

"Charlie, for one?"

The face of Bent wrinkled with malignancy.

"I would have had her," he declared. "Time and a little patience while she forgot the death of the murderer, Destry—and then I would have married her."

"I doubt it," said Destry. "But what made you kill Clifton? Only to chuck the blame on me?"

"I wanted to see you hang," admitted Bent. "I always wanted to see that, from the time when you bested me, when we were boys. Besides, I owed Clifton money, and that was after all the cheapest way of paying him off!"

"Say, I hadn't thought of that! You owed him money? Well, you're a business man, old timer!"

"You stand on top just now, and you gloat a little," said Bent coldly. "But I'll win the game. There are other towns than Wham, other names than that of Bent, other girls than Charlie Dangerfield—though I admit that I've never seen 'em. But better to be a Bent on the wing than a Destry under the ground! Are you ready?"

"You're gettin' tolerable honest, Chet," said the other. "I been wonderin' when you'd try a crooked gun play on me!"

"I don't need to," said the other unexpectedly. "I got you inside the palm of my hand, and I'm gunna keep you there!"

"I reckon that you're in good practice, Chet."

"D'you think that I didn't start preparing for the day you'd get out of prison the day you went into it? Little things are fairly sure to float up to the surface, in time, and there was never a minute when I didn't half expect that I'd have to face you with a gun. The six years that you've missed, I've been working."

A dog yapped shrill and loud across the street; it was silent. And Bent stood at the edge of the table, resting his finger tips lightly upon it.

The very appearance of sleekness seemed to have left him, and the man was hard with muscle as his brain was hard with resolution.

"Knife, or hand, or gun, Destry!" said he. "I'm ready for any one of the three. Which will you take?"

And suddenly fear leaped into the mind of Destry. He who so long had carried the frost of terror to others, now felt it himself. It was not the fear of death, but that much greater dread of being conquered. That which supports the champion is the knowledge that he never has been beaten. Because of pride, he is a superman, until he faces in the ring an equal confidence and feels that stunning impact of the first heavy blow. So it was with Destry. Shaken, chilled, he stared at Bent and saw a faint, cruel smile on the lips of the other. He felt that he could recognize that smile. How often had it appeared on his own lips when he faced lesser men?

"When the dog barks again——" said Bent.

And they waited. There was no attempt on the part of Bent to take an advantage. His finger tips still rested lightly on the edge of the table, his smile persisted, and the cold fire welled and gleamed in his eyes.

Then, shrill and distant as the note of a muted violin, the dog barked again. At one instant the right hands leaped, the guns flashed, and a wrenching impact tore the Colt from the fingers of Destry, flung it back against his body, and toppled him from his feet.

He saw, as he fell, the weapon flashing up to cover him and send home a fatal shot; and he knew that he had met his match at last and had been beaten, fairly and squarely.

All of that rushed through his brain, but as he struck the floor he heard a rapid fire opened from the window. The sheriff, whom he had forgotten!

Straight at the head of Destry, Bent had fired, but the attack from the side sufficiently unsteadied his hand to make his bullet fly wide. It struck the floor and cast dust and splinters into the face of Destry.

Bent, stooping, scooped the crammed saddle bag that carried the cash relics of his fortune from the chair, and ran for the doorway.

He dodged, like a teal in flight, and then the darkness of the hallway received him, while Destry crawled slowly to his knees, to his feet. He could not realize, for a moment, the thing that had happened to him, but stood balancing like a drunkard, uneasy, depressed, fumbling with his mind until the truth drove home.

Beaten, saved only by a masked attack from the side that had routed Bent, he was no longer the man that he had been! He, the conqueror, had been met and conquered! He groaned and struck his fists into his face. Then he sprang for the door.

The world which he knew was now reduced to a great blank in which there lived a single face and a single name—that of Chester Bent. And until they met again and fought to a grim finish, he could not hold up his head and call his soul his own.

Fiercely he ran into the hall, tore open the front door, and crashed against the sheriff, who was lunging in.

"Hey—Harry—are you hurt? Did I hit him?"

"Get out of my way!" gasped Destry.

He hurled Ding Slater roughly from him and leaped down the steps to the gravel of the front path.

When he reached the gate, the violence of his hand upon it wrenched it off the hinges. He left it clattering upon the path before him and turned swiftly down the outside of the hedge toward the horses.

Fiddle, as though she understood, threw up her head and whinnied softly. He whipped the reins up, leaped into the saddle, and started the good mare forward on the run.

From the rear of the house, he guessed, the fugitive conqueror would be riding, by this time, cutting back through the woods and over the rolling highlands beyond.

And so through those woods he drove Fiddle. The trees flicked back on either side. He saw the naked hills, the stars, and against them the shadowy outline of a horseman riding fast before him.

Chapter Forty-two

Much had been taken from Fiddle that day, but she had rested since the strain and now she was willing to run on, straight and swift. And every bound she made lifted the heart of Destry. He felt a cold, hard certainty that unless he overtook his conqueror on this night and fought out the battle with him again, he would never again be the Harry Destry whom other men had learned to fear.

Not that he cared to triumph over them, as he had done before. For now that he had dipped into the valley of humiliation, his heart was softened, and with every pulse of the mare's gallop he swore inwardly that this night would see the last bullet fired from his Colt, whether he won or lost.

It must be a short race, he knew, for Fiddle could not endure another heart-racking effort in this day, but he trusted to her first fierce burst of speed to overhaul the other.

Mercilessly he pressed her on, until her ears flattened, and her head stretched out straight with her labor up the hill, then over it and shooting down a sharp slope at breathless speed. It seemed to Destry like plunging into the dark of a well; and the stars flew back over his head like sparks from a wheel. Then he was riding up the easy floor of a hollow and the trees stood on the ridges at either hand like fenceposts planted regularly.

But all was growing brighter as the moon came up in the east, small and dull behind a rag of clouds. By her light, Destry saw the rider before him far closer than at first and working desperately to drop his pursuer.

It could not be done! With a great upbursting of exultation, Destry knew that the other was surely being overhauled, and Fiddle herself like a hunting dog increased her pace as she saw the race in her grip.

They turned a sharp bend of the valley. The walls of it increased on either hand, and to make surety doubly sure, Destry saw that he had run his prey into a box cañon. Straight before him the way terminated in a low wall over which a stream of water tumbled into spray and showered across the rocks beneath with a continual hushing sound. Beyond the water stood the rim of the moon, so bright that it half dazzled Destry, and made more dim than phantoms the shadowy rocks and trees around him.

But in spite of that dimness he could not but be aware of one form running toward him. It was Chester Bent, who had fled long enough and now turned back to strike at his pursuer.

A bullet clipped the sombrero from Destry's head, the bark of the gun crashed against his ear and the instant echoes repeated it in a harsh jumble. And he fired in turn, half blindly, being desperate with the knowledge that the light was in his eyes, obscuring all things for him as much as it illumined them for his enemy. He was in a thick mist, as it were, while Bent had at least a twilight to strike by. Both weapons spoke again. Pitching down the slip, Bent came, horse and man, like a thrown missile, but the second bullet from Destry at least altered his course.

Up went the mustang on its rear legs. Destry saw the mouth gaped wide under the strain of the reins;

the eyes were fiercely bright. It seemed more like a trained fighting beast than a harmless servant of any master.

However, it reared so high and so far that it passed the balance point, and toppled back as Bent, with a yell of anger and surprise, flung himself from the saddle. Horse and man went down, the crashing body of the big animal seeming to land fairly on top of its master. Yet when Destry sprang down from the back of Fiddle, it was to see Bent rolling over and over, then pitching to his feet.

Destry fired. There was no return. Instead, Bent came running in with a peculiarly rapid, dodging gait, so that Destry was amazed. It seemed as though Bent scorned to use a weapon, but preferred to fight out the battle, trusting to his bare hands.

There was no such folly in the mind of Bent, however. The holster on his thigh was empty; his fall from the horse had disarmed him and his only escape from the bullets of Destry was to get at the source of them.

The truth flashed up like fire in the mind of Harry Destry. The hypocrite, the traitor, the false friend he now held helpless under the nose of the Colt. No dodging could avoid the gun at such a distance, but Destry flung it suddenly from him.

For the fear left him. A sort of madness came on him as he saw this enemy rushing in with empty hands. Out of the past a picture poured upon his mind of the twelve men who had gathered to judge him and to rob him of a portion of his life.

All these years it had seemed a frightful mockery, a frightful sham, that verdict delivered by the "twelve peers." Now, in an instant, all bitterness left him. Whatever weakness and sin there had been among them now was nothing contrasted with the over-mastering sin of Bent. His evil, as it were, was a fire that burned the others clean.

Here was a peer, indeed, a king among men, towering above Destry in keenness of mind, in craft, in all subtlety. Only in one way could he be matched, and that was in strength of hand. So the pride stood up like flame in Destry. He shouted, as an Indian shouts rushing to battle, there was laughter in his throat as he plunged forward. They looked like two old friends, newly met and throwing out their arms to embrace each other. So it was that they appeared, but when they met, it was with a shock that spun them about. Then they fell into a hard grip.

The hands of Destry slipped and glided on the body of Bent. Now he knew for certain that sleekness was not fat but hardened muscle, from which his fingerhold failed. But Bent, in return, drove home his shoulder against Destry's breast, staggering him; then in the excess of his power, he raised Destry floundering in the air. He was a helpless and clumsy child in the grip of Bent. He who had been so proud of his strength was unnerved and half unmanned by the first onset of his enemy.

Yet not beaten!

He was swung in the air, then hurled down, Bent casting his weight forward to fall upon his victim. But Destry, catlike, turned in the air, struck the earth with feet and hands, and dodged from the hands of Bent. His foot tripped on a rock with a violence that cast him head over heels down the slope. More desperately than ever he fought to regain his balance, came staggering to his feet, and braced himself to meet an onslaught that did not come!

Instead, he heard the beating of a horse's hoofs,

and yonder went Chester Bent on the back of Fiddle, rushing up the trail at the head of the cañon.

Vain curses poured from the throat of Destry. he had welcomed this last and greatest battle in a divine frenzy, but even in this he was tricked, eluded, baffled and shamed. He cried out loud, and ran a few stumbling steps in pursuit, until his foot struck the revolver which he had thrown away. He looked blankly down at it for an instant, then scooped it up.

Up the cliff-face on the winding trail went the rider, until at the top he burst out across the face of the moon which now stood just above the rim of the rock. It was an odd and terrible effect, as though Fiddle were snatched into the heart of the sky, racing down the slope of the constellation. Her mane and tail flew out. This was the last instant her former rider would see her, it seemed, and as he rode, Bent waved his hand, laughing.

Loudly, yet as from a distance, that laughter floated down to the ear of Destry, mixed with the ringing beat of the hoofs. It was the laughter that made him recover suddenly from his dream. The gun leaped high in his hand, barked.

And as its nose jerked up with the recoil, Destry saw Chester Bent lurch from the saddle of the flying mare—lurch, so to speak, from the white cradle of the moon. Both his arms were flung out; he dropped at once from view against the rock of the cliff-face.

For an instant, Destry held his breath. In that instant, he told himself that it was impossible. Such a man could not die in such a way, but by a last impossible touch of craft would rescue himself!

Then out of the darkness, Destry heard the impact, horrible, distinct, like huge gloved hands smitten together.

Chester Bent was dead!

Fiddle, in the meantime, had turned back, and coming across the moon once more, she paused there and whinnied anxiously into the dark of the ravine. Only then did Destry raise his head, which had fallen in profound thought. He let the Colt fall from his hand and turned back up the hill, stumbling. Even Fiddle he did not wish near him, for Fiddle had come to him through the dead man's gift!

Chapter Forty-three

Destry went back to Wham, but he did not pause in the town; he went on through it until he came to the Dangerfield house beyond.

He hesitated to approach it. The place seemed dark, until he circled to the farther side and saw the dim glow of a lamp against the drawn shade. Coming up to the front of the old house, he heard voices on the veranda and he paused in the darkness to listen.

It was Docter Whipple and the Colonel. The doctor was saying: "They're like willow. You can beat 'em and bend 'em, but still they're tough and keep their life."

"You mean that he'll come through?" asked the Colonel.

"He's got a tolerable fair chance," said the doctor.

Destry suddenly remembered that there was no call for him to remain sheltered from view in the dark. He was a free man. There was no shadow of legal complaint against him. In all the world no one could give evidence that would place him in danger of the law. A load fell from his shoulders. He came quietly up the veranda steps.

"It's Destry, most likely," said the Colonel. "Is that you, Harry?"

"It's me," said he.

"Set down," said the Colonel. "Ding Slater has just left, and he told us."

"About Bent?"

"He told us everything. You've got him, son, or you wouldn't be back, I reckon?"

"Bent is gone," said Destry soberly. "Did I hear you say that the kid is going to pull through, Doc?"

"If he was ten years older," replied Whipple, "he wouldn't have a chance. But the young ones will bend without breaking. You might go up and see him. He's been talking about you a good deal."

"The fever," said Destry. "How bad is it?"

"Pretty high. He needs sleep and——"

At this, a note of shrill, high laughter came sharply down to them from the upstairs of the house.

Destry listened with a shudder, and started toward the door. The Colonel accompanied him up the stairs to the right door, and there paused with him.

"Charlie is in there with the kid," he remarked, "and before you go in, maybe you'll let me know which turn your trail is gunna take with her, son?"

"Her way is my way," said Destry, "so long as she'll let me go with her."

The Colonel nodded, and Destry tapped at the door. It was opened at once by the girl. She turned pale when she saw the newcomer, but stepped back and waved him in, pointing toward the bed.

Little Willie Thornton lay there, his arms thrown out wide, and looking sun-blackened until they were as dark as a Negro's skin. But his face was pale. He seemed gaunt and old; the skin was drawn tight and looked polished over the cheekbones. And his eyes rolled wildly.

"He's mighty sick," said the girl. "Speak to him, Harry!"

Destry sat on the side of the bed, and took one of the small, clenced fists in his hand.

"D'you know me, Willie?" said he.

"You're Chester Bent," said the boy. "It's you that set me on fire, but Destry'll come and put the fire out. He'll find you, too. There ain't any trail so long——"

His eyes grew vacant.

Destry took the youngster by both shoulders.

"It's me—it's Harry Destry!" said he. "D'you hear me, son?"

Into the eyes of Willie came sudden life and understanding.

"Hey, Harry!" said he. "Hullo! I'm glad to see you. You're safe from 'em, Harry?"

"Account of you, I am," said Destry. "You fixed me up, old son!"

The boy smiled and his eyes closed.

"D'you mean it? And Bent?"

"Bent'll never be seen again."

The boy nodded, his smile increasing.

"I reckoned that you'd tend to him," said he. "Why don't they figger it out with sense? They ain't nobody that ever could give you no trouble, Harry! I reckon that you're the top wrangler everywhere!"

Destry looked back to the swift and desperate fight in the shadow of the narrow ravine and he said nothing, but thought the more. Willie Thornton's closed fist relaxed in the grip of Destry. The haggard tautness relaxed in the face of the boy, and a slight perspiration gleamed on his forehead and moistened his hand. In a moment he was sleeping. Another moment still, and he smiled in his sleep.

"You're the best doctor, Harry!" said the girl.

She had been leaning beside him all this time and now Destry looked up at her through a mist of vast weariness.

"Charlie," said he, "I wonder if this here is the end of the trail?"

She smiled as she looked down at him.

"I mean," he explained, "that I'm plumb tired, Charlie. I'm finished with the game. I'm done up and weary to the bone. But if you still can waste time on a good-for-nothin' gent that never done anything well except the makin' of trouble, I've come back here to ask you to marry me, Charlie."

"You better have a sleep, first," said she. "You're tuckered out and you want to quit now, but tomorrow you'll be on the wing again."

"What makes you think that?" he asked her, too tired to follow her meaning clearly.

"You'll always hunt trouble till you've met a master," said she, firmly. "You gotta ride to a fall, Harry. You gotta fight till you're knocked out."

Destry laughed, and he was so very tired that his head fell loosely back as he laughed.

"I've met my master," said he. "I've met my peer. He beat me to the draw; he beat me with guns, and he beat me hand to hand. I killed him with luck and not with skill. I've throwed the gun away, Charlie. I'm an old man, and finished and done for. A Chinaman could laugh in my face, now, and I'd take it!"

"It was Bent?" she asked.

"Ay, it was Chet."

She drew a great breath.

"I always knew," said she, "that something good would come out of him!"

They were married that month, on the day when Willie Thornton was pronounced able to sit up. Because he expressed a desire to see the affair, it was performed in Willie's room, which was jammed with a crowd that overflowed into the hall and even up and down the stairs.

But, as Ding Slater said, the whole county should have been present, because it meant the end of the old days and the beginning of a new regime in Wham, for Harrison Destry had put away his Colt.

✂

☐ **YES!**

Sign me up for the Leisure Western Book Club and send my FREE BOOKS! If I choose to stay in the club, I will pay only $14.00* each month, a savings of $9.96!

NAME: _____

ADDRESS: _____

TELEPHONE: _____

EMAIL: _____

☐ I want to pay by credit card.

☐ **VISA**　　☐ MasterCard.　　☐ DISCOVER

ACCOUNT #: _____

EXPIRATION DATE: _____

SIGNATURE: _____

Mail this page along with $2.00 shipping and handling to:
**Leisure Western Book Club
PO Box 6640
Wayne, PA 19087**
Or fax (must include credit card information) to:
610-995-9274
You can also sign up online at **www.dorchesterpub.com**.